I0600736

Masquerade

Jeanette Battista

Masquerade

Copyright © 2019 by Jeanette Battista

All rights reserved. Printed in the United
States of America. No part of this book
may be used or reproduced in any
manner whatsoever without written
permission except in the case of brief
quotations embodied in critical articles
or reviews.
This book is a work of fiction. Names,
characters, businesses, organizations,
places, events, and incidents either are
the product of the author's imagination
or are used fictitiously. Any resemblance
to actual persons, living or dead, events,
or locales is entirely coincidental.

Cover design by Marianne Nowicki
ISBN: 978-0-9973197-7-4

First Edition: May 2019

10 9 8 7 6 5 4 3 2 1

MASQUERADE

DEDICATION

For Melissa Marr, the inspiration for this book
and fellow Phantom lover.

Also by Jeanette Battista

The Moon Series
Leopard Moon
Jackal Moon
Hyena Moon
Hunter Moon
Fox Hunt (short story)

Long Black Veil

The Demon's Gate Series
The Iron Bells
The Stone Golem
The Demon's Gate

Played

Books of Aerie
An Unkindness of Ravens
A Murder of Crows

These Violent Delights

ACKNOWLEDGMENTS

The Composer: Gaston Leroux, writer of the original *Le Fantôme de l'Opéra*, without whom this story would not exist.
The Stage Managers: Thank you to Molly Harper and Lish McBride for reading the various iterations of this novel and giving me good feedback, especially the words, "Stalkery but sexy." I love you both.
The Chorus: Thank you to my critique group—Jeremy, Jax, Jennifer, and Rachel—for reading this monster and for humanizing Christine, and for your acceptance of all the ways someone can be a monster. Thanks to the authors at the NOLA retreat where I first conceived of this idea and decided to go for it, especially Kristin, Jaye, Aprilynne, and Rachel V.
The Crew: Marianne for the lovely cover, Bev for her editing prowess, and all the countless people who helped get this book into your hands.
The Audience: Thank you for reading.

CHAPTER *1*

1901 (Present Day)

HIS SEARCH HAD BROUGHT him here, to a public house in a small town along the Irish coast, indistinguishable from all of the other small towns that dotted the landscape. Indistinguishable, except for one thing: Her.

She was waiting for him at a small table set in the far front corner of the pub, the mullioned window looking out onto the green hills and the rapidly approaching storm clouds. Light drops of rain had spattered him on his short walk from the inn, and the wind caught the door and flung it out of his hand when he tried to enter the pub, causing quite the racket.

"Madame Lotte Spöke?" he asked as he

approached, lapsing into his native French before correcting himself. "Apologies. Mrs. Lotte Spöke?"

She looked up at him and smiled. He was sure she was the woman he'd been searching for. Her sublime voice had set the imaginations of the patrons of the Paris Opera House ablaze, and the rumors surrounding her mysterious departure only fanned those flames. The furor abated even though the mystery of the Opera Ghost and the missing soprano was never solved; Parisians found something else to capture their attention and the Swedish soprano and her ethereal voice faded from their consciousness.

It was surprising, then, when ten years later, the Comte de Chagny contracted a solicitor to discover the missing soprano's whereabouts—if she still lived at all—so that she might receive an inheritance from the estate. It was all very strange, but then again, so was so much of time relating to the affairs of the Palais Garnier and its ghost.

He choked on his next words at the sight of her. Her heart-shaped face ended in a stubbornly pointed chin, her blue eyes were large and clear with a fringe of long lashes like spiders' legs, and all of it capped by long, curling hair the color of clover honey. It flowed over her shoulders and down her back, a veritable lion's mane. He found himself short of breath, all his careful thoughts scattering as she stared up at him, a small, secret smile playing around pouting pink lips.

"Mr. Beauchamp," she said in a breathy, almost lilting voice. He caught the faint hint of an unfamiliar accent. His heart was racing for some strange reason. He couldn't fathom it.

"Please, call me Bastien," he replied, shrugging out of his coat and removing his hat. "May I?" He gestured at the empty chair opposite her at the table.

She waved her delicate hand toward the unoccupied chair, reminding Bastien of how a queen directed her subjects. He inclined his head and set down his outerwear in an empty chair before making himself comfortable. "Thank you so very much for coming to meet with me."

"To be frank, it is all terribly curious, your wishing to speak with me. I am no one of consequence, though if I can offer any help in your search I am glad of it." Her eyelids had dropped, just a little, veiling the blue of her eyes with the thickness of her lashes. She appeared a conundrum, a woman who looked much younger than her years and yet exuded a confidence and presence of someone far older.

Bastien signaled to the barmaid for a whisky; Lotte Spöke surprised him by ordering one for herself as well. He smiled, charmed when she turned her head to the side, the faint hint of a blush tinting her cheeks the most delicate of roses.

"You are most gracious to offer your help." He paused while their drinks were placed in front of them, then continued, leaning forward and lowering his voice. She wrapped her slim hands around the heavy glass before her and waited, wide-eyed. "As to what business brings me here: the Comte de Chagny is desperate to find an old acquaintance of his and has tasked my firm to locate her. I think you might have some information about her."

At this mention of the Comte, he thought he saw her face pale, and he hid a smile behind a sip of whisky.

Her voice betrayed nothing of her possible inner turmoil. She adjusted the fingerless gloves she wore fussily, smoothing the fabric over her forearms. "I'm unsure why you think I would even know who the Comte de Chagny is. I fear you've made a mistake."

"Your accent, Madame," Bastien remarked, certain he was on the right path, "do I detect a bit of Swedish?"

He'd had investigators searching cities and towns throughout the British Isles, having exhausted other countries in his hunt to find her. The Comte had told the firm to spare no expense if the information was good, so Bastien had been generous with his hirelings. He did not want to spook the woman he searched for and have her flee before he even gained a chance to speak with her himself.

So he was almost completely certain Lotte Spöke was the woman he sought before he'd even joined her at the table.

The sparkling blue eyes narrowed, her lips thinning into a distressed line. "Swedish?" That faint tinge of an accent had disappeared, but

Bastien wasn't worried. He'd heard what he'd heard.

"With a name like Lotte it seems possible. Are you from Sweden originally or did you have family from there?" He took another sip of his whisky.

"Mr. Beauchamp," she began, pushing aside her untouched glass, "I am afraid you've made a rather large mistake." She climbed to her feet, still slight, her dancer's body swathed in skirts and layers of cloth to keep out the chill wind that had started whipping at the panes.

"Do you recall Erik, Miss Daaé?"

Slowly she turned her head until she faced him, wearing an expression of grudging respect. Her coquettish mask fell away, revealing the feral brilliance she hid behind the innocent shutters of her blue eyes. Honeyed hair tumbled free to frame a pleasing face that concealed a mind sharp as mirror shards and just as likely to cut. She returned to her seat, taking her time. Her gaze never left his face as she surveyed him, again that faint smile playing about her lips.

Bastien breathed a sigh of relief that his gambit to get her to stay and speak plainly with him had paid off. The Comte de Chagny had warned him not to be misled by her innocent looks or her childlike mannerisms. He'd been the one to insist on arming his agents with that one sentence in case their quarry proved recalcitrant. Still, Bastien saw the simple appeal of her as the urge to protect her swelled in his chest even though he'd been told she was more than equipped to extricate herself from almost any situation.

"What is it you want, Monsieur Beauchamp?" she purred, as though she already had an inkling of what he, like most men, would want from her.

"Simply to speak with you so I might carry out the task my employer and our client set to me, nothing more." He watched, startled, as she knocked back her whisky with the ease of long practice. "Another?" he managed to ask when she set the empty glass down.

"We'll see," she said primly, spearing him with the sharp ice blue of her gaze. She frowned, the pale brows drawing down with her scowl. He watched, fascinated, as she waved her hand at him to continue when she grew frustrated at his silence. "Well? Go on."

Bastien blinked, pulling his scattered thoughts back together. Clearing his throat after another sip of his whisky, he said, "Again, my apologies, Miss Daaé—"

"Lotte, please. Christine Daaé has been gone for over ten years now. I do not miss her." Her delicate fingers tapped at the rim of her empty glass as she watched him from beneath her lashes. "And it *is* Mrs." Her lips curled in a sly smile like she held a fascinating secret. "How is Raoul these days? We don't hear anything about him out here."

Bastien straightened with a sharp inhale. Yes, to business. He reminded himself of the warnings, of his reputation and that of his firm. Christine

Daaé or Lotte Spöke or whatever she might choose to call herself was a charming, dangerous woman, but he could navigate these waters safely, he was sure.

She ran the tip of her index finger around the rim of the glass. Bastien watched, mesmerized as a bird was before a cobra, as she brought it to her lips and licked off the faint droplets of the whisky she'd collected. Bastien clasped his hands together atop the table and took a deep, settling breath before he began.

"I am a solicitor from the firm of Foucoult, Abelard, and Charron. The Comte hired my employers to seek out a missing soprano, one Christine Daaé. He kindly provided certain background documents and what information he'd had others uncover over the course of several years. Thus, we've—"

"Why does he want to find her?" she interrupted, her hands clasped on the table in a way that mirrored his.

Bastien frowned. He didn't like to feel rushed or pushed. As if reading his mood, she set her hand on his arm and gave him a gentle squeeze. "I am most curious as to the reason behind your visit. Forgive my impatience." Her cheeks flushed pink with her blush as she lowered her eyes demurely.

He placed his hand over hers and clasped her chilled fingers. They felt like matchsticks in his grip, so dainty that he felt enormous in comparison. The fine wool of her gloves was smooth beneath his hand. When she pulled her hand slowly from his grasp, Bastien had to fight not to hold on tighter.

"I understand," he said, finishing off his whisky. "It is rather startling, isn't it?" He smiled, pleased when she nodded. "The Comte de Chagny has come into possession of some items that he purchased at auction from the Palais Garnier." Bastien reached into his coat and pulled forth the envelope that held the list of contents. "He would like to give you a papier-mâché music box, if you'll have it. He said he saw it and immediately thought of y . . . of Christine Daaé. He remembered seeing it once in her dressing room. He found himself struck with the sudden, inescapable urge to find out how she fared in the world."

Lotte tossed her leonine head back at the sound of that name, reminding Bastien of a fractious horse. "A music box, you say." Her voice was speculative, soft, almost reverent. "It has been a long time if it's the one I am thinking of." Her gaze had turned inward, watching things only she could see.

Bastien pulled another piece of paper from the envelope. It was a rough charcoal drawing that the Comte had included with his instructions, a rendering of said music box. Several masked couples danced in pairs around the circular top of the box, while some kind of composer or instructor stood in the middle, likewise masked but without a partner, seeming to direct the dancers.

She reached out her hand to touch the drawing, her fingers trembling. Bastien passed the page closer, sliding it across the table. Her fingertips hovered over the charcoal curves, not quite touching, and a smile—a natural one, so very different than the ones she'd so far given him—lit her face.

"Raoul drew this," she whispered, then she seemed to snap back to the present. She snatched her hand back as if the page was likely to burst into flames. "I don't want it."

"Lotte," Bastien urged, leaning forward in his chair, "Christine, what *happened*?"

Her face shifted so quickly he barely kept track of the emotions on display: fear, anger, regret, fondness, joy, and grief rushed past him in a dizzying wave. He reached across the table and caught her fingers, holding her as if he thought she'd turn into mist and evaporate. "He wants you to have it," he murmured.

She passed a hand across her eyes and breathed deeply, taking a moment to rebuild the defenses Bastien suspected he'd breached. When she lowered her arm, she wore a bemused expression. "You really wish to know? It's a dark tale and a sad one," she warned.

Bastien subsided back in his chair. He'd volunteered for the assignment, knowing it might take him far from France, knowing that he might never find her. But he'd had to try. The mystery of the Opera Ghost and the missing soprano and the madness of her final performance stirred his imagination. He'd been a young man then, barely out of boyhood, but he remembered the rumors and the talk, the newspaper articles and the questions that arose shortly after the death of the Comte de Chagny, Raoul's brother.

"I do," he answered.

"Then I shall need another whisky."

CHAPTER 2

1889, Paris

THE LOUD THUMP OF MADAME Giry's cane against the boards beside her foot jolted Christine out of her reverie. "Eyes front, Miss Daaé!" the old ballet mistress chided, before slamming her cane to the wood floor once more. "Again!"

Christine stepped to her mark, imagining where she'd like to stick that cane the next time the old witch thumped it at her. She was only a chorus girl, required to sing and dance in the background of the operas performed at the Palais Garnier, but that didn't mean she could shirk. Madame Giry was a feared master and very accurate with her cane. More than one girl came from rehearsal rubbing a thigh or a shoulder after the woman's uncanny aim struck true.

The troupe managed to get through a routine that mollified Giry after their third attempt, which earned them all a brief break. Christine slumped against a wall of the Foyer de la Danse, legs stretched out before her and contemplated the toes of her dancing shoes.

Meg, Giry's daughter, plopped down beside her. "Where's your head at today? Mamá nearly struck you—twice!"

Christine shook her head and began to twist her wild curls back into a semblance of a bun. It wasn't neat, but it was off her neck and that was really all she cared about. "It was a bad night," she said by way of explanation.

"Was it Monsieur le Fure?" Meg asked, wearing a hint of a smirk. "Did he call for you?"

Christine bit back a sigh. Le Fure had been sniffing around her skirts for weeks, another patron of the Palais Garnier who only attended the opera in order to ogle the chorus girls' bodies rather than out of any love of opera. The *petite rats*—as the girls from working class families in the chorus were called—were known to take lovers for coin, but Christine hadn't needed to do that. Yet. Le Fure hoped to be her exception. Meg followed the exploits of the petite rats with a sort of jealous relish, but Madame Giry would never dream of allowing her little Meg to follow in their path. She told anyone who would listen that Meg was destined for greater things than being a low-ranking noble's diversion.

"No. My guardian is sick." Christine rubbed at

one eye with the back of her hand, feeling weariness weigh on her shoulders. Madame Valérius was an aging woman who'd—along with her now-dead husband—taken Christine in after the death of her father, and even paid for her to attend the Conservatoire. Christine didn't particularly care for her outside of a faint gratefulness for the woman's continued gullibility. It gave her a roof over her head and had gotten her a position at the Paris opera, even if Christine hated to sing now.

Meg's hand flew to her plump cupid's bow lips. "I'm sorry—I didn't know!" She acted as if she'd said something hugely offensive, the drama of the imagined slight probably appealing to her.

"She's just old," Christine said, waving away the dramatics with her hand. "She's got a maid, but she likes it when I take care of her."

Meg gave her an odd look. Christine ignored it. She was too tired to worry what some naïve child thought of her. She didn't want to be stuck in the chorus forever, and she certainly didn't want to remain tied to the Valérius purse strings—and the expectations that came with them—for much longer. Perhaps she should allow Monsieur le Fure to take her out. Plenty of dancers and singers had made careers out of being a rich man's mistress.

Little Giry jumped to her feet as her mother swooped back into the practice room like a black bird of ill omen. Christine stood more slowly, already dreading the frustrating minutes that seemed to stretch endlessly before her. Madame Giry called for the troupe to take their places as they began their dance once more.

♩♩♩

Christine tucked her coat more closely around her body as she hurried through the rain-slicked streets of Paris. Vocal practice had been even more terrible than usual. She knew she had a passable voice and that she was capable of more, but Christine didn't see the point in trying anymore. The reason she'd used her voice when she was younger had been the scams she'd run with her father to keep them fed and clothed. With his death, music had lost its luster for her, though it was still an easy way to make money. But when Maestro Abbe pushed her for more, almost as if he knew she was holding back, she resented him and his chiding. Christine had heard Carlotta, the Prima Donna of the Palais Garnier, sing and knew she could not match her, so what was the point of reaching for it only to fall short? Why couldn't Abbe just be satisfied with her adequacy and leave her be?

Adjusting her scarf to more fully cover her head, Christine decided to take a shortcut. Her hair already took forever to dry and Madame Valérius would be waiting for her return. Christine would recount her day while combing out her hair before dinner. This route was usually less populated, as most people preferred to keep to the better lit streets, but Christine wasn't concerned. Her Pappa had taught her many things, not least of which was how to stick a knife in a man's armpit or between the ribs to get to the liver. She carried a sheathed dagger inside her sleeve whenever she walked alone.

But as she encountered more people than expected, especially in this abysmal weather, Christine knew she'd made a mistake. A carnival was in town and had set up its gates adjacent to the street she traversed, the crowd it drew clogging her path. It was probably going to be the last one for a while, what with the Exposition Universelle expected to draw ridiculous crowds when it opened in a few months. Several couples with umbrellas stood before the booth at the gates, buying tickets to what looked like a perfectly ordinary traveling fair. When she was a child, Christine and her father had traveled with several for a time when they needed the anonymity such things provided, and she was not impressed with this one.

At least until the singing reached her ears.

It was faint, hard to make out at first among the din of the people chattering as they waited for entry. But Christine heard the thread of a barely-there voice raised in song and it stole the breath from her lungs. The purity of it, the sheer enormity of the emotions encased in that voice nearly overwhelmed her. Tears sprung to her eyes. She recognized the song as an aria from Mozart's *Idomeneo*. The stunning tenor rose above the background noise, the power of that voice striking her like a blow.

Before she fully realized what she was doing, Christine had crossed to the ticket booth and reached into her purse to pay the entrance fee. She shoved through what looked to be a large family milling about the entrance to the carnival, and then set about discovering the source of that wonderful sound.

The song reached its crescendo and then faded as she continued down the main avenue of carnival games and barkers hawking their rides and wares. Christine froze in place, ears primed to catch even a hint of that amazing voice. The normal hum of the carnival and its patrons mocked her with their ordinary noise. After standing in place for a minute or two without catching another note of the tenor voice, Christine sighed, shoulders slumping.

A voice like that should be showcased in the Palais Garnier, not singing for nobodies in a traveling show. Christine wondered how the singer had come to be here. She began to walk down the alley, head still half-cocked as she listened for any snippet of the tenor's voice.

This carnival was a step above the fairs she and her father once played. It wasn't big by any means, but there were a number of attractions, plenty of games to part people from their money, and one or two rides. She turned a corner and saw the sign advertising the occupant of the tent in front of her:

The Voice of an Angel with the Face of a Devil!

Christine gaped, mouth going slack in shock. A freak? She stepped closer, feeling frustration fill her empty spaces. It was all a con! She and her father had run plenty of them, so she was familiar with most of the common ones.

"Care to see the Demon, mademoiselle?" came a voice at her shoulder.

Christine's hand went to her wrist and the knife she carried up her sleeve before she could stop herself, her heart jumping in her chest. She turned her head to see a balding man in a suit that had been fashionable at least a decade past, the knees and elbows shiny with wear even in the grey light of encroaching night.

"The next performance should start shortly," he said. He pulled back the flap that led to a small seating area.

Christine could see the small stage area that was covered by another curtain, this one threadbare and faded with use. She took a seat at the front, eyes scanning the enclosed space. She didn't see any wires or devices that could amplify voices or pipe in recordings, though if they were good at their con—and she had no reason to doubt they were—such things wouldn't be readily visible. Still, she did a sweep of the floor, especially near the stage and tent poles.

It reminded her of the scams she and her father used to run when she was younger. She hadn't known they were scams back then; it was simply the way her Pappa put a roof over their heads and kept them both clothed and fed. He was an amazing fiddle player with a passable voice, and while he played, Christine often worked the crowd who'd come to watch, her small form and quick hands letting her lighten pockets and purses with ease. It wasn't until she was older that she joined him in singing and dancing as another form of distraction while he worked the crowd.

Chewing on her thumbnail as she waited, Christine took in the scents of the place. Unwashed bodies, the stink of stale sweat made her nose wrinkle. The smell of paint and dust, of rotting cloth and wet canvas made her suddenly homesick. The scent of roasted meat was there, but overshadowed by the smell of live animals and their offal. She lost track of how long she sat there, engulfed in a flood of sense-memories. Finally, unable to keep quiet, Christine stood and began to pace, as if she could outrun the past reaching out for her, ready to swallow her whole.

The curtains shrouding the stage parted to reveal the thick metal bars of a cage. A man stood behind them, his clothes in even worse shape than the barker's outside, his face hidden by the deep shadows of the tent. Christine looked around to find she was alone in the small theatre. She should leave; Madame Valérius would be wondering where she'd got to. But the sudden need she had to figure out the trick, to prove to no one but herself that the magical voice she'd heard was nothing but a faked recording kept her there, in that tent. She took a step closer to the makeshift stage, her gaze settling on the man.

He was a tall man, and thin, reminding her of a scarecrow standing in a field on a county farm she'd passed years ago when her father was still alive. His wrists stuck out of his poorly fitted shirt, the collar of it loose around his neck. His pants were likewise too short, rising up to reveal bony ankles and a bit of calf. His shoes were too tight, digging into the pale flesh of his feet and reddening the skin in angry lines.

She heard some muttering from backstage, what sounded like an angry order, and then the man in the cage lurched forward as though shoved hard from behind. He caught the bars before his face could smash into them, his long, pale fingers wrapping around them in a grip so tight his knuckles turned white. He looked up, and Christine could see his face clearly for the first time.

She jerked to a halt and involuntarily stepped back, one hand coming up to cover her open-mouthed gasp. The man—young, only a few years older than she—flinched at the sound, his head lowering and shoulders lifting as if anticipating a blow. Christine stared, unable to tear her gaze from the wreckage of his face. One side of his face pulled down, heavy with scarring, the eye narrowed permanently. His dark hair appeared shorn on that side, or perhaps it just wouldn't grow, while the rest spread out wildly down his shoulders. The other side of his face was normal, almost handsome though his nose was nearly flat at the bridge and the nostrils pronounced, almost like the holes in a skull. The damaged eye was a cloudy pale color, either grey or blue, while the other was a dark brown.

"Sing!" The whispered order was hissed from somewhere behind the cage and again the young man flinched.

Christine gaped once again at the sound issuing from the young man's throat. It contained such dizzying power, such heartfelt emotion. She recognized the aria—the duet between Faust and Marguerite—though it was like she'd never heard it sung properly before now. His voice held the thunder of command and the despair of heartbreak all at once and she was swept up in the tide of his singing, lost to the music of him and everything his voice made her feel.

Without thinking, she closed the distance between them. She surprised him—and herself—when she took up Marguerite's part, her own bell-like soprano rising as his voice faded. He stared at her, the eye in the scar tissue widening as far as it could go, shocked and frozen behind the bars of his cage as she approached.

Christine blocked out the voices coming from behind the curtain and climbed the riser to stand beside the young man, only the bars separating them. His voice rose along with her hers, merging and melding until it became something ringing and powerful, something beyond the two of them, almost as though it had a golden life of its in own. In that moment, Christine would have sworn she could see the notes floating in the air between them, twinkling like pixie dust. It almost made her believe in magic.

She gazed at his face, watching the emotions play out over the ravaged flesh. His good eye sparkled, alive with joy. The unmarred side of his face lifted in a smile as he sang the duet with her. His hands never left the bars, though they did slide down so they were closer to her, so that if she wanted to reach out, she could wrap her hands over his. Christine didn't, though she did wrap her fingers around a bar close to his. He gazed at her in wonder, in surprise, mirroring her own expression.

Too soon, they came to the end of the piece. As the last notes faded from their throats, silence reigned. "Who are you?" she whispered.

He'd turned his head so that the ruined side of his face was in shadow. "Erik," he answered in a voice as smooth and rich as melted chocolate. "What's your name?"

"Christine." She glanced at the curtain; those behind it had fallen strangely silent.

She glanced around for signs of a con. A good show was made up of lies. Up close, she could see that Erik wasn't wearing makeup—this was how he looked. But the cage? Probably set dressing, just like an opera, to sell the story the barker and the signs were hawking. Not real. In the carnivals she and her father joined with, the freaks were performers just like the rest, their restraints only for show.

Bony fingers closed around her wrist, the icy touch shocking her. "Will you help me?" Erik's eyes pleaded with her. "Please?"

CHAPTER *3*

TRYING TO KEEP THE REVULSION AT his touch from her face, Christine went still. They weren't really keeping this man in a cage, were they? That wasn't how these things worked. "Help you how?"

Erik leaned as far forward as the bars allowed, glancing quickly over his shoulder. "Get me out," he whispered.

Christine backed up as much as she could with him holding her wrist, knowing she could tug free whenever she liked. "This isn't part of the act?" He shook his head, the brown eye wide and desperate. "You're really locked up?"

"So I can't get away," he said, nodding. "I almost did—once. They've been careful since."

"Hey, girl!" A skinny man with a limp and bad

teeth pushed open the curtain and stepped onto the stage. "Get away from it!"

Erik jumped away from her, dropping her wrist in the process. He didn't cower, not quite, but he did retreat from the man as far as his prison allowed. Christine heard a voice behind the curtain say something in a language she didn't recognize, and the man stopped his approach to listen. Erik's eyes darted from her to the man, his back pressed against the bars at the corner of his cell.

Christine gripped her wrist where the knife was strapped, taking comfort in the feel of it beneath her sleeve. She could walk out any time; she wasn't in a cage. The knowledge steadied her, enabling her to put on a small smile to go with her air of curiosity. At least she didn't have to fake it as she waited for the skinny man to continue.

"Were you the one? Singing with it, just now?" The man spoke his broken French with a heavy accent, one she couldn't place.

Nodding, she took a step away from the cell, closer to the man. "Yes. He has the most amazing voice." She pulled the scarf from her head under the pretense of shaking some of the water from it, but Christine knew what the sight of her hair did to men. As her lion's mane of hair tumbled from its confines, Christine watched the limping man from underneath lowered lashes.

"Never heard nobody sing with it before," the man said, his gaze on the wild mane surrounding her face.

Christine saw Erik flinch at the pronoun, but he said nothing. "Oh, that's a shame," she said, making sure her blue eyes were as wide as possible. Let them think her a simple girl, too sheltered or silly for any ulterior motive—that was the first of many lessons her Pappa had taught her. She'd learned it well.

"Everyone's been too afraid to, I'd bet." He wiped his runny nose on the sleeve of his shirt.

"It's just makeup," Christine said with a dismissive gesture towards Erik. "No one could possibly be that ugly!"

The man guffawed. Christine tried not to look at Erik, but she heard the hurt sound that punched out of him at her words. "You're right, miss!" the man said between gales of laughter. "No *living* thing could be that ugly!"

Christine added her tinkling laugh to his, as if oblivious to his joke. Let him think her an idiot, all the better for her. When the laughter died, that foreign voice spoke again, eliciting a strong response from Erik. The young man straightened and yelled, "No! I won't do it!"

"You'll do it if you know what's good for you!" the limping man snapped.

"What did they say?" Christine asked, hands clasped demurely in front of her skirts.

"You wouldn't be interested in earning a bit of extra coin tonight, would you, Mademoiselle?"

Biting her lip, Christine pretended to think the offer over. She risked a glance at Erik, but he refused to look at her. "Doing what?" she asked, voice hesitant.

"Singing, Mademoiselle, nothing more than that. Just as you did before." He smiled, revealing a number of rotting teeth. "Nothing to be worried about."

"Just for one show?" Christine pretended to look around nervously. "I'm already late to get home." She glanced toward the tent flap that led outside and took a tentative step towards it.

The carnival man stepped after her quickly, his hands out in a placating gesture. "Just one show, no more than that!" he assured her, but his eyes gleamed. Christine fought back a grin. He saw money in this and was loath to let it go. He'd agree to practically anything to get her to stay. "You could buy yourself a real treat with it."

She mulled it over, as if the thought of a treat enticed her. "Very well," she finally said, biting back a snarl when he offered her a pittance of a sum for her time. Reminding herself that she wasn't supposed to know any better, Christine simpered at him and accepted the amount.

The man moved over to the cage where Erik now sat huddled in the corner, his head hidden by his arms as they rested on his drawn-up knees. He aimed a kick at Erik's side through the bars.

"We'll need to decide on a song!" Christine broke in, pleased when the man put his foot down without connecting. "Perhaps practice a bit so we get the timing down properly, if that's all right?"

The man nodded and took off toward the back of the tent. "I'll go tell the barker of the change.

Just shout if he gives you any trouble." He threw something back in that foreign language, making Erik flinch again before disappearing behind the curtain.

Christine slumped to the floor of the stage beside the cage with an exhausted sigh. Erik didn't lift his head. As she worked several pins from her hair, Christine thought about what she was doing. Why was she helping this man? What was in it for her? It went against everything she'd been taught, everything she knew about herself. He could offer her nothing, and yet, when she'd heard his voice, it touched something inside her that she'd feared died with her father. She couldn't ignore that.

She couldn't just leave someone with a voice like his in this place to rot. Christine had very few moral compunctions, but this was one. It surprised her.

"Pssst, hey. You there," she whispered, keeping an eye on the back curtain where Erik's keepers were. She held a couple of hairpins in her fist and moved quickly toward the lock on the cage. "Erik!" she snapped when he still hadn't moved.

"What?" he snarled as he raised his head, his face a mask of anger. His brown eye widened when he saw her kneel down, and he scrambled over to her. "What are you doing?"

"Getting you out of here," Christine answered around the pick gripped between her teeth. She bent the metal just as Pappa had taught her years ago. She inserted her makeshift picks into the lock and began to work on opening the cage. "It's what you asked for, right?"

He nodded, black hair falling in his face. "I just never expected you to do it," he said in awe.

"Neither did I," she muttered, but when Erik smirked with one side of his face, Christine knew he'd heard her.

"Where'd you learn to sing like that?" he asked.

"The Palais Garnier," Christine told him, concentrating on listening for the catch of the pick in the lock. She didn't worry about him finding her so she'd told him the truth—if he was smart, he'd put as much distance between himself and Paris as possible. "You?"

Erik shrugged. "I've always sung like this, long as I can remember."

"Sing something now or they'll wonder what we're doing."

"What would you like?"

"Anything!" she snapped, focused on getting the picks in position.

"No need to be surly," Erik reprimanded as though he wasn't the one trapped in a cage. Before she could respond he began to sing a piece from *Carmen*.

Christine wanted to close her eyes and just listen but knew they didn't have time. Still, her voice rose with his without a thought as her fingers did their work. The pick caught. Tongue stuck between her teeth, Christine twisted her wrist and the door sprang open beneath her hands. She pulled it open and moved out of the way to allow Erik room to step outside. He stopped mid-note and glanced at the back of the tent.

Christine beckoned for him to hurry as she reached the end of her line. He stood slowly, his skinny frame tense. He took a step onto the stage, free of the cell and turned to her, smiling.

"Than—"

Christine shoved her scarf at him. "Wrap this around your face and keep your head down. You're lucky it's raining so no one is going to be looking up." When Erik moved too slowly for her liking, she helped him wrap the fabric around his head so that only his eyes were visible.

"That'll have to be enough," she told him as she hurried to the tent flap at the front. Peeking out, she saw it was raining even harder, keeping most people inside tents and off the streets. "Here," she said, shoving her knife into his hand. She had another one stashed in her rooms at Madame Valérius' house and he could use it more right now. "You might need this.".

His fingers closed around the hilt automatically before he tucked it into his pants at the small of his back. His good eye was huge when he stared down at her, like he didn't know what to make of her. "I—"

"Go!" she urged, shoving him out of the tent while there was no one to see. "Before they catch you again!"

Erik gave her one last look before nodding once, firmly. Then he turned on his heel and walked from the tent, as if he was just another carnival guest. Christine followed him out, turned, and went the opposite way, the rain soaking her bare head.

CHAPTER *4*

CHRISTINE SPENT THE NEXT THREE days in bed. Madame Valérius sent for a physician, but the man simply said she'd caught a chill from the weather and they just had to wait for it to run its course. Madame sent word to the opera house of Christine's illness, excusing her until she recovered. At least it meant that she didn't have to wait on the old woman hand and foot so that was a welcome change. Unfortunately, it also meant that Madame Valérius spent all her time in Christine's rooms to keep her company and bolster her spirits. Christine fantasized about stabbing a fork in the woman's thigh—a thought which bolstered her spirits considerably whenever Madame Valérius' chatter became too much.

She was still sniffling when she returned to the Palais Garnier, grateful to escape the too-warm rooms and smothering ministrations of Madame Valérius. It was almost a relief to return to Madame Giry's dreaded cane.

As she made her way to the opera house, Christine wanted out. She felt stuck, trapped by the final con that she and her father had run to ensure her security. Now it chafed at her. Monsieur Valérius had been taken with Pappa's fiddle playing and her father had used the man's delusions of finding the next great musical talent to his advantage. Not that Pappa wasn't talented— Christine had heard enough strangers sing the praises of his voice and his playing to know *that* wasn't a complete sham. Still, Monsieur Valérius had been determined that the rest of the world should know of Pappa's musical genius so he'd paid for them to travel to spread the word.

Pappa hadn't been interested in being seen as a musical prodigy though. His plans were for Christine. With the couple's connections, he'd thought to foster her marriage to a wealthy man, one that would keep them in comfort for the rest of their lives. The Valériuses were only meant to be a starting point in Pappa's plans.

Christine frowned, preferring not to think of the past but unable to help herself. Even when Pappa was coughing up clots of blood, he still played. Christine had taken over the singing by that point, having inherited her father's gift.

Madame Valérius loved to talk about Christine's debut on the stage, dressing her up like a doll, and spending endless hours playing the piano while Christine practiced arias. Before his death, he'd made Monsieur and Madame Valérius her guardians, thinking he was providing for her and giving her more time to find a husband.

Christine had told him she didn't think staying in one place the best idea, especially if it meant she'd end up tied to someone she couldn't stomach but whose bank account made life easy. It was safer going from town to town the way they always had, never staying anywhere long enough to get caught for their thefts. But he'd insisted. "This is a nice deal we have here," he'd told her late one night as she wiped the blood from his lips. "These two were ripe for the plucking and we landed them! Don't go soft on me now."

He'd coughed then, and Christine held the handkerchief up to his mouth once more. Gasping, Pappa said, "Promise me you'll stay, Christine. After I'm gone, you must promise that you'll stay with them and find yourself some security."

"I promise, Pappa," she'd told him, easing his head and shoulders down to the pillows. His skin had taken on a grey cast at the end, sweat plastering the thinning hair to his high forehead. Christine tucked a cool cloth against it and sat by his bedside as he labored for breath.

She'd been around thirteen.

Four years, a move to Paris, and the death of

Monsieur Valérius later, Christine knew she couldn't keep her promise any longer. She had to find a way out from under Madame Valérius' roof. There had been no suitors, and no prospects since that young man she'd met at the seaside. She was tired of being beholden to someone, tired of dancing to their tune rather than the music she heard in her own head.

And if she couldn't find a way, well, she'd just have to make one.

♫♫♫

The chorus was abuzz when Christine arrived. Upon seeing her, Meg broke away from the cluster of girls and grabbed Christine by the elbow, nearly dragging her back to their shared dressing room.

"You have missed practically *everything*!" the tiny girl exclaimed as Christine staggered behind her, unable to even get her coat off.

"I was sick," she told Meg. "From walking home in the rain."

Meg tossed her head so her dark curls fluffed around her face and stuck out her tongue. Christine grinned. "So what did I miss then?" she asked as Meg closed the dressing room door behind them.

As Christine began to change, Meg spoke, her dark face dusky with her flush. "Oh, it's the most wonderful thing, Christine." She moved around the room with a caged, frenetic energy, her high voice breathy. "We have a ghost!"

Christine looked over her shoulder at Meg, lifting one eyebrow skeptically. "A ghost?"

"Yes!" Meg squealed, delighted. "Isn't it exciting?"

"That depends," Christine said, pulling on her skirt. "Does this ghost do anything . . . exciting?"

"Monsieur Buquet said the ghost appeared backstage. Just standing there, plain as day. One moment there and the next—*poof*! Gone!" Meg clapped her hands in glee.

"Buquet is a drunken reprobate who keeps trying to look up our skirts when we practice," Christine said drily. She liked Josef Buquet for the most part. He reminded her of some of the carnival folk she'd grown up around.

"But he wouldn't lie!" When Christine pursed her lips, Meg conceded, "Okay, he would, but not about this. He says he's seen him!"

"The ghost is a him now?"

Meg nodded enthusiastically, getting into her story. "Monsieur Buquet saw him two nights ago as he was putting away some set pieces. He was wearing all black and disappeared behind a flat from *Don Giovanni*."

"And has anyone else seen this ghost?" Christine asked as she fastened her dancing shoes.

Meg nodded. "A couple of the stagehands have mentioned seeing something out of the corner of their eyes, but when they turn to look, nothing's there. Some of the girls have said they've heard footsteps or strange noises." She spun in a circle, dancing skirt flaring wide. "It's just so delicious!"

Sighing, Christine finished with her shoes and stood, brushing a hand down the front of her practice skirt. The girls of the chorus would love this, embellishing this mysterious ghost until he was akin to Satan himself. They, as a group, had imaginations that fed off each other, and Christine expected this *Opera Ghost* would only grow greater with each telling. The Palais Garnier was a massive structure, rife with hidden passages and trapdoors and numerous entrances and exits. Rumors of an underground lake, found during construction, coupled with a staggering number of basements used for storage and who knew what else added to the gothic allure of the place. It was the ideal setting for a ghost story and the chorus girls loved scaring each other.

"How come this ghost only appeared now?" she asked, setting to work on pinning up her hair. "And what does he look like, just so I know to avoid him should I run across him." She was only partly teasing.

Meg pirouetted in a tight circle, as if unable to contain her energy. "Buquet said he was tall and thin and that he didn't have a nose!"

"Everyone has a nose," Christine chided, thinking suddenly of Erik. Meg could have been describing the young man from the carnival if she didn't know any better. But Erik had to be long gone from Paris.

Meg stopped and set her fists on her hips, offended. "A ghost mightn't! They don't need noses—ghosts don't need to breathe!"

Opening the door, Christine shooed the dancer out. "I can find no fault in your logic, Meg. But I don't think your mother is one to excuse tardiness even if the supernatural is involved." The two girls hurried to rehearsal, though Christine wondered if even the Opera Ghost might be afraid of Madame Giry's cane.

Practice proceeded as it always did. Madame Giry worked Christine harder than usual, presumably to make up for her absence of several days. Meg grinned at Christine as Madame Giry made Christine perform the steps again on her own when the rest of the company took a break. It made Christine realize just how much she wanted to get away from the opera house. Being a member of the company was a lot of work for very little reward.

A *bang* sounded from the stage area where the hands assembled the backdrops and flats for the upcoming performance. The girls shrieked and jumped in fright as a loud *boom* followed. "It's the Opera Ghost! He's come to kill us all!" a sniveling girl named Antionette cried, huddling beside another chorus girl. Someone screamed.

Christine rolled her eyes as the girls fluttered and flapped. Meg chattered excitedly beside her, but she didn't listen. Instead she looked up, searching the network of ropes and catwalks that decorated the ceiling of the Palais Garnier's stage. Someone in dark clothes moved carefully above. She couldn't get a clear look at who it was, but she assumed it was one of the stagehands.

"Do you see something?" Meg peered into the darkness above them anxiously. "Do you see *him*?"

"It's just one of the workers," Christine said, turning away as Madame Giry pounded her cane on the floor to get her company's attention. "I'm fairly certain a ghost wouldn't be hanging about in the rafters."

"He might," Meg said with the beginnings of a pout.

"If you were a ghost, would you?" Christine raised her eyebrows.

"No." A sly grin crept across Meg's dusky face. "I'd hang out in the men's dressing room."

Christine raised her hand to her mouth in false shock. Meg nudged her in the side and the two dissolved into laughter. "I bet you would! But what would your mother say, young mademoiselle?"

"How would she know?" Meg returned, dimple winking in her cheek.

"Shush, you. Don't you realize that Madame Giry is all-knowing?" Christine wiggled her fingers like a magician in front of Meg's face. "And that her cane never misses!" She swiped at Meg lazily.

The chorus girl dodged easily. "If I were a ghost, I wouldn't have to be worried about that cane!"

The crack of said cane echoed off the floor once more. "Ladies!"

Christine stifled her good cheer and resumed her place. Madame Giry raised her arms for them to begin, poised to signal the pianist to resume playing, when Joseph Buquet ran in to the salon, white-faced and shaking.

"He's there!" he shouted, pointing up into the rigging.

"Who's there?" Madame Giry looked likely to brain the next person who interrupted her practice.

"The Opera Ghost!" the man said.

The chorus girls descended into excited shrieks and whispers as they all looked at where Buquet pointed. The excitement in the room curled over Christine's skin like a strange caress. No one really believed Buquet, but he did offer something new to brighten up the grind of practices and performances. There was no danger here, just a drunken stagehand making up stories for girls desperate to believe that life still held a hint of mystery and magic.

Christine thought back to her childhood and the tales Pappa used to tell her when she was a girl and they were on the road, looking for their next mark. Tales of ghosts and enchantresses and sea sirens who would lure men to their deaths with only the power of their voices. Haunted tales, some blood-soaked, others less so, but all of them dark and voluptuous and decadent in unique ways that touched some deep place inside of her.

He'd spoken of an Angel of Music too, especially after his illness became too much to hide. He had long talks with Monsieur and Madame Valérius about going to join the Angel after he died, saying his whole line had been blessed by this creature and now he went to join him. One last con in a lifetime full of them.

"Joseph Buquet, you will take yourself away and stop scaring my dancers," Madame Giry burst out as she stalked towards him.

He held his hands up and Christine could see how they shook. "His face," he whispered, his eyes rolling and wild, "I'll never forget his face."

"What did he look like?" one of the chorus girls behind Christine called.

"Thin as a skeleton he was and dressed all in black!" More whispers and titters from the girls, and Christine gritted her teeth to keep from rounding on their foolishness. "His hair—black as death and only on one side of his skull. His face . . ." Buquet trailed off with a shudder.

"Yes, his face! What about his face?" The chorus girls clamored for more. Christine couldn't blame their curiosity, but she felt sick watching it. Would they have gone to the carnival just to ogle the people in the freak tents and giggle?

Buquet suddenly leapt forward, landing in front of Meg and Christine. Meg flinched and screamed, grabbing at Christine's arm in her surprise. Christine recoiled at the smell of cheap wine on his breath and moved a few steps away from him as he gestured broadly.

"Terrible it was. One half of it is normal, which only makes the other side worse. It's the face of a devil!"

Christine's limbs went cold at his words. They

reminded her too much of the sign outside of the carnival tent she'd found Erik in days ago. Erik wouldn't be so stupid as to stay in Paris, and certainly not somewhere as public as the Palais Garnier. Then she recalled his expression as he sang with her while still in that cage. He's been transformed. Even if it was a foolish idea, it made a strange kind of sense. She hadn't risked going back to the carnival, but she'd bet they'd have folk looking for him. He was valuable; they weren't just going to let him go, not if they'd already locked him in a cell to keep him. Erik may not have had money, but she'd given him her knife, so money wouldn't be hard to come by if you had the stomach for it. She glanced up, but saw no sign of a dark figure. It did not comfort her.

As the girls screamed with a mix of delight and fear, Madam Giry interrupted. "That's enough, Monsieur Buquet."

"And his eyes. Oh, his eyes! They burned like the fires of hell!"

"Joseph Buquet, that is *enough*!" Madame Giry's cane slammed into the floor with a deafening *crack*, startling the old man out of his story. Even Madame Giry looked surprised at her vehemence. Her expression changed to one of pity as she took Buquet by the elbow and signaled to the pianist to help her. They escorted the stagehand away with promises of coffee and refreshment.

"See the girls practice, Meg," Giry ordered her daughter as the three exited the room.

"Yes, Madame."

Whispers and murmurings filled the practice space as the chorus girls descended into speculation. Was the Opera Ghost real? How long had it been hanging about before revealing itself? Who was it? The Palais Garnier was a massive edifice and a monumental undertaking of architecture and engineering—could a worker have gone missing during the years of its construction?

One girl, a leggy thing named Giselle, mentioned a theory about a Communist that had died during the revolt, positing it was his restless ghost responsible for the strange happenings. More girls spoke up to offer their opinions, including Meg who trotted out the old chestnut of a young man who pined to death for love of the prima donna. She was shouted down.

"It's just an old drunk seeing things that aren't there and blaming them for his own mistakes," Christine finally snarled, growing tired of the incessant bickering. Her head ached and all she wanted was to be done with practice and back in her own bed. She flounced to her place in the line and stared pointedly at her friend. "Meg?"

As the chorus gathered and took their places, Christine swore she heard a dark trill of disembodied laughter from somewhere above her.

CHAPTER 5

SHE BLAMED MEG FOR this.

Christine turned in the mirror of her dressing room, making sure that she was buttoned and cinched and coiffed to within an inch of her life. She slid on the evening gloves—her one good pair that didn't have holes in the finger seams—and turned to face Meg. "Verdict?"

"Monsieur le Fure won't know where to look!" Meg told her, circling around Christine with a critical eye for detail. "The color would look better on me though."

"You should go out with him then." Christine smoothed the front of the yellow skirt, glimpsing the décolletage the dress displayed. It was one of Madame Valérius' old ones, passed down and tailored to fit Christine. Yellow was not her color, but she didn't have much else to choose from and this dress was the nicest evening one she owned. It would have to do, though Meg was right—it would look amazing against the dancer's brown skin. Christine's shoulders drooped. It wasn't like le Fure was interested in the dress' color, only its contents.

Meg snorted. "Like my mother would ever let me. If she has her way, I won't ever go out to dinner with a man until I've lost all my teeth and I need to drink my food." She adjusted a piece of hair over Christine's shoulder. "There, perfect."

Christine patted at her coif, making sure the pins holding it were secure. Glancing in the mirror, she supposed she looked presentable. The yellow of the dress washed her out, but her blue eyes sparkled above her pert nose and she'd artfully applied some of the makeup they used in the chorus to flush her cheeks and stain her lips.

"Be glad your mother watches out for you," Christine admonished, trying to keep the fear and resentment from her voice. She had finally accepted le Fure's invitation because the feeling of being trapped in a life she didn't want had become unbearable. She wanted out of the opera, away from Madame Valérius before it became too late for her. If having a wealthy patron enabled her to make a future that was hers and not governed by her dead father's schemes or her guardian's dreams then she had no choice but to take it.

"But you get to go and dance and drink and have a handsome man compliment you and spend money on you," Meg dreamed, still in her costume from the last act of *Jérusalem*.

"That's not all I'll be doing," Christine said sourly, then bit her lip at revealing too much. It was a mistake she couldn't afford. She smiled to cover her misstep.

Meg's dark face turned serious and she placed a gentle hand on Christine's arm. "If you don't want to do this, you don't have to, Christine."

Christine turned, pulling away from Meg as she did so. She couldn't bear to see the pity in her friend's eyes. "Yes, I do," she told Meg.

"Is it really so terrible, being here?" Meg fluffed the back of Christine's dress even though Christine doubted it needed it.

Leaning into the mirror, she checked her makeup, clearing a small smudge at the corner of one blue eye with the pad of her ring finger. Keeping her expression neutral, Christine met Meg's eyes in the mirror. "Not all the time, and not with you here," she said to soften the harshness of her previous words. "But I don't want this to be my life."

"I don't understand you sometimes," Meg said, watching her worriedly. "I've heard you sing— *really* sing—before, but you don't do sing like that here. Why not? You could be really good!"

"Really good isn't good enough." She shook her head gently. "You have to be great to be a Prima Donna. I know I can't match Carlotta, not without a teacher, and I don't even know if there's one good enough who would want to take me on." A knock at the door interrupted her. "If I want out," Christine said, breaking eye contact with Meg as she crossed the room to open the door, "I have to find another way."

She saw Meg's mouth open in protest, but Christine opened the door to cut her off. Monsieur le Fure stood at the threshold holding an obscene amount of flowers cradled in his hands. He passed them to her with a deep bow. "Mademoiselle Daaé, you are breathtaking as always."

Christine made sure to coo over the flowers even though she hated the things. To her it was stupid to pay money for things which grew freely only to have them die after a few days. A walk in a garden was far preferable to vased corpses, or so she thought. She bustled about for a container with Meg's help.

Le Fure was a stocky man in his middle thirties. He still possessed a lustrous head of dark hair and wore a neatly groomed beard and mustache. While not nobility, he'd become accepted by the upper echelon of Paris society due to his wealth and financial investing acumen and his patronage of the arts. He had a name for being a collector of beautiful things, the more esoteric the better. He had never been married, though a number of well-connected women had tried their hands at seducing the entrepreneur with no rumored success.

He was also an inveterate social climber. Everyone who was anyone held boxes in the Palais Garnier, so of course, le Fure had done his best to secure one. The best ones were already spoken for, but le Fure had managed to gain one of the lesser boxes. Many in the nobility had mistresses among the actresses and singers in the company; le Fure had set about securing one of those as well.

Christine had been amused when he'd first begun to pursue her. She'd even encouraged him, falling into the same patterns she and her father had once used to ensnare others. A smile here, a fleeting touch there, laughing at his witty remarks, breaking away to leave him wanting more, pretending to a vulnerability she didn't feel. But soon his persistence grated on her nerves and she tried to distance herself from le Fure only to have his ardor for her increase. The more unavailable and intractable she became, the more patient he seemed to become in response. She hid her distress, knowing at the back of her mind that one day she might want to make use of his feelings for her, continuing to play the game of hide and seek that le Fure so loved.

When the flowers were dealt with, Meg approached Christine with her evening wrap as Monsieur le Fure offered his arm to her. "Thank you, Mademoiselle Giry," Christine said as she lifted the section of hair that she'd kept loose.

Meg fussed a bit, leaning in close. "Just remember, you can always change your mind,"

Meg whispered in her ear as she helped Christine on with the wrap. "Be careful." She kissed Christine on the cheek.

Christine wanted to tell her it was well past the time for care. She was seventeen, no longer a new face in the chorus. Time slipped through her fingers. Instead she returned Meg's kiss, barely brushing the other girl's cheek with her lips so as not to mar her makeup and returned, "Everything will be fine. Don't fret."

As she left the room with her hand resting on Monsieur le Fure's forearm, Christine tried to feel like she hadn't just crossed a bridge over which there was no returning.

The feeling only grew stronger as they made their way to the Grand Foyer. Attendees of the evening's performance congregated and mingled in the opulent space. As she descended the massive staircase on le Fure's arm, Christine couldn't help but scan the faces of those assembled. Gathered here were the uppercrust of Parisian society, rubbing shoulders as they tried to impress each other. Christine's fingers twitched with the thought of all the pockets she could pick among the press of people.

They'd nearly reached the main floor when her attention was caught by the call of a familiar name. She turned her head as the patron cried again, "Comte de Chagny!"

Christine watched the corpulent man trundle toward an imposing gentleman dressed in impeccable evening wear. The company's premiere dancer, La Sorelli, graced Phillipe's—the Comte de Chagny--arm in a fashionable green gown. His dark skin and light eyes were similar to his younger brother, Raoul, and Christine glanced around—both hopeful and anxious—to see if he had attended along with Philippe.

"You're clutching my arm rather hard," Monsieur le Fure chuckled, patting her hand. "Don't worry, my dear. I have no intention of leaving you."

Drawing in a calming breath, Christine consciously relaxed her grip on le Fure's arm and gave him a weak smile. A confusing mix of disappointment and relief filled her to find that Raoul was not among those with the Comte's retinue. It had been years since she'd seen him—she might not even recognize him now, though a part of her doubted that. Pappa had taken a special interest in Raoul—and his title and money—so Christine had been forced to as well. It didn't mean she hadn't enjoyed his company for its own sake.

"Mademoiselle? Are you feeling well?" le Fure asked when she'd paused her steps for too long.

"Quite well, Monsieur," Christine assured him smoothly, shaking herself from her memories. She allowed him to lead her out of the Palais Garnier without a look back at the Comte de Chagny, vowing to put Raoul out of her mind.

♫♫♫

49

Christine dipped her spoon into her bowl of potage á la crécy and did her best not to yawn in Monsieur le Fure's face as he droned on and on about fabric dyes. She smiled and nodded at what she deemed appropriate times during his monologue and asked leading questions that enabled him to expound on his knowledge while she lost herself in memories of a much more innocent time.

She didn't know why she'd been surprised to see the Comte de Chagny in the Grand Foyer as she left the Palais Garnier with le Fure. It was common knowledge that de Chagny's mistress numbered among the singers, but Christine had only ever glimpsed him in his box. Seeing him as she walked out on le Fure's arm had been a shock but seeing Raoul would have been worse.

They'd been children, playing together on the beaches of Brittany. Raoul had been out with his governess on the day Christine lost her scarf in the sea. Well, on the day her father had plucked it from around her neck and let the wind carry it away. Raoul had gone wading in, ignoring the protests of his governess, to get it back for her. They'd been fast friends ever since.

At least until the day he'd suddenly left. Christine didn't know what had caused him to depart the coast without even a word of goodbye, but her father had suspected it had something to do with Raoul's growing friendship with Christine. She'd cried herself to sleep that night, resentment of her father and his ways adding another brick in the wall around her heart.

"My dear, you've hardly touched a thing," Monsieur le Fure admonished as the waiter swept her soup away and replaced it with the next course.

"I'm terribly sorry," Christine apologized even though she rankled at the tone in his voice, like her lack of appetite was an affront to him. "I find I don't have much appetite after a performance." A polite lie, but acceptable. Usually she was starving.

"You need to keep your strength up," le Fure admonished, his expression barely avoiding that of a leer.

"I just find your conversation so fascinating that it completely skips my mind to eat," she complimented, doing her best not to retch.

The lamb shank with creamed pearl onions and leafy greens turned her stomach, but she forced herself to eat. Prompting the man with questions helped distract him as she carved off pieces of meat and moved them strategically around her plate to make it appear like she was eating. She hated lamb, but le Fure hadn't asked for her preferences when he'd ordered for her.

Her thoughts strayed to Erik suddenly and the rumors of the Opera Ghost. Buquet's description had been uncannily like Erik. Had the man been to the carnival before Erik's escape and seen him? Had Buquet's alcohol-addled brain used that experience to fill in his hallucinations? Or had he actually seen someone who looked like Erik on the catwalks of the opera house?

The idea was ridiculous. Erik would have been foolish to stay in the city, no matter how well-hidden he might think he was. He'd have to go out eventually and when he did, everyone who saw him would remember him. Lord knows, she did.

It wasn't that she was worried he might be found and offer up her name as an accomplice to his escape. No one would believe him anyway. And his face, while hideous, didn't frighten her, not as much as cold or hunger did. Those she'd experienced and she knew just how harrowing they could be. A scarred and twisted face was not particularly frightening in comparison. It was the feeling that seeing him in that cage filled her with that was so unbearable. She felt a strange kinship towards him, trapped as he was in a life not of his choosing. She felt she owed him somehow, and she hated that feeling more than almost anything else.

"—heard of the Exposition," he said as Christine dabbed at her lips with her napkin, "which is sure to bring even more people than last year. You'll be attending, of course?"

She'd only been halfway paying attention. Christine smiled and nodded, having no idea what she was supposed to be attending.

"Perhaps you'd care to accompany me?"

"To the Exposition?" she asked archly, widening her eyes slightly.

Le Fure shifted in his seat. Christine smiled,

slow and sweet as honey dripping from a comb. He cleared his throat, then leaned forward to close the distance between them. He reached and ran a finger down her gloved hand. "To many places, my dear. But first, to the Exposition Universelle."

Christine suppressed a shudder at his touch. She lowered her gaze, dropping her eyelids to veil her eyes shyly. "I hear they've got a female sharpshooter from America at a Wild West show. I expect that would be quite fascinating to see," she murmured.

"A woman with a pistol? Nonsense!" He laughed heartily, dropping his napkin to the floor. As he bent to pick it up, he also slipped a hand beneath Christine's skirt to slide a hand up her ankle and calf.

She bit the inside of her cheek, but managed not flinch out of his grasp. The touch only lasted a moment, but to Christine it felt like a year. What would being his mistress feel like? How was she supposed to get through a night with him when she could barely tolerate the briefest of his touches?

When he returned to the table, le Fure wore a suggestive grin. Swallowing, Christine gave him a shaky smile before quickly downing the rest of her wine. She was going to need some liquid courage to get through this evening. Le Fure refilled her glass.

"Drink up, Miss Daaé. The night is still young."

They finished their meal, though Christine

hardly tasted any of the little she managed to choke down. She'd slowed down on the wine once her head started to feel a bit muzzy. Monsieur le Fure helped her into her wrap and suggested they take a carriage ride.

"That sounds lovely," she answered smoothly though she didn't feel like sharing any enclosed space with the man. Climbing into the coach, she worried that she was getting herself into a situation she couldn't handle. She went over everything her father taught her to calm her nerves. She settled, smoothing her skirt over her legs as she released her held breath. The carriage began to move.

Christine shifted nervously on the coach's velvet seating. Le Fure had instructed his coachman to drive around the circle of the opera house so they might enjoy the night air a bit longer, but Christine knew the unspoken meaning behind the request. Besides, it was drizzling.

It was time for her to earn her dinner and a bit more besides.

The disappointment she felt at the location surprised her. Christine wasn't sure what she'd been hoping for—perhaps a hotel suite or somewhere with a bed, at least—but she supposed inside a moving coach made a certain amount of sense for their first time. She hadn't expected him to bring her to his lodgings right away.

Le Fure took her hand. Christine allowed him to, lowering her lashes and giving him an encouraging smile. She could do this. Being his mistress meant gifts: jewelry, clothes, things she could sell for money. She kept telling herself this was a scam of a different sort, though not much different than those she and her father had done. It was almost like his plan to marry her off to a wealthy man—just another trade of goods for services.

It wasn't *that* different at all.

"You must allow me to tell you again how ravishing you look this evening," le Fure whispered against the silk of her evening glove. He pressed kisses to her knuckles, before moving up her hand. He turned her arm so that he could mouth at the underside of her wrist. She suppressed a shudder as his humid breath and the dampness of his mouth made the fabric stick to her skin unpleasantly.

"You have already said so a number of times, Monsieur," she told him, trying to pull her arm from his grip surreptitiously and failing. "But a woman never tires of hearing she's beautiful."

Le Fure slid closer until his hip was pressed against hers through the layers of her skirts. He kissed his way up her arm to her shoulder, pushing aside her wrap as he went. Christine tried to stay relaxed, but her body tensed of its own accord. Her shoulders rose until they nearly touched her ears, denying him access to her neck.

"Monsieur, please, you overwhelm me," she gasped, placing her hand against his chest and pressing him back. She needed a moment to brace herself for what was to come. If he would just give her that . . .

"Good," he whispered in her ear, his tongue tracing the edge of it. Christine closed her eyes as her stomach turned, the food she'd managed to eat at dinner in danger of making a reappearance. "I want to overwhelm you."

Rolling her eyes would have killed the mood almost as quickly as that terrible response, so she refrained. Still, what little enthusiasm Christine might have mustered for this enterprise died a grisly death then and there. Meg's words rattled around in her head: *You can always change your mind.*

"You flatter me," she whispered, wiggling away until she was trapped against one side of the carriage in a bid to gain time. Her calculating brain screamed at her that this was no different than when she and Papa used their musical talent to draw people in to make money and then pick their pockets.

"I'll do more than that, my dear," le Fure replied, inching forward until he was once again crowding her. "Just one word and I'll shower you with anything you could ever want."

Christine's lips curled in a smile. She could want an awful lot.

Still, their first coupling should be somewhere nicer than a cramped coach cabin in the rain. Christine decided to risk it: le Fure would either order the driver to take them to a hotel or they'd agree on the date of their next assignation. Either way, it bought Christine a space of time to get her thoughts in order.

"Gustave," she said, wincing when he bit down too firmly on her earlobe. If he kept that up, he was going to swallow her earring, and she liked the pair, cheap paste jewels though they were. She pushed at his shoulders lightly, just a touch too hard to be playful. "I really would prefer waiting for a proper bed."

Le Fure reached up between their bodies. Christine thought he might cup her cheek or brush the hair from her face; she wasn't expecting him to grab the lower part of her jaw in a painfully tight grip, his fingers and thumbs digging into the hinges of it.

"I think I've waited long enough, Miss Daaé." His brown eyes were dark, his face in shadow as he lowered his head to kiss her.

With his hand on her jaw, Christine couldn't close her mouth to deny him. Instead, she reached down, hooking her fingernails so her hands looked like claws and grabbed at the spot between his legs. His breeches were thick so Christine couldn't get a good hold, but she yanked at what she could grab. Le Fure choked and jerked away from her.

"Harridan!" he snarled, his arm flying out in a backhand that struck her cheek.

Christine gasped, more surprised than hurt. Using her rising anger, she shoved him as hard as she could. Le Fure sat between her and the door to the carriage which was still rolling despite the fracas inside the cab. It likely wouldn't stop unless le Fure ordered it to, and he was unlikely to do that.

"I *changed* my mind," Christine snapped, breathing heavily. Ridiculous dresses made fighting nearly impossible in cramped spaces like this. Her range of movement and ability to draw breath were severely curtailed.

"I won't be made a laughingstock by some chit of a chorus girl who thinks she can get something for nothing." His hand covered his privates for protection.

"You bought me dinner, not the Imperial Diamond!" she countered, hopping over to the opposite bench. From there, she could at least raise her leg and get to her knife, currently strapped to her thigh under layers of skirt. Christine wished she'd worn a hat; what she wouldn't give for a hatpin right now.

He lunged toward her, not giving her a chance to get her hand even close to her knife. Christine flung herself at the door's handle, one hand closing around it even as le Fure's arms tightened around her waist. He tried to drag her back. She held onto the handle with both hands, kicking and bucking to free her lower body from his grip.

She heard le Fure curse as she managed to kick him in the chest. His grasp relented, giving her the chance to pull herself further away from him. Panting, Christine swung the door open. The wet night air was a welcome relief after the closed heat of the carriage interior. Rain splashed her face as she hauled her body away from him.

Christine looked down. She was now half-in and half-out of the coach, one hand braced against the side while the other still held the door handle in a tight grip. The ground looked very far away.

"Get back in here," le Fure snapped, still holding onto one ankle.

Christine thought quickly, her mind working to assess the situation. Whatever gentleness might have accompanied their first encounter was gone now, as was whatever hope she might have for a continued, mutually beneficial relationship. She'd begun this endeavor as a way to get out of one situation she had little say in; Christine had no intention of going into another that offered her even less control. All of which left her few options.

"I wish you a pleasant evening, Monsieur le Fure," she said sweetly as she reclaimed her ankle from his loosening grasp.

"Are you mad?" he shouted as she gathered her feet under her and jumped from the still-moving carriage.

CHAPTER 6

JUMPING OUT OF A CARRIAGE did not fall on a list of things Christine ever wanted to try. She knew enough to leap out rather than just letting herself fall so that she didn't get caught under the back wheels of the coach, but that didn't mean she was at all prepared for the experience of actually doing it. Or for the pain that came with it.

She tried to roll as she landed hard on her knees but only managed to bang her chin on the cobblestones even as her palms slapped down to break her momentum. Her mouth filled with blood when she bit the side of her cheek and tongue. Christine barely felt it; instead she pushed herself back to her feet and took off when she heard the coachman pull the horses to a stop.

Rage and terror propelled her forward. How dare he touch her like he had any right to at all! She was not a thing to be collected, a pretty doll that could be bent and shaped to another's will! What if she hadn't been able to fight back? Did he really think he had the right to force something on her that she did not want?

Her booted feet pounded against the earth, a percussive counterpoint to her spiraling thoughts. The dress made it hard to breathe, but Christine didn't care. She had to get away from that coach, away from le Fure. It didn't matter that the clatter of hooves and the rattle of wheels no longer followed her. She knew in the darkest part of her soul that he could still come after her, still find her if he wanted to, and he could . . .

Christine cried out as her heel got stuck on an uneven cobble causing her ankle to twist painfully. She fell, off balance, and landed on her hip and shoulder. She lay there for a moment, gasping, as tears and sweat ran unheeded down her face. Her ankle throbbed in time with her racing heartbeat. She reached down and rubbed at the soreness through the leather of her boot, feeling a sob work its way up her throat.

She squeezed her ankle tightly and swallowed down the burn of pain. The sharp burst of sensation calmed her clamoring mind, giving her a new clarity. It was something to focus on, to use. Christine took a few noisy breaths and ordered herself not to weep. Crying was useless.

Her dress was ruined, at least that was

something. She'd ripped the skirt in several places when she'd jumped from the carriage and landed on the cobbles. The yellow silk was water-stained and filthy. If anyone saw her, they'd think she was exactly what she almost became tonight. Her laugh held a hysterical edge, and she wanted to hang her head and cry for some indeterminate period of time.

Instead, she rooted through her skirts to find the small knife strapped to her leg. Holding it in her hand made her feel better. Christine took several watery breaths, and then looked around to get her bearings. She couldn't go back to Madame Valérius' house in this condition, and certainly not with this ankle. But she wasn't far from the Palais Garnier, thank goodness. The gate at the Rue Scribe was only a short walk to her right which would let her inside the lower level of the opera house if it was unlocked. She could make her way to her dressing room through the warren of backstage and subterranean passages once inside.

Christine's knees shook as she climbed painfully to her feet, trying not to put too much weight on her turned ankle. Knife clutched in one hand, she began to hobble toward the back gate. She could rest in her dressing room, change clothes, and clean up a bit. That was the best she could do with circumstances being what they were. The methodical approach helped her keep her growing panic at bay.

The gate appeared, sooner than she was

expecting, lost in her thoughts as she was. Christine sighed with relief as she sagged against the metal, her free hand clutching one of the bars. The gate moved beneath her hand, soundlessly, causing her to stumble. She caught herself before she fell, but she put more weight on her bad ankle and her leg buckled. Her eyes watered with the pain, teeth burying themselves in her lower lip to stifle her outcry.

She closed the gate behind her as she hobbled along, too focused on not doing further damage to her ankle than to pay attention to her surroundings. Madame Giry was not going to be pleased if Christine couldn't dance on it in practice, though that would be nothing in comparison to her rage if Christine couldn't perform.

A dark shape reared up in front of her, grasping her upper arms in a tight, painful grip. Christine couldn't stop the scream that escaped her as someone yanked her close. She dropped her knife. The heavy scent of cheap wine stung her nose. She saw wide, wild eyes, the whites standing out from the shadowy darkness of the corridor.

Terror struck Christine. Her mouth went dry and her heart slammed against the walls of her chest. All the creatures from her father's strange tales reared up inside her imagination. Dark things, monsters, giants, and ghosts clutched at her. Her breathing sounded labored in her ears and her throat closed up, making it hard to breathe. The darkness rattled her, combining with the violence of the night, and she struggled fiercely to break free.

"You've seen him!" the creature that held her shouted, shaking Christine until she feared her head would snap from her neck. "What he is?"

"Let go!" This was too much like what had happened in the carriage.

He began to drag her by her arms, pulling her off-balance. Christine tried to right herself, putting more weight on her bad ankle. Pain ripped through her, all the way to her knee. She screamed again, and would have fallen if not for the hands forcing her upright. Tears spilled down her cheeks. Panic blinded her.

"What do you know of the demon!" the monster raged. "You're in league with him!"

"Nothing!" Christine shouted back, the wetness of her tears chilling her face in the subterranean tunnel. "I don't know anything, I swear!!" What demon was he speaking of? Was he mad? How would she know anything?

The pain of his grip became excruciating as he continued to drag her forward. Christine fought against him, throwing her weight backwards with all her strength to slow their progress. She jerked hard, sending them both toppling over. Her breath blasted out of her as she hit the ground— for the third time that night—and her head bounced off the compacted earth when the man landed on top of her.

Her hands scrabbled out in search of anything

that could be used as a makeshift weapon but found nothing. The man sat on her legs, pinning her beneath the weight of his body. Grabbing at her shoulders, he continued to shake her, slamming her back into the floor with every frenzied movement.

"Tell me!" he shouted into her face, eyes gleaming with madness and horror. "What does he want with me?" His hands wrapped around her neck.

Christine recognized the twisted face of Joseph Buquet above her. He bore little resemblance to the stagehand she knew: his lined face twisted in fear and suspicion, the skin sallow with drink and lack of sleep, his eyes red rimmed and bloodshot. The stink of his breath in her face made her choke. His body held a manic strength, and Christine flailed around for anything that might get him off her. His hands slowly tightened around her throat.

She felt something rough and hard beneath her straining fingertips. Wrapping her hand around the loose brick, Christine brought it up with all of her might, the fear-driven strength powering her right arm. She brought the brick down onto Buquet's temple as hard as she could, striking with a dull thudding sound. Buquet immediately went limp, falling to the side with the momentum of the blow. Something dark and wet slid from his hairline into the dry ground.

Scrambling out from beneath him, Christine scooted backwards on her bottom until she hit something hard and could move no further. Her gasps came out more like sobs and she couldn't seem to stop shaking, even while she clutched the brick in her hand. She was going to throw up or faint, the panic filling her mouth with a sour taste.

Another, darker shadow detached itself in the dim light. The scarred face of Erik stared down at her as she trembled, before he knelt just out of arm's reach and said in a wondering voice, "Christine? What are you doing here?"

She surprised Erik—but most of all herself—when she answered him by bursting into tears.

"What are *you* doing here?" she half-sobbed, half-screamed, unable to stop her hysterics. Seeing him there, in the Opera House, was the final shock in a night full of them. "You were supposed to get away from Paris!" Sudden fury filled her. Why had she even bothered to free him if he was only going to be stupid enough to stay where he could get caught again?

He ducked back, good eye widening in surprise. "If I tell you, will you put down the brick?"

She hadn't realized she'd still been holding it, let alone brandishing it at him. It fell from her nerveless fingers, hitting the ground with a *thunk* similar to the noise it made when she struck Buquet. Christine flinched, bile climbing up the back of her throat. Her hands flew to her mouth and she swallowed hard.

"Thank you," Erik said when she was disarmed, and she found his solemn politeness terribly funny. Her choked laughter bubbled around her fingers, and she felt unable to stop it.

Erik leaned forward now that the danger of her braining him with a brick had passed and peered into her face. He glanced back at the man lying on the ground before turning back to her. "Did he hurt you?"

Christine shook her head with a hiccup, her fingers still pressed to her lips. "No, I don't think so," she managed to get out, speaking softly. Her back and head ached, but she didn't think anything was broken. Her throat felt sore. Her ankle still bothered her more than anything.

"Is he dead?" she squeaked, doing her best to shrink into the wall at her back.

"I'll check." Christine watched Erik walk over to Buquet's prone form and feel around the man's neck for a pulse. He stilled, a darker shadow hunched over a body, like a vampire from a penny dreadful. He said nothing for a long moment.

After a minute or two, her mounting frustration got the better of her. "Well?"

"He's dead." Erik looked over at her from his crouch by the body, his black hair falling across the scarred part of his face. "Definitely."

Christine clapped her hands back over her mouth. "I think I'm going to be sick," she moaned.

Erik hurried to her side, kneeling before her. He placed gentle hands on her drawn-up knees and soothed, "Hey, *hey*. Just breathe. You need to breathe."

At first his words made little sense to her, just a jumble of noises in the cacophony going on inside her skull. As he continued to talk softly to her, Christine felt the panic ebb away, leaving her wrung out and exhausted. Her hands fell into her lap as she slumped against the wall. The events of the evening finally hit her with the force of a falling tree, leaving her with no reserves. Her eyelids drooped and it was all she could do to keep them open.

Erik seemed to understand. He moved slowly, carefully gathering her up in his arms and rising smoothly to his feet. Christine nuzzled into the warmth of him, only realizing how wet and cold she was from her walk in the rain. Shivers wracked her and she felt Erik's arms tighten their hold.

"I've got you," he murmured into her hair.

"Hmmmm." Christine fought the weariness that pulled at her, desperate to keep her eyes open to see where Erik was taking her. It was funny, she felt safer in his presence than she'd felt the entire night in le Fure's.

Then Erik raised his golden voice in a gentle lullaby and Christine fell into sleep.

CHAPTER 7

CHRISTINE WOKE TO THE most amazing music she'd ever heard. She didn't move at first, thinking she must be in her dressing room, listening to a rehearsal of some new opera she was unfamiliar with. As she listened, she soon realized that there was no way Signor Piangi, the tenor who always sang opposite Carlotta, could sing something of this complexity and power.

Upon opening her eyes, Christine realized she had no idea where she was. She took a moment to just be still and look around for clues as to where she might be. The room was dark, lit only by a few oil lamps. She could barely make out the walls of the room in their dim light. An old trifold screen separated this part of the room from the next—a discarded prop from an opera fallen out of favor. There was a tear in the left-most side, and through it Christine could make out someone moving in the space beyond this one.

She sat up slowly, mindful of her aching body. She'd been asleep on a cot, wrapped in an old blanket she thought she recognized from Carlotta's dressing room. It had gone missing while Christine had been ill and recovering at Madame Valérius' house, but Meg had filled her in on the drama the soprano had caused with her accusations of the chorus girls stealing it out of jealousy. Meg had offhandedly mentioned a ghost having done it, but Christine hadn't paid attention then.

She was paying attention now.

The air was humid, making her still damp clothes feel clammy against her skin, despite the warmth of the worn but heavy fabric. Her stomach twisted as she swung her legs over the edge of the cot and wondered how she'd gotten wherever she was. She coughed and thought her head might explode as pain made colors dance across her closed eyelids.

The singing stopped and Erik's frightening face appeared from the other side of the screen. "You're awake," he said, his gorgeously rich voice echoing in the chamber strangely. "How are you feeling?"

"Better," she told him. "Where are we?"

"Were you aware there's a lake beneath the opera house?" He grinned like an excited child.

"There's an island with a small house—really more of a big room—on it. I think it might have been where the architect or master builder lived when the Palais Garnier was being built. That's where we are—several basements beneath the actual opera house." His good eye narrowed as he assessed her, before it crinkled in a small smile. "Forgive my manners. Would you like something to eat?"

Christine nodded, thinking food might help with the headache, if she could keep it down. She'd known the Palais Garnier was huge—there was a stable set up in one of the lower basements where they kept the horses used in performances—but this was beyond what she'd ever imagined. Just how extensive were the Palais Garnier's secret corridors and did anyone know the extent of these subterranean spaces?

Erik ducked behind the screen again, only to reappear a few minutes later with a plate that contained half a loaf of crusty bread, two apples, a small wedge of cheese, and a pear. In his other hand, he carried a bottle. He sat and placed the plate and bottle on the floor between them.

Christine slid from the cot, shivering when the cold of the floor seeped through the blanket. She ignored it in favor of being closer to the food. Reaching out, she grabbed the bread and ripped a hunk out of it, then went back for a piece of fruit, eyeing Erik the entire time. He simply watched and waited.

"I thought you would have fled Paris at the first

opportunity," she said after several minutes of silence while she demolished the bread. She bit into a pear. Her teeth broke the thin skin, tearing into the pale flesh of the fruit so that juice dribbled from the side of her mouth. She wiped it away with the back of her hand.

Folding his long legs up so he appeared smaller, Erik shrugged. "I didn't have money," he told her. "And I remembered you saying you were with the Opera. I thought I could hide here, perhaps make a little coin. I have a good voice."

"They'd never hire you," Christine said before she thought better of it. "And I gave you my knife. You could have gotten money."

Erik's good eye went wide, like she'd said something shocking. "I'm not going to kill someone!" he protested.

Christine rolled her eyes at his affronted expression, as if he were too good for robbery. "You don't have to kill anyone. Just wave the knife in their faces and they'll give you whatever they've got on them." She licked the fingers of one hand clean of juice. "In a situation like yours, one can't afford to be picky."

"No," he said, his head low. "I won't be a bully." Both of her knives rested on the floor beside the nearly empty plate. He must have gone back to pick up the one she'd dropped when Buquet grabbed her.

Chewing absently, Christine tapped her finger against her lips. No, she supposed he wouldn't, not after his time in a cage. "How badly did they treat you at the carnival?" She remembered the way his keeper had shoved him and the threatening words spoken in a language she didn't understood.

He sighed. "Not badly, not at first." Erik drew music notes in the dust on the floor with his index finger, humming softly. "But then I didn't understand much of what was said."

"But you do now," she confirmed, and he nodded. "How did you come to be with them anyway?" Asking him questions meant she didn't have to answer any uncomfortable ones he might have for her. She settled the blanket more securely about her shoulders and moved so she had a better view of his face. It was unsettling to look at—one half perfectly formed, the other half a horror, but his hair thankfully hid the worst of it.

He wouldn't look at her directly, angling his face so the worst of it was hidden mostly in shadow. Every time she moved, he adjusted unconsciously, as if he were so used to hiding he didn't know how to stop. "My father sold me to them."

Christine choked on her fruit. Erik jerked to his knees, hands outstretched to help her, but she waved him away. He offered her the bottle of watered wine instead. She accepted it with another cough and took a swig. "What?"

He glanced up, holding her gaze with his mismatched eyes. "My mother had died a few months before we went to the carnival. She'd been the one who'd gone to doctors to see what could be done for," Christine watched as he gestured toward his face, "this, but the operations never helped much. My father just made me wear a mask when we went out."

Taking up a knife, Erik began to carve slices out of an apple. He held one out to her. Christine took it from between his fingertips, watching him as he went back to slice a piece for himself. "It came loose as we were walking. I remember some woman screaming—I think someone fainted. People crowded around me. It scared me—you see, I wasn't allowed out much because of my . . . condition." He shrugged. "So I ran."

"Your father didn't search for you?" Christine asked, disgust and understanding warring in her chest. Her Pappa would never have gone anywhere without her; she was simply too valuable. She supposed he loved her too, but most of their cons were easier to run with two people. Though if she looked like Erik, he might have been less sad about parting.

Shaking his head, Erik put down the knife. "One of the carnival people talked to him when he was picking up my mask. Asked him about me. Said there was a lot of money to be made off a face like mine." As Christine watched, Erik bit his lip and lowered his head. "My father was upset after my mother died—it hit him hard. He wasn't thinking clearly. And it was hard, I think, looking at me."

Christine couldn't help the shocked squeak

74

that escaped her lips at Erik's words. He was making excuses for his father abandoning him in that place? She saw the points of his jaw tighten with the clench of his teeth and forced herself to calm down. It made sense, the lies people told themselves to live with the unthinkable. She suspected Erik had to make up something to keep from going mad when he'd been caged. A made-up story to excuse the inexcusable, to protect the mind and heart and make horrors easier to bear seemed ideal.

"So he sold you?" she asked, still not quite believing it.

"They told him they would take excellent care of me," Erik said. He seemed composed, but Christine saw the long, graceful fingers of one hand drumming across his knee. "And they did, at first."

"How old were you?"

A shrug. "Perhaps nine. I'm not entirely certain." He snagged the bottle and took a drink. Christine watched his long throat work as he swallowed. What must it have been like for him?

"All I really understood was that my father was gone, just like my mother. I tried to escape several times, but they were always watching me. It got worse when they discovered I could sing."

"What happened then?" Christine leaned forward, wanting the rest of the story, fascinated by the details, and by the lilting cadence of Erik's voice. How could someone sound like he did with a face like his?

He gathered up the plate, empty but for some crumbs and the fruit cores, his face shuttered and dark. "I've talked enough," he told her in a stern voice, and Christine knew better than to press, even though she wanted to. There was a coiled tension to his body that she was wary of. "How is your ankle?"

Christine went still. Her ankle. The carriage and le Fure. The cobbles and the gate. Then Buquet and the darkness. Until, finally, Erik. She remembered it all in blazing detail once again and felt queasy.

She turned it slowly, teeth gritted to stifle any outcry, but all she felt was a twinge. It surprised her, considering how much it had hurt when she'd twisted it. "I think it's all right. A bit sore," she said, relief filtering into her voice. Madame Giry would cane her if she couldn't dance on it for the performance.

"How did you injure it? Was it that man—Joseph Buquet?" Erik moved behind the screen. Christine heard him setting things down and slowly climbed to her feet, using the cot to steady herself. She put some of her weight on her bad ankle and it held firm. It ached, but not terribly.

"No, it was before that. I jumped out of a moving carriage."

Erik's head popped back around the screen, his brown eye wide. "That's not terribly safe."

"Neither was staying in the carriage."

"Ah." He came back into the room and leaned his shoulder against a wall, waiting for her to continue. He surprised her by not asking invasive questions.

Christine shifted out of the blanket to look down at her ruined dress with a sigh. "How long have I been here?"

Erik twisted around to consult a small clock on a crate. Most of the items in this hovel looked to have been scavenged or stolen from dressing rooms or forgotten props in the depths of the opera house. Meg's talk of the Opera Ghost began to make much more sense now. "Not quite twelve hours."

Christine sank down onto the cot with a groan, threading her fingers into her wild mass of hair. It had come undone in all of the struggles of the night before. "I'm ruined."

Erik cocked his head in confusion, stepping closer. Christine noticed that he took pains not to loom over her despite his height. "Ruined? Why?"

"I missed practice and did not send a note." Madame Giry had expelled girls for much less. Christine had no doubt that the woman would have already begun the search for her replacement. "And if Meg told her who I was seeing, I'm sure she assumes the worst of me." And Meg would tell her mother of Christine's dinner with Monsieur le Fure, of that Christine had little doubt. The girl was an unapologetic gossip.

"The carriage?" Erik asked, understanding. At her nod, he moved until he sat at her feet. "There's got to be something we can do."

"Short of saying the chorus girls' Opera Ghost abducted me, I can't think of anything that will explain my absence," she told him absently, already working through and discarding possible excuses.

"Well, why not?"

Christine inspected her dress, wracking her brain for ideas on how to get out of this mess. Madame Valérius only allowed her out of the house to attend rehearsals and lessons and performances—if she didn't have those, she'd be trapped taking care of the woman until Madame finally died. She was only half-listening to Erik. "Why not, what?"

"Blame it on the Opera Ghost."

She dropped her hands in her lap. "You can't be—" but he was nodding firmly, his black hair flying about his head. Well then.

It had potential. Meg and the other chorus girls were already keyed up with mentions of the ghost to the frustration of all of their instructors. Strange sightings were passed around with relish. It might do the job, but it would need a bit of work to convince Madam Giry.

"Do you have an idea?" she asked. She had the inklings of one, but wanted to hear what Erik thought first.

When he shook his head, she grinned and nudged his leg with her foot. "How do you feel about notes?"

♫♫♫

Christine timed her re-emergence for maximum effect; she worked in the theatre so she knew how to manage a scene. This was a scene, no doubt about it, and Christine had to put on her best performance. After working herself into a suitably sweaty frenzy, she staggered into the rehearsal area backstage, the note she and Erik had so painstakingly worked on clutched in her fist. Gasping as though she'd just swum the Channel, she collapsed in a heap at the far end of a line of girls, shaking with suppressed sobs.

Pandemonium erupted as the controlled chaos of the rehearsal evaporated like morning mist. Meg had reached her first, gently touching Christine's shoulder as she tried to catch her breath and get herself under control. A babble of voices surrounded them, making it hard to hear what anyone was saying.

Even the heavy banging of Madame Giry's cane on the studio floor couldn't completely quell the outburst, especially when Meg asked, "Christine, what happened to you? Where have you been?"

It was here that she really had to sell it. Moaning, she grabbed at Meg's shoulders as tightly as she could, pleased when the girl winced in her claw-like grip. "I saw him, Meg! When I was lost beneath the opera house. I saw the Opera Ghost!"

Cue fainting. Christine collapsed in Meg's arms as the other chorus girls screamed and scuttled around like crabs looking for the ocean.

"Someone get salts," she heard Madame Giry order. "Take her to the manager's office."

Christine felt herself being swept up roughly and bounced in strong arms as whoever had her ran toward the closest set of offices backstage. She made sure to keep a tight grip on the folded paper, and wondered if Erik was watching from somewhere. She hoped he was.

That thought sent her mind back to when she'd left him. He'd rowed her back from the house on the underground lake. The boat had been rickety but didn't have leaks. As Erik poled them toward the dock, Christine had gazed into the dark water, watching her reflection ripple. He'd steadied the boat while she climbed out and waited for him to alight. Her heart was beating fast at the con she was going to pull—it had been far too long since she'd tried one, and this was ambitious. But if she could pull it off, perhaps she wouldn't feel so adrift, so cut off from who she'd always been.

Erik's feather touch on her shoulder pulled her from her musings and suddenly she was struck by a question that she desperately wanted to know the answer to. Christine tilted her head up to search Erik's mismatched eyes, and asked, "Why are you doing this for me?"

"Why did you help me back at the carnival?" he'd returned, and then paused, as if actually waiting for her response, as if there was a right one.

Christine opened her mouth to give an easy

answer, then paused. Why had she helped? It wasn't what she'd been taught, and she hadn't really thought her actions through. She'd simply done it, not even planning it out, unsure if it would even work. She didn't have an easy answer for him. Christine just knew that something she saw inside of him called out to that same thing inside of her and she was helpless to deny it. She had known with a frightening certainty that she could not leave him in that cage.

"Because you let me," she finally told him, surprised at how sincere she sounded.

Erik nodded in absolute seriousness, and led her back to the upper levels of the opera house.

She felt herself placed on a soft, velvety surface, much nicer than the cot she had slept on the nights previous. The bustling noise of people hurrying about filled her ears, the rustle of their clothing and the heat from their bodies making Christine want to twitch. Instead, she held herself still, waiting a few moments before opening her eyes with a sigh. She saw Madame Giry, Meg, the chorus master, and one of the managers, Monsieur Debienne, staring down at her. She gave a small terrified shriek of surprise.

"Where am I?" she said, looking around frantically.

"Mademoiselle Daaé, you fainted," Debienne explained gently. "And no one has seen you for nearly two days."

She gasped, clutching the note to her chest, then looked at it strangely since no one else seemed inclined to mention it. "What's this?" She held it up curiously, pleased when her hand trembled ever so slightly.

Meg snatched it before anyone else could grab it, the smaller girl sliding between crouching bodies. "It's a note! I bet it's from the ghost!" she cried. She studied the page and cried, "And it's to you, Mama!"

Christine took a moment to savor the varying expressions everyone present wore. The manager looked like he'd swallowed a bad oyster, Madame Giry's face was sour enough to curdle milk, Meg appeared delighted, and the music master seemed to wish he were back at his piano surrounded by twittering girls rather than be dealing with this foolishness.

Everyone spoke at once, talking over each other. Christine subsided against the arm of the sofa, content to watch the drama play out, pleased that things were going so well. Chaos ensured that people didn't think through things fully and fairly obvious questions ended up not being asked in favor of everyone expressing their strongly felt opinions.

Madame Giry stomped over to her daughter and plucked the missive from her hand. Christine held her breath, shoulders tensing as she closely observed the woman's face. This is where the whole thing could fall apart if Christine had misjudged the dancing mistress. Her pappa had taught her the importance of reading people, of determining what they wanted most, what they hoped for and what they feared. Once you knew that, it was remarkably easy to nudge them along in the direction most advantageous for you.

The woman's eyes roved over the letter. Christine and Erik had spent the longest on this one. He'd doubted her at first.

"Do you really expect this to work? It's a rather large reach," he'd said as he concentrated on the words she was dictating. Christine had stolen some paper and a pen from an empty dressing room while Erik found a bottle of red ink. The scratch of the pen's nib as Erik scrawled across the paper was the only noise in the small house.

Christine kept her leg elevated on the cot, wrapped in a blanket on the floor, but she tilted her head to stare at Erik upside down. "Madame Giry has *aspirations* for her little Meg," she told him, doing her best to remember all of the gossip from the opera that the chorus girls loved to share. "This will feed into them nicely. Read it aloud to see how it sounds."

Clearing his throat, Erik began. As he spoke, his voice took on a booming quality, carrying to all corners of the house. He read:

MADAM:

1825. Mlle. Menetrier, leader of the ballet, became Marquise de Cussy.

1832. Mlle. Marie Taglioni, a dancer, became Comtesse Gilbert des Voisins.

1846. La Sota, a dancer, married a brother of the King of Spain.

1847. Lola Montes, a dancer, became the

morganatic wife of King Louis of Bavaria and was created Countess of Landsfeld.

1848. Mlle. Maria, a dancer, became Baronne d'Herneville.

1870. Theresa Hessier, a dancer, married Dom Fernando, brother to the King of Portugal.

1895. Meg Giry, Empress!

"Ooooh, the voice is good. I like it," Christine told him, chin resting in her hand. She could use that voice. There was power in it.

Erik dropped the letter to his side. "But Empress? Really?" He glanced up at Christine with a dubious expression, his hair tucked behind the ear on the good side of his face.

"Trust me. She believes her daughter is bound for great things. It's part of why she doesn't let her associate with any of the patrons—it's in case one of them wants to woo her for his mistress. Meg *hates* the way her mother protects her." She rolled over onto her stomach and propped her chin on her fists so she could watch him without getting a headache.

When he still didn't look convinced, Christine continued, pushing up onto her elbows for emphasis. "We need someone to act as a go-between for us and the managers if we want this Opera Ghost con to work. And we need it to be someone who's opinion they trust and who is above reproach. Giry's been with the opera a long time. She's got no life except for dancing and Meg and everyone knows this. She's the perfect candidate."

Pride was what made Madame Giry tick, what drove her. The woman prided herself on her training of the chorus girls, she prided herself on her ability to keep them in line and on her own sterling reputation among the rest of the staff at the Palais Garnier. That pride demanded that Giry—or Meg—rise above her station, rise higher than any other chorus girl or diva ever had in the opera house.

Christine could work with that.

"As you say, Christine," Erik said, returning his full attention to the letter.

Now she studied Madame Giry's face closely, looking for a sign that their bait had managed to tempt their prey. The woman's frown intensified for a moment, only to relent slightly a few moments later. Giry ignored the manager when he asked, "What does it say?"

As Christine watched, Madame Giry's gaze shifted thoughtfully to Meg, and then back to the letter in her hand. Covering her mouth with one hand, Christine hid her smile. Giry's fingers clutched the paper so hard it crinkled.

They had her.

"Mama—" Meg began, only to be cut off by a loud bang and then screaming.

Christine couldn't have asked the timing to be better. As the rest of the group ran from the manager's office, she followed more slowly. She already knew what they'd find.

The body of Joseph Buquet lay in the center of wide circle of onlookers. A noose and the frayed rope attached to it slithered like a snake across the wooden boards. The girls screamed and sobered as they were shepherded away by a few of the matrons, while stagehands milled about, looking frightened and confused.

"What happened here?" Monsieur Debienne demanded. He pushed forward, stopping short at the body and craning his neck upwards.

"We don't know, Monsieur," said Bertrand, one of the prop handlers. "One moment we were working and then next, he came falling past us!"

As more witnesses began adding their voices to the tale, Christine moved behind Madame Giry and slipped a second note into her pocket. Her sleight of hand skills had grown rusty with disuse, but she was confident enough in her distraction to risk it. With it done, she moved away from the rest and screamed.

Pointing upwards into the rafters of the building that held the series of catwalks that the stagehands used for the elaborate effects of a performance, she shrieked, "There he is, the Opera Ghost!"

Meg looked up and screamed as well, which set off all of the remaining chorus girls. Shouts of "I see him!" and "There!' filled the space.

Christine promptly pretended to faint once more.

CHAPTER *8*

CHRISTINE RETURNED TO ERIK and the small house on the underground lake the first moment she was left alone. She couldn't believe how well everything had worked out! The chaos with Buquet's body had derailed any questions that Christine might not have been able to answer and had done more to cement the existence of the Opera Ghost than any number of notes could have done.

Erik waited for her at the dock, sitting cross-legged and trailing his fingertips along the top of the water. His pale skin nearly glowed in the dim light of his lamp against the pitch blackness of the lake's surface. He stood when she approached, and she noticed he was wearing different clothes.

These fit better—the pants covered his ankles and the shirt he wore didn't bag around his thin frame. He'd also found a solid pair of work boots that she suspected a stagehand might miss in the coming days. His thick black hair still hung in his face, covering the worst of his deformity and scars.

Erik smiled. In response, she handed him the sack she was carrying, which he accepted and placed in the boat before helping her down into it. He stepped in after and began poling them across the lake. Christine focused on him rather than the dark water surrounding her and clung to the side of the boat with a knuckle-cracking grip. The boat made her nervous so she tried not to think about it.

"I heard everything!" he told her as he poled them out. "You were right about Madame Giry." He sounded impressed.

Christine preened. Of course she'd been right. It was all about knowing what people wanted most and making sure they had a good enough excuse to go after it. Her father had taught her that from the time she was old enough to sing. "I think Buquet helped a bit with that."

Erik turned his head to stare at her sharply, his body easily balanced in the shallow boat. Christine swallowed and hoped he didn't pitch them both into the water. "Yes, well, when I helped you move the body, I didn't think you were going to do *that* to him."

Sighing, Christine clenched her hands into fists, watching the ripples from the boat's progress before replying. "He was already dead. He might as well have been of use one last time."

Erik regarded her strangely. It was similar to the look Meg sometimes gave her when she said something the other dancer didn't understand. "He was a *person*, Christine."

"*Was*," she reminded him. "He was also a drunk who attacked me," Her voice climbed higher, sounding strained to her own ears. She didn't like feeling scared and Buquet had frightened her badly. She hated that she was still affected by the encounter days later. "No one was going to miss him anyway." She lifted her hand and shook water droplets from it.

"You don't feel at all bad about it?" Erik asked, expression curious and hesitant.

Christine knew what she should say, just as she knew what she didn't feel. But Erik didn't need to know any of that, not if she wanted to keep him as part of her plan. So she lowered her voice and cast her eyes down and said, "Of course I feel bad about it, Erik! I didn't mean to kill him."

She swallowed around a lump in her throat, remembering how terrified she'd been in those frantic moments before her hand had closed around the brick. She hadn't meant to kill him but she wasn't particularly sorry that she had. "But he was choking me—hurting me. He was drunk and crazy. I don't feel bad for protecting myself."

She watched Erik out of the corner of her eye as she spoke again. "And he'd seen you, Erik. He'd become obsessed with you. In a way, you were the one that drove him mad." Buquet's ravings had certainly paved the way for the Opera Ghost fabrication she'd spun, but she needed Erik on board for it to work. Having him get second thoughts was not an option she could allow.

"So it's my fault he's dead then?" he asked in a scornful voice. She heard the wood of the pole creak beneath the strength of his grip. "You are unbelievable."

Turning his face from her, Erik poled them on in silence for a few long minutes. Christine clasped her hands tightly together in her lap, fingers interlaced so firmly the bones ached. Erik didn't deserve that, but she couldn't have him leave, not now, not when she was so close to getting away from this pre-made life that she never wanted.

When he finally spoke, she gave a silent sigh of relief that she hadn't angered him enough to drive him away. "How did you plan the timing of it?"

Ducking her head so Erik wouldn't see the relieved smile that flitted across her features, Christine relaxed. She felt like she'd just navigated a trapped labyrinth and come out the other side unscathed. "I didn't," she admitted, sheepish. "I just sawed through the rope enough to weaken it and figured either one of the stagehands would find him hanging there or the weight of the body would cause it to break. It was just luck that the body fell when it did."

Christine remembered her father once telling her that they made their own luck, right after he'd first encountered Monsieur Valérius after they'd been run out of a particularly unfriendly town when one of their cons had been discovered. The meeting had felt fortuitous at the time; now she wondered how much her father had engineered to put them in the music lover's way. The man had obviously heard of Pappa's playing and had been scouring the local fairs for them. She wished she could claim that kind of forethought.

Erik hummed as he piloted the boat, lost in his own world. Christine was grateful for the quiet, needing space to think after the chaos of the opera house. The upside of the body slamming into the stage was that the damage to his head had been such that no one suspected he hadn't been hung. While Christine had been "unconscious" she'd listened to the wild speculations, and one thing became incredibly clear: everyone was primed to believe in the existence of some specter haunting the Palais Garnier.

The second note that she and Erik had penned and that Christine had snuck into Madame Giry's pocket had been well-received considering that it amounted to a politely worded blackmail notice. It had been Christine's idea to ask for a monthly stipend for the O.G., split evenly between her and Erik. He could use the money for whatever he liked and Christine could facilitate her escape from the drudgery of the chorus that much faster. It had been Erik's own idea to ask for a box in which to view the performances. He'd asked Christine if there was one that had an excellent view of the stage, and she'd immediately recommended Box Five.

"They took the second note surprisingly well," she told him, unsure if he'd stayed after the initial outcry surrounding Buquet's body.

"Tell me of it."

Madame Giry and the rest had ended up taking Christine back to Debienne's office and laying her out on the same couch. It was there that Madame Giry discovered the second note and read it aloud to the assembled group. Christine had 'woken up' shortly after the managers ordered everyone but Giry and the music master out of their office.

"The managers at first thought the whole thing ridiculous," Christine explained. "Until Madame Giry helpfully reminded them of what just happened to Joseph Buquet for daring to speak ill of the Opera Ghost."

"Really?" Erik asked archly.

Christine felt the beginnings of a flush heat her cheeks. "Well, I might have helped that story along. A bit."

Erik's deep chuckle was the only response she received. The hair on Christine's arms stood up at the darkly decadent sound of it. Glancing at the good side of Erik's face, she shivered. She could almost imagine him whole and handsome, and what might that be like?

She suddenly remembered the Comte de Chagny's dark, handsome face in the audience milling about the staircase of the Palais Garnier and thought of Raoul. What did he look like now?

Was he as handsome as his brother, as handsome of the promise of his youth led her to believe? Would he remember her from their childhood jaunts at the sea? Did she even want him to?

"Did they agree to it?" Erik's voice intruded on her private thoughts.

Shifting uncomfortably in her seat, Christine pressed the back of her hand to her cheek. She felt warm. Goodness, what was wrong with her! "Not yet," she told him. "But they will." It was only a matter of time.

"How can you be so sure?" he asked.

"People aren't particularly hard to figure out, Erik," she told his back. "Once you realize what drives a person—like I did with Madame Giry—it's pretty easy to manipulate them into doing what you want."

Erik went still, pole clutched tightly in his hands. His shoulders hunched, making him seem a black blot in the dim light of the lantern. "Are you doing that with me?" His magnificent voice was taut with warning.

"What? No!" She widened her eyes to plead with him if he should turn around to look at her. "I wouldn't do that to you. You're my friend." She cursed her carelessness silently. She'd been thinking about something else, flustered at the memory of Raoul.

She needed to remember that Erik was smart—smarter than his scarred face made him appear and that she couldn't judge him on appearance alone. He might seem simple and interested only in music, but he'd been raised in circumstances similar to hers, surrounded by people of questionable moral fiber and brutality. Christine suspected he could be just as mercenary as she—and it would not do to forget that.

He glared at her over his shoulder, as if he knew the path of her thoughts. "Don't lie to me," he growled. His sudden movement made the boat list alarmingly.

Christine froze, her heart lurching inside her chest. She wasn't afraid of him, but she was wary. She was alone in a boat with a relative stranger and no one knew where she was. She was confident in her abilities—and the knife in her sleeve—but she didn't want to anger him. "I'm not lying. I would *never* lie to you."

"See that you don't." The threat in his voice made Christine wonder what she might have gotten herself into. Controlling Erik might not be as simple as she'd originally thought.

"I swear, I won't."

He breathed out and the tension left him with the air in his lungs. "Forgive me for my harshness," he apologized in a whisper. "I've had . . . few friends."

She thought it best to change the subject and struck out with the first thing that came to mind. "Why do you want a box anyway? You can just sit anywhere backstage and hear the opera."

Erik continued poling, so that all Christine could see was the muscles of his back moving beneath his ragged coat. But his voice sounded wistful when he answered. "I've never seen one before, for all that I've sung the parts of them. I want to experience the whole spectacle of it."

Christine held her tongue. She could tell him about the sweat and greasepaint, the acrid smell of the painted backgrounds and ripe costumes, the whispered threats and muttered curses. That was what she knew of opera, but she hadn't spent years in a cage, singing songs and imagining what it might be like to witness it. There was no need to take this away from him, and it seemed unusually cruel to do so.

"You can't just sit in the box," she reminded him, because she couldn't help herself. Christine might feel bad for him, but there was still her plan to consider. "People will see you. And I imagine the managers will set up some kind of guard to see if they can catch the Opera Ghost."

Now Erik did turn his head to look at her, the ruined half of his face in shadow. Christine was grateful that he kept it hidden, that she didn't have to look at it. "Do you know of all of the trapdoors and hidden tunnels in this place?" When she shook her head, he smiled slyly and said, "Neither do they."

That made sense. Erik had to fill his time somehow and he'd become quite the expert at navigating the Palais Garnier unseen. She knew he'd been stealing food and clothes since his escape from the carnival without getting caught. She wondered how many secret ways he'd discovered and whether he would show them to her.

The boat bumped against the shore of the island. Erik hopped out nimbly and hauled the boat up, then offered Christine his hand to help her out. Once she was steady, he grabbed the sack she'd come with and the lantern, and led her to his house.

"I brought you some things I thought we might need," she told him as they crossed the rocky ground. She stumbled once, and Erik reached out to steady her, hand on her elbow. She could feel the chill of his grip through the fabric of her blouse.

He kept his hold on her as they walked, as though fearful that she might stagger and fall on the uneven ground. Her heart beat so fast and loud in her chest it was a wonder Erik didn't hear it. Part of her wanted to pull away from his touch, remembering his frightful visage, but it warred with the part that appreciated his solicitous care of her. Remarkably, she felt safe when she was with him. Most of the time.

"Like what?"

"More red ink and parchment for one." She'd also included other things she thought he might like: black ink and pens for transcribing music so he didn't have to write in the dust, some dried meat and fruit, another loaf of bread, chocolate, a few spare shirts that she'd pilfered from Monsieur Valérius' remaining things, and some toiletries.

"We're sending more notes?" He opened the door to the shack and ushered her inside.

Nodding, Christine noticed he'd procured two chairs from somewhere in the opera house, probably raiding forgotten stores of props. He'd also stolen a set of velvet draperies which he'd secured to separate the room into two spaces rather than relying on the screen. There were other touches about the space—a few bowls and a pitcher, a low table, and several more lanterns and candles in holders.

It looked rather homey.

"Did you get into any trouble when you finally went home?" he asked.

She turned in a circle, taking in the changes with an appreciative eye. "Not once I explained to Madame Valérius that I'd been taken by the Angel of Music."

"The Angel of Music?" Amusement colored his voice. "I find that hard to believe."

"Not at all. Pappa used to talk about sending me an Angel of Music once he died. He'd been sick for a while and Madame and Monsieur Valérius agreed to be my guardians when he finally passed. They heard my father say such things often in his final months. And Madame does love a good story. When I told her of the opera ghost and the Angel of Music, she was thrilled that I'd been chosen!"

Erik set down the sack and turned to Christine wearing a thoughtful expression. "Why don't you sing like you did at the carnival?"

His question rocked her. There was no way he could pick her voice out of all the others.

Christine bustled past him and began unpacking the things she brought. "Whatever do you mean?"

"I've been wondering," he said, and she heard his footsteps as he moved closer to her, "since I came here. You don't sing the same."

Her fingers clutched at the rough canvas. She didn't know what to tell him. The music had soured when her father died, when she'd realized what he'd used her for. She'd lost the joy in it when she realized it was just another way to con people. She'd been left empty, angry with him for what her childhood had been but missing him terribly all the same. Music was tied up in all of that, a Gordian knot that she couldn't hope to unravel.

"I'll never be good enough," she said instead, staring down at her hands and forcing them to relax her death grip on the fabric. "I don't see the point when I'll never oust Carlotta."

She felt Erik's presence close at her back, so she wasn't surprised when she felt his hands on her shoulders, turning her to face him. "Christine, you can be more than Carlotta could ever hope to be. I think you know that."

"You don't *know*." She refused to look into his face.

"Yes, I do." His voice was warm, mellow, reminding her of mulled wine after a cold walk. "I've heard you, remember. That was *you* I sang with. No one else. Why won't you let everyone hear you?"

His fingers lightly touched her chin, lifting her

face so he could stare into her eyes. Christine swallowed, out of her depth now, and completely unsure of what the right answer was. A part of her longed to show the world what she was capable of, to be something beyond what her father had planned for her.

"With a voice like yours, you could be a Prima Donna in any company you choose. The world would fawn over you, throw itself at your feet. You are magnificent. Why do you hide that?" Wonder and confusion filled his eyes as he gazed at her, a gentle smile on his lips.

"What if I only sound like that with you?" she asked him before she thought better of it. Christine felt small and cold suddenly. The chill of his hand didn't bother her anymore, not when she felt carved of ice.

"Then I will always be there to sing with you," he whispered, the smile reaching his one eye. "But the world deserves to hear you as you are."

"Will you help me then? Train with me?"

His smile widened, blossoming like a flower. "Of course, I will."

CHAPTER 9

1901 (Present Day)

"YOU WERE THE OPERA Ghost!" Bastien exclaimed, staring at the slight figure across from him in shock. "It was all your idea!"

Christine inclined her head, a faint smile playing about her lips. He thought she looked inordinately pleased with herself for a moment before she finished the whisky in her glass. He signaled the barkeep for another for her.

"Thank you," she murmured, and Bastien watched her pink lips move, helpless to stop himself.

Clearing his throat, he tried to bring himself back under control. He clasped his hands tightly around his own half-full glass, grounding his thoughts. "You killed a man," he said in a quiet voice, reminding himself as much as her.

"In self-defense," she answered quickly, refusing to look at him, "when I was already in fear of my life." She ran her finger around the rim of her empty glass, chin perched on her hand.

"Still," Bastien began, then snapped his mouth shut. What did he want to say? That there was no way she appeared capable of it? "The Opera Ghost. Why tell me?"

She offered him a mirthless smile as her fingers plucked at the back of one fingerless glove. "Raoul warned you about me, didn't he?" Her blue gaze locked with his and he saw the hard glint of a survivor in their depths. When he nodded, she leaned back in her chair. "Then you ought to realize that even if you were to say something about what I did no one would believe you." She gestured broadly, her hand sweeping out to encompass both her face and body. "Who would believe this could do all of *that*?"

Her words held a sharp edge, hard and unforgiving as steel. Bastien polished off his whisky. He knew she was right. Too many people would take one look at her slight frame and her doe-eyes and her wild hair and dismiss the prospect of a mercenary's brain lurking beneath it.

"And you asked for the story of what happened at the Palais Garnier," Christine reminded him. "This is a part of it."

Bastien rolled the glass between his palms. "You fooled everyone."

"Not everyone." A wistful expression crossed her face, like clouds skudding across a sunny sky. "There was one person who always knew who I was."

"Erik."

She nodded, gaze unfocused as she looked inward. Bastien subsided, giving her a moment to compose herself. "What happened to him?"

Before he could prepare himself, her charmingly rakish smile returned. It drew him in despite his better judgment, and he could finally understand the way she captivated people with seemingly no effort. He wanted to press for more, to learn her secrets, to feel like he was the one she could turn to in distress.

But Christine Daaé had never been in distress that wasn't of her own calculated making. He was coming to realize that from the tale she'd told. Only two people knew that on a fundamental level, and one of them had created her.

Both were dead.

"Listen and I will tell you."

Bastien leaned forward in his seat as Christine began to spin her tale once more.

CHAPTER *10*

1890, Paris

CHRISTINE PRESSED HER HANDS flat against her stomach in the vain hope of stifling the butterflies fluttering about as she waited for the knock at her door to signal it was time to take the stage for the finale. It was a newer dressing room than the one she'd shared with Meg and a few other chorus girls. She'd been installed in this particular room, ousting La Sorelli—one of the principal dancers—at the Opera Ghost's behest.

Tonight was a gala night, offered up by the Palais Garnier's managers Debienne and Poligny in honor of their impending retirement. She'd already sung from Romeo and Juliet, which she'd performed adequately, but now was the true test: *Faust*. La Carlotta had taken ill—a dose of a particularly strong diuretic in her wine had seen to that—and Christine had been offered the role of Marguerite to replace her at the last minute.

This was everything she and Erik had been working towards the past six months. Countless hours spent in his house on the lake, sleep lost to practice as he pushed her beyond what she thought her limits were. His voice rose with hers, spurring her on to greater heights as she clawed for notes only dreamed of in her range before. They fell into her hands like jewels, glittering and precious.

If she could perform tonight in front of an audience as she did in the privacy of Erik's house, she would be the talk of Paris. She would be a sensation!

The managers had fallen into line easily once Christine had arranged for another "accident" and Erik had provided Madame Giry with one more red-inked note. The monthly stipend of twenty thousand francs had begun appearing regularly for pick up in Box Five. Christine had discovered that Erik could throw his voice, so she'd had him use the trick occasionally when it seemed like Debienne and Poligny were beginning to doubt the presence of the Opera Ghost. Seeing the chorus girls run screaming from whatever room they were in simply added to her amusement.

The dressing room's mirror opened up to admit Erik from one of the many secret passages honeycombing the opera house. He wore evening dress and a papier-mâché mask that covered the ruined half of his face. It was made up in flesh tones to better blend, and Christine had to admit that with his long hair down, he could pass for normal so long as someone didn't get too close.

"You're going to be incredible," he assured her as he stepped closer. He carried a cloth-covered object in his hands. "You have nothing to worry about."

She smoothed down her costume's skirts again absently. "I'd like to believe you."

He grinned and Christine found herself answering it with one of her own. "What's stopping you?"

A million different things, she wanted to answer. What if she got onstage and she froze, unable to make a sound? What if her voice cracked? What if she couldn't hit the highest notes like she had in practice? What if she fell? What if the chandelier crashed down on her head? What if she failed?

Instead, she tilted her head to indicate what he carried. "Is that for me?"

Erik nodded and placed it on the dressing table with care. Christine moved closer to get a better look as he pulled away the cloth with a magician's flourish. She gasped in surprised pleasure at what was revealed. Carefully crafted papier-mâché figures in gloriously detailed painted outfits danced in pairs around the circular top of the box. They were dressed for a masquerade, each of their faces hidden by intricately embellished masks. In the center stood a figure in black evening clothes but without a mask. His arms were raised as though conducting the dancers in their movements.

Erik reached beneath the box and turned the winding mechanism. When he stepped back again, the dancers began to spin around the man in the center, moving in a circle on the perimeter. The conductor's arms rose and fell in time to the music, an almost hypnotic waltz that Christine didn't recognize. She couldn't tear her gaze from it. She'd never seen anything so beautiful.

"Does it please you?" Erik asked softly.

"Very much," Christine told him, breathless. "It's the most wonderful thing I've ever seen."

He smiled proudly. "I am glad."

"Is this—did you make this?" She shifted her gaze so she was staring into his face and she saw the bashfulness in his expression. "You did, didn't you?"

At his nod, she threw her arms around his neck and hugged him, overwhelmed. It was the nicest present anyone had ever given her. Her father's gifts always had another purpose besides just bringing her joy. This music box was solely for her enjoyment and nothing else.

"Thank you," she whispered into his neck.

He'd gone stiff and still as she held him. After a few moments, she felt his hands on her back. There was a tension in him that hadn't been there before, almost as if he didn't know whether to pull her closer or push her farther away. Instead, he held her tentatively where she was.

"You are quite welcome, Christine." His voice

sounded choked to her ears, his diction painfully formal.

The knock sounded at the door to her dressing room, signaling it was time to take her place onstage. Christine jumped away, the nerves she thought she'd banished returning with a vengeance. Erik opened his arms and let her go.

"I won't wish you luck," he whispered to her, his forehead nearly touching hers as he bent over to speak in her ear. "You don't need it."

"Will you be watching me?" she asked, her voice sounding small and fragile.

He took her hand in his cold one and squeezed gently before dropping it again. "Always. Now go. Be brilliant."

Christine hurried from her dressing room and took her mark. It was dark behind the massive velvet curtains that closed off the stage, making her feel wrapped in warmth. She saw Meg in the wings, her dark face alight. The dancer waved at her and Christine waved back. Then the orchestra swelled with music, the footlights sparked, the curtains parted, and Christine sang like she never had before, her gaze trained on Box Five. She knew Erik was singing with her.

♫♫♫

She returned to her dressing room in a daze, having little memory of the performance. It almost felt like an out of body experience. Every one of her fears fell away with each swell of her voice. And through it all, she heard Erik's honeyed tenor, just as she had in practice, intertwining with hers, urging her higher, louder, stronger. The applause she heard when the final notes fell into silence was a crescendo, a crashing wave surging over her senses. As she accepted the audience's accolades, Christine was certain Erik's mismatched gaze bored into her. She was overwhelmed and undone, close to tears, as Meg and the other chorus girls swarmed over her after her bows, and it was only the threat of a thump from Madame Giry's cane that enabled Christine to retreat. Only Meg was bold enough to follow Christine back to her dressing room.

"*What* was that?" the dark-skinned girl asked, dodging through the clogged backstage arteries of the theatre.

Christine's heart beat wildly, almost as if it were trying to get away from whatever propelled her forward. She didn't want to attend the reception in the Grand Foyer. All she wanted was to get out of this costume and collect herself before having to face the crowd of her admirers. The idea wasn't so appealing now. Meg was just making her feel more anxious.

"What are you talking about?" Christine snapped, rounding on Meg when she grabbed her wrist. "It was just singing!"

Meg quickly took her hand from Christine's arm and dropped back a step. She eyed Christine incredulously before stating, "There's singing and then there's *singing*. What you did tonight was the latter."

"You're being ridiculous," Christine told the dancer, waving her away.

"And you're lying," Meg countered, following after her. "Who's been teaching you?"

"No one!"

"Liar," the dancer replied, a smug smile on her face. "If you could have sung like that from the beginning, you would have replaced La Carlotta long ago. So who is it?"

"Someone you don't know!" Christine returned, grateful when she spied the door to her dressing room. Hurrying through it, she turned and stopped Meg from following her with a shove to her shoulder.

"Now leave me be!" She slammed the door in Meg's startled face.

Heavens, she needed some peace. Singing on the stage had been wonderful, the feeling like nothing she'd ever felt when she ran cons with her father, but now she wanted Swedish comfort food: kroppkakor, a loaf of crusty bread, a pot of lingonberry jam, and no one to speak to her for at least an hour. The high she experienced when singing had left her wrung out and wasted, the need to tumble into sleep nearly overwhelming.

She growled at the knock on her door. Meg needed to go away immediately, or Christine was liable to shatter a vase full of the flowers that filled her dressing room over the dancer's head with no regrets. Throwing a robe over her costume, Christine stalked to the door and flung it open.

"I told you to go away!" she shouted into the surprised face of Vicomte Raoul de Chagny.

He looked much the same as he had when they were children, playing on the shore and listening to her father spin tales for their amusement. He was still brown of skin, curly of hair, with eyes of surprising blueness, making his face look more open and naïve than any face had a right to look. His shy smile had fallen away at the suddenness of her outburst. He'd grown tall, though not as tall as Erik, but Raoul was broader in body. His suit was impeccably tailored and his shoes gleamed with a high shine.

Christine gaped, hand pressed to her breast in surprise. "Oh," she breathed, completely confounded at this new development. "I'm terribly sorry. I thought you were someone else."

The shy smile returned. When he spoke, Christine noticed that his voice had deepened from that of the boy she'd once known. "I must say that I am quite glad I am not that person, Mademoiselle Daaé. Angering you is the last thing I'd ever want."

Keeping one hand on the doorknob, Christine extended her hand to Raoul. She couldn't decide which was the better course of action: pretend she didn't know him or acknowledge that she did. It had been years since they'd seen each other, since he'd left her waiting for him on the beach only to find out much later that his brother, Phillipe, had suddenly summoned him back to Paris. Perhaps he did not recognize her anymore, though she would have thought her name different enough to warrant notice.

Her father had been disappointed when she'd returned to him with the news of Raoul's departure. He'd been hoping she would have had more time to secure Raoul's affections, hoping for childish love to lead to other, deeper feelings. But when he'd noticed how sad she seemed at the loss of her playmate, he'd picked up his fiddle and played a rousing dance to make her feel better.

"Again, my apologies, Monsieur...?" She let the question hang between them. She remembered that desolate feeling of abandonment as she'd waited at their favorite spot on the bluffs overlooking the water until her father came to fetch her. She and Raoul had whiled away hours there, playing games, singing songs, and telling stories. And he hadn't even considered her worth a proper goodbye.

His leaving had stung her then. Now she realized she was grateful for it. If he'd stayed, Pappa would have pushed for her to somehow force an introduction to Raoul's brother, Comte Phillipe, and Christine hadn't wanted a friendship she'd valued turned into yet another source for coin. She wanted one relationship that wasn't about what it could do for her or her father. She knew her father's plans and Raoul had been an attractive target. But Christine would never have used him in that. She'd valued his friendship, at least until he'd proved unworthy of such feelings.

Raoul looked stricken though he hid his

expression quickly. "Raoul de Chagny. It was presumptuous of me to expect you to remember the boy who fetched your scarf from the sea years ago." He bowed.

Christine feigned surprised recognition with a gasp, her hand shooting up to cover her mouth. "It was a blue scarf!"

"It matched your eyes," he said, glancing down shyly.

Christine allowed a smile to curl her lips, encouraging him. He was a noble, and it never hurt to encourage noble favor. It was a widely known secret that his brother, Phillipe, had taken La Sorelli as his mistress, ensuring that at least one de Chagny would often be in attendance. "Raoul? Is it really you?" she asked, putting warmth in her tone. It pleased her when he blushed.

"Yes, Christine." He nodded. "I remember those stories your father used to tell us about Little Lotte and the wonderful music he played for us. How is he doing these days?"

Christine lost her smile. Mentions of her father still caused her stomach to tighten with a low-level dread she couldn't quite name. "He took ill some years ago and died shortly after," she told him. The feeling of the walls closing in on her, of her life telescoping slowly into this stage and this room backstage nearly caused her to faint for real.

"My condolences, Christine. I am sorry to bring up such a painful subject. I'm sure you miss him terribly. He was a wonderful man." Raoul spouted platitudes the way he'd been taught. Such a good little gentleman.

Christine loved her Pappa dearly, but she did not believe in lying to herself. Her father was not a wonderful man. He might have played the fiddle well enough to make Satan himself jump, and sing to make an angel weep, but talent didn't equal goodness. Most people didn't understand such distinctions; most of her father's marks certainly hadn't.

Suddenly the conversation exhausted her. She hadn't seen Raoul since they were children, and Raoul was still very much a boy despite his years. He even looked younger than his age—his fresh-faced naivete and his wide eyes conspiring against his maturity. Christine felt like a crone in the face of it.

"You'll forgive me, Monsieur de Chagny," she said, closing the door halfway to indicate the conversation was over, "but I am very tired from my performance and I would like to rest."

"Oh, of course, Christine. How foolish of me!" He glanced around as though he was preparing to impart a salacious secret to her. "May I tell you how magnificent you sang? Your voice was a revelation!"

She gave him a tired smile. "Thank you for your kind words." She spoke the words she'd say to any admirer. He was no one special after all, just another patron. "I am pleased that you enjoyed the performance."

"If I might be so bold," he continued as if she hadn't spoken, his words leaving him in a nervous rush, "might I have the privilege of seeing you again? Perhaps after your next triumphant performance?"

Christine barely came to Raoul's shoulder, but she drew herself up with all the haughtiness she could muster. "I am afraid, *Monsieur*, that you have the wrong impression of me," she replied in a chilly voice, expression as frosty as her tone.

She'd heard no rumors about her ill-fated night out with Monsieur le Fure, but that didn't mean the man hadn't shared or embellished details of their evening. She supposed she shouldn't be surprised if he had—men loved to gossip as much as women when it came to their conquests, but she'd thought Raoul better than to listen to drivel like that.

The young man blushed, the flush making his dusky skin darker. He raised his hands in surrender, realizing his mistake. Christine bit back a chuckle at his horrified expression—he couldn't have looked more scandalized than if he were a nun at a brothel.

"Good Heavens, Mademoiselle Daaé, I implore your forgiveness if it sounded like I . . .," he floundered awkwardly, unable to even say the words. "All I meant to say was that I hoped you would take the time to speak with me again, as old friends ought. That is all. Please say you forgive me for my poorly chosen words."

Christine hid one hand behind her back so she could dig her fingernails into her palm to keep from smiling. She'd heard tales of Phillipe's wooing of La Sorelli, but it seemed that the Comte's brother was not cut from the same cloth if his fumblings and stutters were any indication. It would not do to laugh outright, and she had no wish to alienate Raoul. He might prove useful.

His next words made her rethink her assessment of him. He ducked his head and murmured, "I don't know if you are aware of how much I enjoyed our time together when we were playmates."

She was intrigued. Why would he mention his sudden departure now of all times? "Did you think of me at all in all these years?" she asked.

He looked up then, meeting her gaze. His dark skin was flushed still, but his eyes were clear, almost adoring, when he looked at her. Christine's heart beat faster and it made her angry. "Nearly every day."

His answer made her insides twist with a longing she'd never known before. Raoul's expression was open, guileless. It unnerved her, and she reverted to the only thing she knew—her father's teachings. "Then I wish you good evening, Monsieur de Chagny." She began to close the door.

Raoul reached out his hand, arresting the door's closure. "But may I see you again?" he asked, and she could hear the pleading edge in his voice.

Always leave them wanting, her Pappa had told her. *Make them work for what they want. You can't give it to them too cheaply or they won't value it, and eventually, neither will you.*

Smiling shyly, remembering the happy, quiet boy from the shore, Christine whispered, "We'll just have to see, now won't we?" She closed the door with an emphatic click.

"Who was that?" Erik asked as he emerged from the mirror, still wearing his evening clothes and mask.

CHAPTER *11*

CHRISTINE LEANED HER BACK against the dressing room's door, shoulders slumping. "No one." She did not want to talk to Erik about Raoul now, at least not until she figured out what she was going to do about him. "Just another opera lover." She tilted her head and gave him a tired smile. "Did you enjoy yourself? It wasn't a proper opera, I know."

Erik raised his eyebrow not covered by the mask but said nothing. He stepped into the room, a wide smile crossing his lips. "You were incredible!" he enthused.

From the various corners of the room came Erik's voice. "Brava!"

She gave him a tired smile. "Thank you," she

said as the echoes of his voice died away.

"I prepared a feast for you. You must be famished," he said, gesturing to the mirrored passage from which he'd emerged.

"I could eat," she told him. "I need to get out of this costume first."

Erik served as her dresser, his long fingers helping her with the various fastenings and laces. He took no liberties, not that she expected him to, and he turned away when she stripped to her underclothes. Once she was free of that costume and had slipped into her robe, Christine felt immeasurably better.

"All done," she said, holding out her hand when Erik turned around. "Lead on before my stomach declares war on my backbone!"

"Your wish is my command, Christine."

He took her to his house by way of the lake, poling the boat through the black water with ease. She was getting used to the sensation even though she still hung onto the sides of the small craft until her knuckles ached. It helped that Erik sang from *Aida* the entire time.

She gasped when he led her into his house. The place was awash in candlelight; Christine wondered how he'd managed to steal so many candles without anyone noticing. His little collection of glass and stone figurines stood arranged in a row, reflecting the light. The tapestries and carpets he'd raided from the various prop storage rooms helped the space feel warm and inviting, and he scavenged various pillows to a make a comfortable picnic area.

As she settled herself on a stack of pillows, Christine stared in awe at the lovely meal Erik had provided. Cold roasted chicken with sprigs of rosemary and sage still tucked under the crackling skin, cold blueberry soup, boiled new potatoes seasoned with dill, thin slices of salmon with onions and pickled herring, an array of hard cheeses with a loaf of bread, chocolate pastries, and two bottles of wine, one red and one white.

"You did all of this?" she asked as he set out plates and utensils and cloth napkins.

Erik hummed, nodding. "I thought you deserved something special after your performance. And since I can't take you to a fancy restaurant, I thought I would bring the fancy restaurant to you."

Christine snagged a pastry and bit into it. "You got me my favorite," she said around a mouthful of flaky dough.

Inclining his head in acknowledgement of her words, Erik uncorked a bottle of wine. "Red or white?"

"White, please." Christine closed her eyes as she polished off the pastry in a few more bites. Sighing, she said, "That was delicious."

Handing her a glass, Erik filled his own and then raised in a toast. "To Christine Daaé. May she have many more triumphs to come!" He looked in her eyes as they clinked glasses.

Christine nearly forgot her manners, almost looking away from the intensity of his gaze before remembering it was bad luck to not meet eyes when toasting. She smiled at Erik over the rim of her glass as she took a sip. Then she dug into the offered feast with gusto. As they ate, they spoke of this and that: favorite moment of the performance, best loved operas, childhood foods, strangest ghost stories they'd heard.

She's just finished off a piece of dark chocolate when Christine turned to Erik and asked, "Who taught you music? You have a remarkable depth of knowledge."

Erik put down his glass of red wine, the laughter fading from his eyes. Christine wondered if she'd made a mistake, but it was too late to back out now, and she was curious. He played a number of instruments, could read and write music, possessed a breathtaking knowledge of opera, and had an incredible voice. He might be a prodigy, but someone had to have taught him the basics. He hadn't learned them in the carnival.

He ran a hand through his hair, gaze abstract. He read his memories like pages of sheet music. His head was cocked as though listening. Just when Christine gave up on him ever answering her, Erik spoke. His voice was soft, wistful.

"My mother—she was an incredible talent. She gave voice lessons in our home. I grew up surrounded by music. And her voice," he shook his head, "I've only heard the like once." He stared at her.

She put her hand to her chest. "Me?" At his slow, reverent nod, she felt herself blush. "I'm flattered you think so highly of me." Christine paused, then asked, "Why didn't she ever go on the stage?"

Erik picked up a half-eaten piece of bread and began to pull it apart into tiny bits. "I'm not sure. She married my father when they were very young. He was a clerk at some shipping firm." He stopped tearing the bread and leaned his chin in his palm as he thought. "My mother was a quiet woman—almost shy. She never seemed to seek out the limelight, always more content to fade into the background."

When his smile came again, it was tinged with sadness. "But when she sang . . .," he shivered. "It was like she possessed this power that she could turn off and on, like one adjusts a gas light. Suddenly she was so big, her voice filling up every iota of space in any room. I remember sitting on the floor and just staring up at her as she sang the aria from *Aida*."

"You must have loved her deeply." Christine felt a surge of jealousy. Nothing she felt for her father was so pure and clear. She hoped she kept the bitterness from her voice.

He nodded. "I surprised her one day. She was playing the music on the piano for something—I don't remember what now—and I began to sing, just as she had. I don't remember how old I was, but I was little." He took a deep breath and released it slowly, like he was managing some phantom pain. "From that point on she taught me everything she knew. What she didn't know, I picked up on my own."

"You didn't go to school?" she asked him.

He gestured to his mask. "With this face?" Erik's laugh was mocking. "No. I barely left the house save for doctor's visits."

"Doctor's visits?"

"Surgeries. To fix my face. To make it look, well, if not normal then at least something that wouldn't cause people to scream in fear and horror." Again that pained smile. "As you can see it didn't work. It made it worse."

"How did she die?" Christine couldn't help but ask.

"Fever, I think." His hair, disrupted from its neat style, fell about his face. He tucked strands behind his ear absently. "My father wouldn't let me see her in case it was contagious. So I sang to her through the closed door." He closed his eyes. "When she stopped singing back, I knew she was gone."

Christine gasped, hand flying up to her mouth. "Oh, Erik."

He waved her concern away, his shoulders hunched as if buckling under the weight of a great burden. Slowly he straightened, giving her a tremulous smile. "Enough about me. What was your growing up like?"

Christine thought about spinning a fanciful tale of wonder about her youth, and found the thought of doing so made her queasy. Erik had shared his history with her without reservation, offering it up to her safekeeping. He didn't realize, or maybe he didn't care, how it made him vulnerable. For some reason, she found she didn't want to do any less for him.

"Pappa and I moved around a lot after Mama died," she began slowly, choosing each word carefully, like a jeweler choosing stones for a necklace. "He'd never really wanted to be a farmer, but Mama had insisted he settle down and try. He loved her, so he did." She paused, staring down at her hands. How relieved he must have been to finally leave that plot of land behind.

"But as soon as he'd buried her, Pappa sold the land and took to the road. He loved it out there— getting rides on carts, sleeping in barns, playing for his supper. At first, I thought it a grand adventure."

"And then?"

"It is a terrible thing to be cold and hungry and shivering in a hayloft not knowing if you'll be able to eat tomorrow." She rubbed at her wrist, needing something to ground her in the present.

Erik's hand covered hers, stilling it. When she looked up in surprise, he smiled at her. "I understand."

She thought that he did. If anyone could, it was Erik. The experience was as far beyond Raoul as the stars in the sky, but Erik knew that special kind of fear.

"Pappa began to play for money. He also talked people into outrageous bets. Sometimes he outright stole from them. He taught me how to pick pockets, how to pick locks, how to distract people so he could steal food from their cart. He always kept us on the move, working our way around the festivals and fairs where he could always find work and easy marks."

"That doesn't sound like much of a childhood."

"It wasn't all bad. Pappa managed to make everything feel like fun when I was younger. He had stories for every occasion." She slid her hand from beneath his. "I couldn't stay angry with him. No one could." It was one of the things she most resented about him. If she could hate him without feeling guilty, she might be able to resolve the division inside of her, but it was beyond her. She'd adored him as a child; it was only as she grew older that she realized what he'd turned her in to.

"Did you have any friends during that time?" he asked.

Christine thought of Raoul, knocking on her dressing room door earlier in the evening. She remembered him as a young boy, running into the ocean after her scarf, and then as a young man, stopping by the cottage in Perros several years too late to explain that he would never be able to see her again. "Not really, no."

He nodded, as if he understood what she wasn't saying just as much as what she was. "You have one now," he whispered, picking up her hand and kissing the back of it.

"And this celebration has become entirely too solemn," he said, rising to his feet and pulling her along with him. "What now, La Daaé?"

"I'm not the opera's diva yet."

"It is only a matter of time, my dear, until you triumph over your rivals and bring Paris to its knees before you."

She blushed and turned her head away, strangely undone by his words. Desperate to change the subject, she said, "You have so much confidence in me. And yet none in yourself even though you are so much better than I could ever be. Why?"

He pointed at his face. There was something sad and resigned in his voice when he said, "The only way anyone would want to hear me is through you, Christine. We both know that."

"In a way, I'm just another mask," she said, narrowing her eyes, unsure whether she approved or not, then deciding it didn't matter. Erik was committed to helping her for whatever reason and that was all she needed to know.

"A beautiful one, yes." He ducked his head shyly. "And one I am proud to wear."

She felt her face grow hotter with her flush. He needed to stop saying such things. Her insides swooped, turning strange and tight and tingling. His flattery felt true, nothing like what le Fure had said in hopes of wooing his way into her bed.

"Then let us sing together," she said. "The mask and the man."

He grinned and took up his violin. "Gladly."

CHAPTER 12

CHRISTINE SHOULD HAVE KNOWN it was too good to last. As soon as word of Christine's triumph reached La Carlotta's ears, the Spanish diva descended on the Palais Garnier in a fury of scalded pride and silk bustles. Erik had listened to her histrionics with the new managers, Monsieurs Moncharmin and Richard, and reported her demands of them—which ranged from a new dressing room to Christine never getting a part with greater than three lines again—to Christine.

"Lovely," she snapped as she paced the length of her dressing room. "If that old bitch won't let me sing, I'm as good as sunk."

Erik lounged on the sofa, his head thrown back over the arm on one end while his long legs dangled off the other. Christine found herself staring at the lean line of his throat, fascinated by the twitch and jump of muscles as he sang to himself. He'd taken to wearing the flesh painted mask that covered the less pleasant part of his face regularly, even when it was just the two of them. It annoyed her for some reason, like he was cheating by keeping part of himself hidden from her. She smothered her irritation—it wouldn't do to lash out at Erik just because she was furious at being blocked by Carlotta.

"We'll send the managers another note," she told him, speaking louder so he would hear her over his own humming.

Erik nodded, his foot tapping out a cadence in the air. When he didn't move, Christine crossed her arms and waited, pointedly staring at him until he finally looked over at her.

"I'm sorry," he said, blinking at her. "Did you say something?"

She wanted to snap at him. He wasn't taking any of this seriously. He might be happy staying in that drab little house on the lake, but he'd spent years in a carnival's cage. It was probably a step up for him. Christine had greater ambitions. She wanted to be done with the plans everyone else had for her. "Oh no, do continue," she said, sweeping into a broad bow. "I would hate to interrupt something *so* important."

Levering himself upright on the sofa, Erik swung his feet to the floor and glared at her with his brown eye. "What is bothering you so much?

You've been practically insufferable since you performed at the gala and it has nothing to do with Carlotta! If all you are going to do is snipe at me, I'll leave you alone."

The irritation that she'd trying so hard to stifle burst into a conflagration of anger. How dare he speak that way to her! If it wasn't for her, he'd still be wasting away in that cage, singing beautiful songs to people who couldn't appreciate them, who only wanted to gawk at his face for the cost of a few measly coins.

"Fine!" Christine shouted at him, flinging her hand in the direction of the mirror. "Go then! Hiding is all you're good for anyway!"

She knew as soon as the words passed her lips that she'd made a terrible mistake. Erik stood slowly, like a giant bird unfurling its wings, staring at her all the while. The cloudy blue eye blazed almost unnaturally behind the mask as his dark eye bored into her. He stood as tense as a wound spring, all quivering, barely restrained violence.

"And without me you'd still be slaving away in the chorus with all the other miserable little girls," he whispered in a deadly voice. "Good luck unseating La Carlotta, Christine."

He bowed mockingly. As he did so, he plucked the mask from his face and flung it at her feet before his heavy steps carried him through the dressing room mirror and down the secret tunnel that led to the bowels of the opera house.

Christine called after him, panic rising inside of her chest, a monster devouring her from the inside out. "Erik!"

He gave no acknowledgement that he heard and the mirror swung closed, cutting off sight of him. Walking over to the mask, Christine picked it and cradled it to her chest. She hadn't meant what she'd said, but she'd been frustrated by the foolish machinations of Carlotta. Christine worried that her plans were doomed to fail. She regretted the words as soon as she'd given them voice, but she couldn't take them back now and she certainly wouldn't apologize if she seemed ungrateful for his help.

So why did she feel so bad? Erik was a convenient tool, an acquaintance at best. She'd told him they were friends, but Christine didn't have friends. Did she? Dropping to sit on the sofa, she tried to think her way around the chorus of voices in her head.

Carlotta needed to go. If Christine had a hope in hell of becoming a prima donna, Carlotta needed to be forced to step aside. The only problem was that Carlotta wouldn't leave until someone pried her cold, dead hands from their grasp on that title at the Palais Garnier. Christine could send another note to the managers, but without the Opera Ghost to back up the threats, she might as well not even bother.

She could try to find another way out of her predicament. Christine's attempt at becoming a wealthy man's mistress had ended in disaster, but perhaps there was another way. Marriage might work out better for her. It might take a bit of doing, but Christine felt certain she could find someone suitable whom she could "convince" to marry her. Perhaps her father hadn't been wrong after all.

A knock sounded at her door. Setting aside Erik's discarded mask, Christine crossed the room. Raoul, the Vicomte de Chagny stood on the other side of the door, in a state of supreme agitation. "Hello, Raoul," she greeted, allowing a shy smile to cross her face. Perhaps her father was watching over her after all.

He brushed past her, surprising her with his rudeness. Stalking around her dressing room, he appeared to be looking for something as he poked his head into every corner. "Where is he?" he burst out, his eyes wild when he turned around to face her.

"Where is who?" Christine asked, though she felt a shiver of fear chill her limbs. She had to remain calm. No one could find out she and Erik were behind the fraud that was the Opera Ghost. With Erik angry at her, Christine couldn't trust him to be loyal if he were caught.

"The man! Where is the *man*, Christine?" Raoul sounded positively frantic.

She stepped back, gasping in surprise. He couldn't have heard, could he? Best to deny everything than risk being discovered. "I have no idea what you are talking about."

Raoul rounded on her, grabbing her upper arm in a firm grip. It wasn't tight enough to bruise her—he was still careful in his anger—but it did shock her. He must be terrifically upset to touch her in such an intimate way. That thought had her almost slipping into a grin.

"I heard a man, Christine—just now and on the night of the gala. You were talking to him in your dressing room! I demand to know who that man was! What is he to you?"

"You listened at my door?" Christine's fury returned at her privacy being invaded so cavalierly, her anger igniting like paper put to a matchstick. She jerked out of Raoul's grasp and shoved his chest so hard he stumbled away. "How dare you make demands of me like I'm some kind of common criminal? You have no right over me—you don't own me!" Her mind went to Erik, locked in his cage and another surge of anger crashed over her. "You, sir, are no gentleman!"

Her words seemed to strike Raoul hard enough to jolt him from his frenzy. The Vicomte approached her slowly, hands at his sides and contrition on his face. "Please, Christine, I must know. I've been going mad with the thought of it these past days. You must tell me who was in here with you. And I think I heard their voice again, just now."

He sounded so apologetic and sorry that Christine clasped her hands to keep them from shaking in her excitement. This she could use. Such jealousy and adoration made for a powerful aphrodisiac. Perhaps there was another use the Opera Ghost could be put to—one that would secure her liberation from the Palais Garnier into the bonds of marriage.

She made her decision.

Bottom lip trembling, Christine looked around the room, as though searching for something. She saw how closely Raoul watched everything she did and again bit back a smile. His eyes lingered on the music box Erik had crafted for her. He stepped over to it, examining it carefully. Christine watched him, body taut as violin strings, wanting to call him away from it. She jumped when he turned and looked at her curiously, as though afraid to ask the question he so desperately wanted an answer to.

Putting her finger to her lips, she gestured to the sofa, indicating he should sit. He did so, his eyebrows raised in wordless questioning. When he was seated, she joined him, taking one of his hands in hers.

"I don't know if you remember the tales my father used to tell us," she began hesitantly, as if searching for right words.

"Of course I do!" Raoul assured her.

She made a shushing motion, glancing toward the mirror. She expected Erik had returned to his house on the lake, taking refuge in his music after their disagreement. Still, she didn't want him to overhear what she was telling Raoul until she'd gotten a chance to speak to him about it first.

"The Angel of Music?"

At his confused look, she shook her head. "Never mind," she told him, moving to the edge of the sofa in preparation for getting up. "You wouldn't believe me anyway." She turned her face away from him, making sure to stare for just a moment too long at the mirror.

Raoul slid off the sofa so that he was blocking her exit. "Christine?" She felt his closeness as he knelt down on the floor before her. "Talk to me, darling, please."

Endearments. Delightful. He was already half-hooked. She just had to be careful reeling him in and then she wouldn't ever have to sing again if she didn't choose to. She wiped at imaginary tears, and met Raoul's gaze with a haunted expression.

"We can't talk here," Christine whispered, gaze darting around the room. "I'll send a note with details of where we can meet to speak."

"But Christine . . .," he began. She pressed her index finger to his lips and watched as his eyes slid closed at the touch of her hand.

"Not now, Raoul. You must trust me on this." She stood in a silken rustle of skirts and walked to the door. "Good day, Vicomte," she said in her normal voice as she opened the door to her dressing room.

"Good day, Mademoiselle Daaé." As he came even with her, he leaned down to whisper in her ear. "But are you safe, Christine?" His gaze lit once again on the music box. He raised an eyebrow in question.

Christine nodded. When he scowled, she put her hand on his arm, drawing his attention away from the music box. "My angel would never hurt me," she answered, a frown on her lips. "But it does not do to anger him."

At Raoul's horrified expression, she closed the door and stifled her laughter in her hands. She had him!

Now she just had to manage Erik.

CHAPTER *13*

"I HAVE AN IDEA," she called as soon as she entered Erik's house after giving him several hours to calm down. They'd discovered another way to the house on the lake from a tunnel in the backstage area where the large scrims were stored and now she could come and go as she pleased so long as she was careful not to be seen. It also meant Erik didn't have to ferry her across the lake which had always unnerved her. She hated being in that boat, surrounded by the cold, dark lake with fears of drowning and dying rose up inside of her.

She didn't see him at first. His dark clothes and hair blended a little too well into the shadows cast by the lamps and candles. He sat hunched in the corner of the house in the space curtained off as his bedroom. He held another mask in his hand, one she didn't remember seeing before.

"Erik?" she said, just loud enough to get his attention.

He jerked, nearly dropping the mask from unsteady hands. He turned his head in her direction, his pale face looking like it was floating in the air as the darkness hid his black clothes. "What do you want, Christine?" His voice was raw, ragged. Like he'd been screaming.

She felt odd, filled with something very like guilt. What had he been doing since he'd left her dressing room? Was he still upset at their argument? She'd long ago forgotten what had even started it. "To talk to you."

"I don't have anything to say to you," he said, climbing slowly to his feet. He wiped at his nub of a nose with the back of one hand and stalked past her to heat water for tea. "Go away."

"No."

"Get out!" he shouted and pointed to the door without turning around.

"No!"

His hands clenched into fists. "I don't want you here," he snarled.

"I don't care!" Christine knew that she shouldn't push Erik, but she couldn't help herself. She needed him on board with her plan for it to work.

With a roar, he grabbed the nearest, breakable figure from his ever-growing collection—a small crystal horse from heaven knew where—and flung it at the wall. It shattered, raining shards of glass. "Why don't you ever listen?"

"Because you're not saying what I want to hear!" she yelled back, not willing to admit that Erik's rage filled her with a dark thrill. She was the cause of that. It was a heady kind of power.

Erik laughed mockingly. "At least you're honest about some things."

"Don't be like that," Christine chided, stepping closer. "Why are you so upset?"

He swung back around suddenly, glaring at her. His body thrummed with barely leashed rage. Christine smiled up at him, refusing to show how his reaction unsettled and delighted her. "Why am I upset?" he snapped, rasping voice like rough stone against her ears. "You dare ask me why I'm upset?"

Christine rolled her eyes skyward. He could be so dramatic. "Yes, I *dare*." She placed the mask he'd flung at her on one of the tables he'd scavenged from the props languishing in storage. "I brought you the mask you *threw* at me."

"The things you say sometimes," he started, then shook his head as if thinking better of his words. "It's like you don't care that you hurt people."

She had been hoping he would have gotten over his insulted feelings by now. Christine didn't have time to wait until Erik decided he was done sulking over his slights; she needed his help with her plan now. "I do care."

His inelegant snort as he turned back around to

deal with his tea had her wanting to pick the mask back up and lob it at his head. Why must he be so difficult?! "I do!" she insisted. "It's just that—sometimes—my mouth runs off before I can think about what I am saying."

Leaning forward so she could see around him, she noticed that he'd only prepared one cup of tea, subtly telling her that she wasn't welcome to stay. Cautiously, wary of being shaken off, she placed her hand on his shoulder. She felt the muscle twitch beneath her fingertips, going taut with tension.

"Let me make it up to you," she murmured, thinking quickly. She needed to get Erik's help with Raoul. Men liked to feel powerful, like protectors. Raoul was eighteen but seemed much younger, so achingly naïve that it made Christine wish for a different kind of past. She needed him to see Erik as a credible threat. She had her story ready for Raoul, but she'd need a little something extra for him to buy into it like she wanted him to.

Erik frowned. Christine reached out and flicked his earlobe, earning her another glare. Huffing out a frustrated breath, he pulled out another teacup and began to fill it with tea from his pot. "What is it?"

His voice was still cold, but Christine thought she detected a faint thaw in it. She could work with that. "The anniversary of my father's death is coming up. I thought I might visit his grave this year." She paused, swallowing nervously. She hated it, the act of going to visit her father's grave as though she missed him, but she couldn't think of any place else that her plan would work.

She had his full attention. Erik turned to face her, slumping against the wall so he didn't loom over her quite so much. "What does this have to do with making something up to me?"

Christine reached up, tucking the black hair that hung over the good side of his face behind his ear. She hated when his hair fell into his good eye. It made it difficult to read his expressions.

Erik went eerily still at the touch of her hand. She heard his breath catch in his throat as he froze in place. His good eye was wide and dark when he met her gaze, and Christine was struck by how pleasing he could look if one ignored the other half of him. His hand came up, as if to catch hers and press it to his cheek, but Christine stepped away to say, "I want you to come with me."

Erik stared at her, stunned into gaping silence. When he finally recovered himself, all he managed to gasp out was, "Me?"

Smiling at his reaction, Christine nodded. "Yes!" As a wide grin split his face, Christine knew he'd forgiven her, or at least forgotten about her venomous words from earlier, which worked just as well.

"I've never really gone anywhere before," he told her in an awed voice. "At least not anywhere that I got to see. We went lots of different places with the carnival." His voice dropped to a low mutter at the mention of where Christine had found him.

"We'll take a train," she told him. "I have a few days off from the theatre—we can go then."

"What about . . .," he gestured toward his face.

"We'll figure something out," she assured him, her mind already working on what she would write to Raoul to get him to Perros so she could further the next step in her plan.

Erik's gentle hand on her arm surprised her. Startled, she glanced up at him, a question in her eyes. "Thank you, Christine," he whispered, smiling down at her with something warm and fond in his gaze.

She placed her hand atop his, feeling an answering warmth blossom inside of her. "You're welcome, Erik."

♫♫♫

The letter she sent to Raoul a few days later was vague, short, and perfectly calculated to light a fire of agitation under the Vicomte. She sent it late enough that he would already have missed the train she and Erik were taking.

Monsieur:

I have not forgotten the little boy who went into the sea to rescue my scarf. Today I journey to Perros to visit my father on the anniversary of his death. He is buried there, with his violin, in the graveyard of the church at the bottom of the slope where we used to play as children. It is beside the road where, when we were a little bigger, we said good-bye for the last time.

Pleased that Raoul would come running at the reference the unfortunate circumstances of his leaving Perros years ago, Christine set out. She had saved most of her share of the stipend money from the Opera Ghost con, as had Erik. He insisted on paying for a private car for the trip to Brittany rather than risk people staring at him— or worse, recognizing him from the carnival— and Christine had not objected. They'd passed the trip playing hands of écarté. She taught him bezique, which he picked up quickly, making her regret suggesting it. Erik laughed at her frown and collected the cards, easily shuffling them through his long fingers.

"I've been meaning to ask, but I didn't want to make you upset," he began, flipping the ace of hearts over his knuckles.

"So you've picked now, when I can possibly throw you out of a moving train in a fit of pique?" she answered with a grin. "Brilliant plan."

Erik ducked his head, but she saw his lips twitch in a half-hidden smile. "I never said I had a good sense of self-preservation." He folded the card back into the deck.

"I noticed." She leaned back in the seat, stretching out her sore neck. "Why else would you hide out in the opera house rather than leaving Paris entirely?" Glancing in his direction, she noticed the top of one of his ears turn red. He was blushing.

He coughed into his fist. "Yes, well, I wanted to

ask you about this trip. The things you've said about your father have me wondering why you'd come to his grave on the anniversary of his death. It seems—to me at least—that you've been trying to distance yourself from him as much as possible." He shuffled the deck again and dealt out a game of solitaire.

Staring out the window, Christine let her gaze drift to the darkness surrounding them. She felt like a burrowing animal, safe in a hole with earth pressing in on every side of her, keeping her warm and safe. Even though she'd vowed never to return to Brittany, she didn't feel anxious or upset at breaking her promise to herself. There was a part of her that wanted to go, that had been wanting to return for quite some time.

"I'm not sure how to explain it," Christine said aloud, although whether she was speaking to herself or Erik she was no longer certain. "I loved my father dearly, even when I hated the way we lived. Is it possible, do you think, to love someone and hate them at the same time?"

Erik nodded, his lacquered hair falling in his face after he ran a hand through it. He'd asked her to cut his hair for the occasion of their trip and she hadn't done too poor of a job on it. He'd told her he wanted to look neat when he went with her to see her father's grave. "Yes, I know that it is possible." His teeth worried at his lower lip, face twisting unpleasantly as he thought of something upsetting.

"Your parents?"

He turned to stare out the window, giving her his masked profile. "My father." Sweeping up his game of solitaire, he absently shuffled the cards as he spoke. "There were times when I was in that cage that I dreamed about killing him, of what I would do if I were ever to have him at my mercy." The visible part of his face tightened with rage. "Just as there are times when I wonder what I might do should he ever come to me to beg my forgiveness." He shrugged. "There is a part of me, I think, that will always want to see him again just to end things between us, one way or another."

"How do you not go mad with trying to make sense of what he did?" she asked him. Christine couldn't understand such things. If her father had treated her as Erik's had treated him, she thought she wouldn't be able to rest until she'd made him suffer for it.

Setting the cards aside, he leaned forward in his seat facing her. Christine likewise shifted, the air heavy with shared confidences. "Sometimes I wondered if I had," Erik whispered. "In that cage. I feared I had imagined having a mother and a father, imagined I'd had any home besides the bars behind which I lived." The broken sound that emerged from him was half-laugh, half-sob. "But then I would remember my mother and the way she used to sing."

He smiled softly, sadly. "There was always music in our house. Until the day there wasn't."

Christine nodded, thinking she understood. Her mother had died when she was young so she'd only known the love of one parent for most of her life, but she too had a childhood filled with music. When her father died, it had felt like he'd taken the music with him.

"One of my clearest memories is of Pappa playing the violin," she said dreamily. "It was the *Resurrection of Lazarus* and he played it magnificently. I always loved it when he played just for me."

Erik's hands stilled. "You make it sound like it didn't happen often."

Christine shifted, feeling the press of memories that she did her best never to think about. "I suppose he played all the time," she hedged.

"But not for you."

"Not *just* for me," she clarified. "When I was a child, I didn't notice it as much. But as I grew older, I realized how rare it was for him to focus his playing just on me and my enjoyment." Christine swallowed, the sudden lump in her throat surprising her. She'd said good-bye to her father years ago. She didn't understand why talking about him now would affect her so.

Erik said nothing, just watched her with hooded eyes, a quiet, comforting presence in the closeness of the private car. He reached out his hand, as if he wanted to touch her, but then seemed to think better of it and subsided back into his seat, his hands returning to rest on his knees. Christine tried not to let the burn of disappointment show on her face.

"It was almost always about the con, rarely about what I might want to hear or sing. What I wanted didn't really enter it, not when we had to eat." She looked down at her hands, lost in her memories. "But when he did," she smiled, "I felt like I'd gone to heaven."

"He was that good?" His voice sounded wistful.

Christine had never been inclined to false modesty for either herself or her family. "Yes. The best I ever heard."

"But that made you resent him more, didn't it?" he asked softly.

The darkness outside the window caught her eye. She didn't want to answer aloud because she knew what it would sound like, even though she knew Erik wouldn't judge her. Christine nodded.

"I know it sounds terrible," she finally admitted, "but I was almost relieved when he died. I thought it meant that I was free."

Erik cocked his head, one hand holding the cards delicately. "You don't strike me as feeling particularly free," he said hesitantly, like he was afraid of offending her.

Shaking her head so her wild hair bounced on her shoulders, Christine laughed bitterly. "I wonder if I'll ever truly be free," she said. At his questioning look, she continued, "Pappa made the Valérius couple my guardians and they loved his music even more than I did. To stay in their good graces, I had to keep up with it, even though a part of my love for it died when he did. They sent me to the conservatory where I was a passable student, completely mediocre because I never wanted this life."

"Why stay in it then?"

"You've been hungry before, have you?" At his nod, she pressed further. "And cold? So cold that your entire body never stopped shivering because it was the only thing keeping you warm?" Again came his slow nod. "Then you'll understand why I never want to experience those pleasures first-hand again."

"Even if it makes you miserable?" he asked.

"Miserable is relative," Christine answered quickly. If things worked out the way she hoped with Raoul, she would never have to sing again if that's what she wanted. She regarded Erik curiously. "I'm surprised you want anything to do with music after that carnival."

"Music was the only thing that brought me comfort," he told her after a few long moments of contemplation. "It was a way for my mind to escape that cage, the only escape I had on the really terrible days."

"But they made you sing! How was that an escape?"

"They didn't know I could sing, not at first. They just bought me from my father for my... for the way I looked. The first time I escaped, they forgave it, but after the second and third times, they punished me. To gain back some of the *privileges* I'd lost," Christine caught his grimace before he continued, "I let them 'catch' me singing so I had something to bargain with. They never knew that providing me with music was the thing I wanted the most."

"Oh," Christine exclaimed, eyes wide with admiration, "that's brilliant! And I bet you made them think it was their idea to add it to your shows!"

Erik ducked his head, ear flushing red at the tip and she knew she'd guessed correctly. Perhaps they were more alike than she'd originally thought. They'd both understood what needed to be done to survive and they both had figured out enough of human nature to understand how to manipulate people to their advantage. Perhaps Erik would understand what she was trying to do with Raoul and she didn't have to fool both of them.

"Erik," she began, reaching out to touch his knee across the seat.

"I think we're here!" he said, shifting closer to the window so he could watch as the train pulled into the small station.

Christine sat back in her chair and kept her thoughts to herself.

CHAPTER 14

ERIK INSISTED ON HIS own room with a window at the top of the inn. Christine's room was on the second floor, though she did check on him once they were settled and suggested food be sent up to their rooms rather than have him sit in the main room for meals. He acquiesced gratefully, agreeing that it was probably for the best.

Before they'd left Paris, Christine had checked the train schedules to determine when Raoul might be expected to arrive. If he took the train immediately after he received the letter, he'd be there that evening or possibly the next morning. She and Erik had the better part of the day to explore Perros before she had to worry about Raoul showing up.

Erik left well before she did, an instrument case strapped to his back. Christine circled around the rear of the house and met him there. "Are we going to see your father?" he asked as soon as he saw her.

It was the last thing she wanted to do, but Christine knew that she should get it over with, so she led Erik to the small cemetery beside the church where a large stone angel loomed over the headstones. As she knelt and tried to order her thoughts into something approaching coherence and respect, Erik opened his case and took out an old violin.

"Where did you get that?"

Tucking it beneath his chin with the ease of long practice, he said, "There are lots of abandoned instruments just waiting to be reclaimed throughout the opera house. You'd be amazed what you can find if you really look. This one was still in decent shape. It just wanted new strings."

"You know how to play?"

He nodded, hair flopping across his forehead. His mask covered the misshapen half of his face. "I've been practicing—it's been some time since I've played."

When he set bow to strings, Christine swore she forgot how to breathe. The aching, trembling wail of the violin hit her like a horse-hoof to the chest, blasting the air out of her. Tears filled her eyes at the impeccable rise and fall of the notes, the sweet whine of sound that swirled out from

Erik. He stood before Pappa's grave, swaying with the music as he coaxed out the gorgeous voice of the old violin, just as he coaxed out Christine's true voice. It was his special kind of magic, that he seemed to make the ordinary extraordinary, that he elevated the plain into something sublime.

Recognizing the song, Christine raised her voice in song, weaving her voice into the aural tapestry that Erik wove. It was a tribute she wasn't sure her father deserved, but she couldn't deny that she appreciated Erik's gesture. She watched him, his lanky frame bent over the violin like a witch stirring magic in a cauldron. His face split in an ecstatic smile as his music transported him somewhere truly other, a paradise he created with his talent. She'd never seen someone look more beautiful.

Stepping forward, she let her tears fall on Pappa's headstone. A festering darkness she'd kept close to her like a rotting shadow broke open and she dropped to her knees with a sob. "I'm sorry, Pappa," she whispered, hands clutching the grass that had grown up around his headstone.

Erik's playing screeched to a halt and he dropped down beside her, his sharp knees digging into the mushy earth. The smell of green, growing things and rich mud filled Christine's nostrils. She closed her eyes and leaned against Erik, tremors still shuddering through her.

"I'm sorry, I didn't mean to make you upset," he whispered, his lips against her hair.

Shaking her head, Christine let out a watery

laugh. "You didn't, I swear it. Your playing was the greatest honor you could have paid him. I'm sorry I interrupted it."

"I can play it again," he offered, a worried frown on his half-visible face.

Christine stood, steadying herself on her father's headstone. "Not now," she said, a glimmer of an idea forming in her mind. Holding out her hand, she said, "Let's take a walk to the shore. You can play again tonight. I'm going to have a mass said for him."

Erik took the offered hand. Christine didn't flinch at the cold flesh; she'd grown used to him. "Very well, Christine. If that's what you wish."

"It is, Erik," she murmured as they walked away from her father's grave arm in arm. "Very much so."

♫♫♫

Christine returned late in the afternoon to find Raoul sitting downstairs at the inn, drawing on a piece of paper. She'd requested a mass be said for her father earlier that day and had gone to hear it. Raoul must have only just arrived—he looked harried and windblown with his flushed cheeks and coat in disarray, younger than his eighteen years. He'd clearly been in a hurry to get there from the station. Christine welcomed him with wide eyes and a shocked expression.

"Raoul! I did not think you would actually come!" she lied, smiling prettily. She glanced over his shoulder to see what he was working on.

It was a sketch of her. She stared for a long moment, surprised at the simple beauty and accuracy of the drawing. She'd had no idea that Raoul could draw so well. What else might he surprise her with?

"How could I not come, Christine?" he chided her, rising so he could pull out a chair for her. He signaled for a glass of wine before folding the sketch and sliding it into his jacket pocket. "Especially when you hinted at answers to the mysteries of the Opera House!"

"You'll have your answers," she assured him, settling into her seat. "How was your journey?"

"The man's voice, Christine," Raoul reminded her, unwilling to be distracted. "You said you'd speak of that."

Glancing around the nearly empty room, she pretended to consider. She already knew the story she was going to spin, but there were layers to every good con that made it believable. She didn't want to make a sloppy, careless mistake.

"Yes, of course," she answered reluctantly. Christine paused while Raoul's glass was set in front of him, and began again once he'd taken a sip. Widening her blue eyes as much as she could, she said, "My father always told me that once he died and reached Heaven, he would send the Angel of Music to me to continue my education. Well Raoul," she put a note of breathless excitement into her voice, "Pappa did die and the Angel of Music finally appeared to me some months ago!" She clasped her hands together tightly in front of her chest. "Isn't it remarkable!"

She worried that she might be overplaying the wide-eyed innocent, but Raoul's expression of concern convinced her otherwise. "What do you mean 'appeared to you,' Christine?" His voice held an edge of jealousy and worry.

Exactly what she wanted.

"A voice, Raoul—what did you think I meant?" She blinked at him confusedly. "I thought I was the only one who could hear him until you told me you'd heard his voice the night of the gala."

"So you've never seen him in person?" He sounded relieved. She couldn't have that.

"At first, no." Christine sunk her teeth into her lower lip. "It was just his voice, giving me singing lessons in my dressing room at the opera house. He told me to keep it from everyone, but I had to tell my guardian, Madame Valérius. She was so excited when she heard the news!"

Raoul twisted his body in his chair, almost as if he couldn't bear to keep still. He looked like he wanted to move, to jump out of his seat and pace, but refrained in case he frightened her. Perfect. "And then? Have you seen him simce?"

Nodding, Christine leaned forward, as if she couldn't stop the story pouring out of her. She spoke quickly, tripping over the words in her haste. "He revealed himself to me after you came to my dressing room the second time." Raoul flinched at her phrasing. Christine had deliberately worded it so it sounded more risqué than the visit had actually been. "He told me that I'd earned the privilege of seeing him but that I must remain loyal if I ever hope to ascend to the heights I'm capable. Then he took me to where he lives—it's beneath the opera house!"

He gritted his teeth. "You're still a good girl, aren't you, Christine?" Raoul asked, his face going a strange, ashen grey.

There it was. Christine felt the dull thud of disappointment deep in her chest. Raoul asking if she was spoiled goods was exactly what she'd expected to happen, but her indignation was real regardless. She jumped to her feet, hands clenched into fists. This, at least, she didn't have to fake. "Of course, I am," she practically yelled at him, pulling backwards and away from his grasp.

"How dare you even ask me such a question!" She took a step closer to his chair; eyes narrowed with rage. "We just sang, Raoul, but thank you so much for expecting the worst from me."

She spun around before her true feelings could be revealed on her face. Raoul was giving her so much to work with. Now, though, was the time to expeditiously retreat. As he called out a bereft, "Christine!" she fled upstairs.

"I knew you wouldn't understand," she tossed over her shoulder to torment him just a bit more.

She waited for an hour or so in her room. Erik was resting and Christine didn't want to disturb him, so she paced restlessly, going over the next portion of her plan. Raoul was inexperienced with women and he already had a connection to her.

Christine could work that angle, especially since he was protective of her innocence.

Christine snorted, then covered her nose and mouth with her hand. Asking if she was still a good girl? She knew exactly what he meant by that question. She imagined Raoul would not only be upset over their fight, but also that he had been so forward to ask that of her. Still, it spoke of his interest in her, his forgetting his manners like that.

When she'd thought she'd given him enough time to calm down, Christine left her room to journey downstairs. The Inn's mistress directed her to the path that led up to the bluffs. She knew it well—she and Raoul had played there as children. Tying a blue scarf around her head, she had supper sent to Erik's room while she went to look for Raoul.

The Vicomte wasn't hard to find. He sat on the cold ground, knees drawn up to his chest as he stared at the waves breaking below him. Christine stopped and watched for a few minutes. He was so perilously young-looking. His innocence shone through his blue eyes. She knew he'd been protected by his older brother, Philippe. It left him unprepared for the less savory elements in the world.

People like her.

When he turned his head to look back at her, she couldn't help but flinch at the misery in his eyes. Raoul might be easy to manipulate, but Christine knew he felt things deeply. She felt momentarily bad for her anger, when he'd come to the cottage and told her he could no longer see her. As much as she knew those were his brother's orders, his words had still hurt her. But seeing him like this, she wished suddenly to be someone different. Someone who didn't immediately look at another person and figure out what use they could be put to.

She walked over to join him. The wind was cold, whipping in off the water. Christine had no idea how long Raoul had been out there, but he was chilled to the bone. He hung his head as she lightly touched his shoulder.

"I am truly sorry to have overstepped my . . .,"

She placed her gloved hand over his lips. "Don't talk, Raoul. I already forgave you," she assured him. "He's my teacher and that's all he is. You needn't worry."

Raoul subsided into quiet. Christine settled beside him as gracefully as she could. When Raoul spoke again, it wasn't what she was expecting. "What were those tales your father used to tell all those years ago?" His expression was wistful as he looked at the sea crashing against the rocks below.

Christine laughed, remembering those stories. "Little Lotte," she said and began to recite the words they both knew by heart from hearing them from her Pappa. "thought 'Am I fonder of chocolate or ribbons or frocks.'"

"Your father always knew the best ghost stories," he said. "I remember us huddling together as children while he told us frightening

156

stories from the north. Then he'd play his violin for us to lighten the mood."

Christine stared out in the direction of the churchyard where her father was buried. She shivered, second thoughts about the events she'd planned for tonight leaving her cold. Maybe she should give up this whole idea, let Raoul go where he wanted rather than force him along a path that might not be right for him.

"Do you really believe your father sent you an angel, Christine?" He sounded tentative but determined to see the conversation through.

Christine blinked at the sudden subject change. "Yes, of course I do."

He turned hang-dog eyes on her. "I know it is going to upset you, but I think someone is having a laugh at your expense."

Jumping to her feet, Christine gathered her skirts roughly in mock-fury. "Never mind! It was a mistake to invite you! Just go!" She stomped off in huff, a secret smile on her face.

Now he'd be more determined to prove the ghost false. Which would lead him right to Erik.

CHAPTER 15

WHEN CHRISTINE LEFT THE inn by the main door at half past eleven, she felt sure Raoul would follow her, and he did not disappoint. Affecting the air of a sleepwalker, she was still able to keep tabs on the Vicomte as he stumbled along the darkened road behind her. He was right to think her mad; were she in his position, she would have thought the same. Hopefully after tonight, he would have no further doubts as to her sanity. Raoul was a sweet young man, easily trusting and relatively sheltered. Christine vowed she would protect him from people like her when they were married. She slowed when he seemed in danger of falling too far behind, but when she arrived at the low stone walls of the cemetery, Christine hurried to her father's gravestone.

The moon hung like a silver coin in the sky, almost full, the air chill with late winter. The snow had mostly thawed except in shaded areas or where it had piled against the corners of the church. As she grew closer to the gravesite, the stone angel loomed large, swathing Pappa's tombstone in its shadow. The wind had died. The scent of rain mixed with the lush smell of growing grass. Christine thought a storm likely. A few stars managed to peek through the heavy cloud cover, offering diffused light that allowed her to pick out certain parts of the statue, as if viewing a half-solved puzzle. She didn't see Erik, but she trusted that he was there. All according to her plan.

Christine stopped in front of her father's tombstone and began to speak. "Pappa, you were right," she said with as much girlish excitement as she could pour into her voice. She suspected Raoul couldn't hear her, but it didn't do to be sloppy. Cons had gone south for less.

"The Angel of Music—he came to me. I've never heard such singing." She hadn't seen Raoul, but suspected he lurked nearby. She hoped he was close enough to hear her words, but knew they weren't the important piece of this particular performance.

"Thank you for sending him to me. I miss you so much, Pappa." A lie, but Raoul didn't need to know that. So much of this speech was performance, one of her best. "I wish you were somehow here again. I know you can hear me when I sing, Pappa, but it just isn't the same."

As if on cue, Erik's violin sang out from the statue. Christine had told him what she wanted him to play, though she hadn't elaborated on why. It was a piece Pappa had often played for her and Raoul when they were children, the melancholy *Resurrection of Lazarus*. They'd spent hours listening to her father play on the beach, the colors of the water and sky drawing out his homesickness for his native Sweden. She was certain Raoul would recognize it.

"Thank you, Erik," she whispered, knowing he wouldn't hear it, but overcome with the urge to acknowledge him for the beauty he coaxed from bent wood and strings. Her eyes filled with tears once again. Christine felt like she'd cried more with Erik than she had in her entire life before meeting him.

She stayed where she was, her face tilted up to the statue. When the last note of the song faded, she stood and began to make her way back to the Setting Sun inn. The cold had settled into her bones, seeping up through the thin soles of her shoes. The emotion of the day and the stress of maintaining her façade made her steps sluggish. Holding up the hem of her sleeping gown, she shivered as the cold wind skirled around her ankles. Hopefully Raoul had witnessed Erik's virtuoso performance and would now give credence to her Angel of Music story. She'd done as much as she could tonight and all she wanted to do was sleep.

It didn't take long to return to the inn, and she let herself in with the key the innkeeper had given her. She left the door unlocked for Erik, hung the key on the nail near the bar, and took herself up to her room. Wrapping the quilt tightly around her, Christine huddled in the bed and tried to get warm.

She must have dropped into a doze because she jerked awake at the soft knock on her door. Still clutching the quilt around her, she opened it to reveal Erik, his clothes and hair in disarray. His eyes were wild and he clutched his mask in one hand, and the broken neck of the violin in the other.

"What happened to you?" she asked, pulling him into the bedroom. He offered no resistance, a dazed expression on his face.

She led him to the only chair in the room and pushed him into it. He sank down without protest. "He attacked me," Erik muttered in disbelief. He stared down at the broken violin in his hands, stunned.

Christine gently slipped the mask back over his face. "Raoul?"

Erik nodded and held up the neck of the instrument. "He broke it."

There was a part of her that wanted to laugh. He looked so bereft, so utterly confused! Christine found it funny in a strange way since he appeared so offended. Carefully she took the remnants of the instrument from him and placed it on the floor beside the chair.

"I was leaving, being quiet just like you told me," Erik said, "and I was going around the side of the church like you said to do." He reached up and pressed two fingers to his mask, as if assuring himself it was there. "He saw me near the pile of skulls near the back wall of the church and chased me. I ran inside to try to get away, but he followed and grabbed onto my coat."

Christine made a choked noise in the back of her throat. Erik didn't look injured, but what about Raoul? Erik wouldn't have killed him, would he? She'd told him a little of what she planned for Raoul, so she hoped he understood how important the Vicomte was, but what if Erik lost his temper? There was a rage simmering inside him that he rarely let out, but Christine had seen its aftermath.

She took a deep breath to calm herself. She was being silly. Raoul was probably fine. "What did you do then?" she asked, doing her best to keep her voice calm.

He gave her a look like he was questioning her sanity. "I hit him, of course!"

A bolt of fear speared her. "Did you hurt him?" No one was supposed to get hurt. What if Erik scared Raoul away?

"Probably!" Erik flung up his hands. "I didn't really stop to ask if he was okay!"

Christine tried to keep calm—no need for both of them to be upset. Keeping her voice even, she soothed him. "It's all right, Erik. What happened next?"

Swallowing hard, Erik dropped his hands into his lap. "We struggled. He tried to hold onto me." Erik wore a strangely lost expression. "All I wanted to do was get away, but he kept grabbing at me. I dropped the violin and he stepped on it—I heard it crack." He glanced down at the ruined violin, a frown crossing his face. "We crashed into some pews and ended up near the high altar. He grabbed at my face and ripped off my mask."

Christine gasped, hands going up to cover her sudden smile. This had worked out even better than she could have hoped! Raoul had caught a glimpse of Erik's face. While it wasn't exactly what she'd planned, Christine knew she could turn this to her advantage. If she spun the story the right way, she could have Raoul eating out of the palm of her hand.

"How did he react?" she asked when she could school her expression back to seriousness.

"The look on his face!" Erik shuddered, scowling. "It overwhelmed him. I pushed him backwards and he staggered. He finally let go of my coat. I ran and I didn't look back."

"Did you come straight here?" She did her best to speak in cool tones, keeping her excitement hidden as best she could. "No one followed you?"

Erik shook his head. "Not that I noticed. I didn't come directly back just in case though."

She nodded her approval. Raoul would likely be fine. It sounded like a minor scuffle. The shock of seeing Erik's face probably frightened Raoul more than Erik's punch had. She stood, brushing her hands, intending to usher her friend back to his room.

But when she glanced at him, Christine noticed how tightly Erik's arms were wrapped around his middle. He hunched over, looking miserable. "Are you all right? Did you get hurt?" She knelt down so she could peer into his face.

He was so young, his expression open and terribly vulnerable. Christine imagined him as a boy, sitting in that carnival cage, hoping that someone would look at him and see not a monster, but a frightened child. How much time and growing had he lost to the carnival? How many experiences had he been deprived of, singing in that cage and being gawked at by people who couldn't look beyond his appearance?

"No, I'm not hurt," Erik whispered, but she could see how pale he was and how he shook. Her insides ached for him. "I'll be fine." His teeth chattered.

"Silly boy," Christine chided, standing. "Scoot over."

He raised his head then, dark bangs falling across the flesh colored mask. "What?"

Sighing in exasperation, Christine nudged his legs with hers. He finally responded by moving over as far as he could. Raising her quilt up like a cape, she draped it over the back of them both and squeezed her body next to Erik's in the chair. She wrapped her arms around him and settled her head beneath his shoulder.

"What are you doing?" His rich voice sounded

terrified.

"Do be quiet, Erik, and let me hold you," she soothed.

After a few still moments, she felt his hand come up and rest on top of her head. A few fraught minutes more and Christine felt those long fingers begin to card through her lion's mane of hair, caressing her scalp. She hummed lazily, an aria from *Romeo and Juliet*, as she felt him relax more and more beside her.

Christine dreamed of her father.

They trudged up to the door of the farmhouse, cold and wet. They were still at least a day's journey from the next festival town, but night was falling as was the rain. They'd been slogging through it all day. Christine's short legs were mud spattered up to her knees and she shivered beneath her coat. Her father at least hadn't made her carry anything—he shouldered their packs and his fiddle across his back as if they weighed nothing.

She sniffled. She missed the farm and her mother. It had been two years since her mother died, but Christine always missed her more when she was sick. No one made her feel as warm and safe as Mamma. Her throat hurt and her head pounded, but Pappa had promised a warm meal and a fire at the end of all their walking. It was the only thing that had kept her putting one foot in front of the other as her nose started leaking snot that mixed in with the water from the rain.

An older man opened the door. He was perhaps Pappa's age, maybe a few years older. But his face was deeply lined and weather beaten where Pappa's was still cheery and soft looking, ready with a smile a moment's notice. He scowled at them as they stood shivering in the wet and cold.

"What do you want?" the man said.

Christine let her father speak, but her stomach fell. This wasn't the face of a man who would let them warm themselves by his fire. Everything Pappa promised for the night might as well have been flushed away by the rain.

"My little girl and I seek shelter for the night."

"I don't take in strangers."

Her father smiled his charming smile. Christine peered around his leg to get a glimpse at the inside of the house. It was a small, rough farmhouse, but it held a fire that burned brightly in the hearth. She wanted nothing more than to curl up in front of it and fall asleep.

"I notice you have a barn." Pappa gestured toward the neat building a short distance from the main house. "We could sleep in the hayloft if you'd allow it. Just something to get out of the wet." He tugged Christine closer so that the farmer could get a look at her. She gazed up at the man piteously, not needing to act tired and hungry.

The famer sighed, rubbing a hand down his face. "Very well. You can stay the night there."

"Bless you, sir. We have nothing to pay you with, but perhaps a song? My daughter has quite the lovely voice."

The man regarded Christine with a sour expression. She could only imagine what he saw when he looked at her: a bedraggled urchin, covered in mud, drenched to the bone, with hollow eyes and a red nose from wiping it on her sleeve all afternoon. In that moment, she hated her father for making her a pitiable spectacle, her discomfort and sickness something to be gawked at and leveraged for a night's rest in a barn. She missed her mother desperately.

Pappa's knee nudged her back, signaling for her to begin. Christine opened her mouth, but all that emerged was a ragged, broken cough. Once started, she couldn't seem to stop, bending over at the waist. Pappa made an embarrassed noise.

"She's ill," he said by way of apology. "But if you let me see her settled, I will come back and play for you and your family myself."

Christine glanced up at her father through eyes that brimmed with tears. Her throat felt like she'd swallowed broken glass, but Pappa stood smiling at the man at the door as if there was nothing to worry about. She shrank back, fever sweeping through her. Her thin body burned and froze all at the same time.

The farmer nodded. The smell of something roasting hit Christine's nostrils then, and her stomach grumbled loudly. Tugging on her father's arm, she tried to get his attention, but he shook her off.

"I'll return presently," Pappa said. The farmer closed the door, leaving them in the rain.

She slogged behind her father, breathing a sigh of relief when they were finally out of the wet beneath the barn's roof. She dropped to a pile of hay, not even bothering to take off her wet coat. She wished her Mamma was there to comfort her. Instead, her father coaxed her out of her coat and boots and wrapped her in a dry blanket. He shook out their wet things and hung them to dry.

Brushing her hair from her face, her father said, "I'll be back soon with something for you to eat."

She tried to nod, but Christine slipped into exhausted sleep before she could do anything.

She woke up later, not sure what time it was. Her father was not back yet so she hadn't slept long. She shifted on the hay as a few pieces dug into her through the rough blanket, and snuggled back down. She felt warm and clammy, but glad to be out of the wet. She barely lifted her head when she heard the barn door open.

"Christine?" her Pappa called softly.

He carried a small bowl in his hand with one of his handkerchiefs draped over it. The smell of stew carried to her and she managed to sit up, suddenly ravenous. Her father handed her the bowl with a chuckle, watching with amusement as she shoveled the cooling meat into her mouth with her fingers.

"Do you feel well enough to travel tonight?" he asked as she licked her fingers clean.

She thought for a moment. The nap helped, but she still didn't feel her best. She told her father so and he shook his head. "There's nothing for it though. We'll need to move quickly."

"Why, Pappa?" she asked, burrowing back into her blanket.

"I found where they stashed their savings," he said, looking pleased with himself. "I only took half, but we need to be well shot of here before they notice."

Christine gaped at him. He smiled down at her and patted her shoulder. "Get as much sleep as you can. I'll wake you before dawn."

Too full and tired to do anything else, she did as her father said.

Christine jolted awake at the frantic knocking on her door. She rubbed at her face, angry and unsettled by the dream of her past. She didn't want to be reminded of her childhood spent sleeping in barns and relying on the kindness of strangers. Her father had loved the challenge of it, so much that even when Monsieur Valérius took them in, Pappa still dragged them around the countryside during the summer fair season. He had the nerve to act like she should be grateful for the experience. Getting back to their roots, he'd called it.

Erik roused almost immediately and jumped away from the chair where they'd slept like he'd been in danger of catching some wasting disease from her. Ignoring the hurt she felt at his reaction, she gestured for him to stay out of sight and went to answer the pounding at her door.

Her hostess stood in the threshold, hands clutched nervously together. "Mademoiselle, you must come downstairs at once," the woman urged.

"What is the matter?" Christine asked, keeping the door half-closed and blocking the rest of the doorway with her body to allow Erik time to hide.

"Your young man—the one you spoke with in the common room yesterday—he has been found!"

"I wasn't aware he was lost," Christine answered worriedly. She blinked confusedly at the woman.

"He was found this morning, Mademoiselle, passed out in front of the altar of the church. Some men have just brought him round and I've sent for the doctor. But I thought you'd like to know since you seemed to know each other."

"Thank you," Christine simpered. "I'll be right down as soon as I dress."

As soon as the woman disappeared back down the stairs, Christine closed and locked her door and rounded on Erik. "I thought you said he was fine!"

Erik stood from where he'd been crouched behind the chair they'd slept in, and he still looked groggy. He grabbed the quilt and folded it neatly. "Forgive me that I didn't stay to check on his well-being, Christine. Especially after he attacked me. It's not my fault if he fainted dead away at the sight of me unmasked," he growled, practically lobbing the folded quilt at her bed.

"I have to go see to him," she told him, gathering up her dressing things.

Erik raised his head, capturing her gaze with his. His eyes were sad and angry by turns. "Why must you?"

"I'm at a key moment in the plan, Erik," she told him, unable to keep the condescension from her voice. "It's important that mine be the first face he sees when he wakes."

"What plan?" he asked, suspicion turning his voice hard. The line of his jaw firmed as he clenched his teeth.

"Never mind," Christine dismissed, not in the

mood to argue with him. "I don't have time to waste—turn around so I can change. When I know how much he remembers of last night, we can make ready to return to Paris."

What was visible of his face flushed a dark red. Erik took a deep breath and held himself stiff, shoulders thrown back proudly. "I'll do you one better, Christine. I'll leave you to it." He stalked to the door, opened it, and strode up the stairs to his room.

Gritting her teeth in sudden anger, Christine just barely managed to not slam the door behind him. Why must Erik get so upset? It was ridiculous that he should make her feel bad for doing what she needed to in order to survive. If Raoul could be persuaded to marry her, she wouldn't have to bother becoming a diva, and she'd be taken care of in comfort for the rest of her life. She knew Erik wanted her to be happy, so why was he acting so childish?

Throwing on her clothes as quickly as she could, Christine tried to put Erik out of her mind. She needed to be focusing on Raoul—he was who was important right now. But the more she tried not to think of Erik, the more rage-filled she became. All she wanted to do was march upstairs, bang on his door, and yell at him until he saw her way of things. Why did he have to make things so difficult?

By the time she'd finished putting up her hair, she'd leashed her temper. Vowing to focus only on Raoul, Christine hurried downstairs to find him sprawled on a couch, covered in blankets. Knowing that eyes were upon her, she gasped and raced to his side.

"My dearest," she said, taking his limp hand in hers and lifting it to her cheek. "Oh, my darling Raoul." She pressed an earnest kiss to the back of his hand.

She stood beside him, waiting for him to wake. It took several minutes of her calling his name and entreating him to open his eyes, but eventually he did. His skin was ashen and clammy to the touch. His tightly curled hair had become even curlier in the sea air.

When his eyes finally cracked open, she gave a small sigh of relief. He gazed up at her, blue eyes blearily focused on her face before he recognized her. When he finally did, he grabbed her hand in both of his and spoke in hushed tones, pulling her down so the rest of the room didn't hear.

"I saw him, Christine! That monstrous face— I'll never forget it! You must believe me, Christine. It is not an Angel of Music that visits you, but a demon from hell!"

"Shhhh, Raoul." She extricated one hand so she could pet his hair soothingly. He leaned into her touch, and Christine crowed internally. Last night had been a success beyond her wildest hopes! "You've been through quite the ordeal. You must rest now."

He sighed, eyes sliding closed. "You must believe me, Christine," he murmured. "I fear you are in grave danger."

"Hush now, my darling," Christine whispered, squeezing his hand. She wanted to shout for joy, but suppressed her elation, though a fond smile still curved her lips. "The doctor is coming to make you well again. You mustn't tax yourself."

Raoul's eyes opened once more, their crystalline blue almost shocking in the pallor of his face. "You'll stay with me, won't you, Christine."

Pressing a gentle kiss to his forehead, she assured him, "Of course, Raoul."

His eyelids drooped. The tight grip on her hand loosened, though Raoul did not let it go even in sleep. Christine looked around and found the matron ushering the doctor in.

As the doctor approached, Christine gathered herself and stood. Hurrying up the stairs, she climbed to the third floor and knocked on Erik's door. "It's me," she whispered at the jamb.

Slowly, the door opened to reveal his brown eye. He said nothing, just stared at her for a long moment. When it didn't seem like he would ever say anything, Christine ordered with a roll of her eyes, "Gather your things. We're going back to Paris."

CHAPTER 16

CHRISTINE BIT BACK A yawn as Madame Giry inspected their held positions. She and Erik had arrived back in Paris late the previous evening and he'd disappeared into the underbelly of the Palais Garnier while Christine had gone to Madame Valérius' flat. Madame Valérius had been overjoyed to hear that Christine's Angel of Music had appeared to her in Perros, accepting it as proof that Pappa Daaé still watched over her from his seat in Heaven.

Christine had a hard time choking back her laughter. If her father was watching her from anywhere, it was from his spot in Hell. She wondered what he thought of her now. Would he be proud how she'd taken his lessons to heart?

She'd told Madame about Raoul too, just in case he came looking for her, as she suspected he would. Christine had done an adequate job of building a mystery to ensnare the young man, but she needed Madame Valérius to corroborate her story. Thankfully, the credulous woman was more than willing to believe in the existence of the Angel of Music, and serve as a stumbling block for Raoul's pursuit of her.

"If it is between the Vicomte de Chagny or your Angel, your music must come first!" the old woman had said. Christine had agreed with a small smile.

While she was pleased at the outcome of her visit to Perros, the trip had left her exhausted. She wasn't given a chance to rest before having to report back to the Palais Garnier for rehearsals. Christine slumped in relief when Madame Giry finally dismissed them.

As the chorus trooped back to their dressing rooms after rehearsal, she heard Meg complaining about the managers barring her mother from doing anything with Box Five. That was news.

"The Opera Ghost won't be happy to hear about this, let me tell you!" Meg announced while several girls expressed their solidarity with the dancer. Meg had been using her mother's 'relationship' with the Opera Ghost as a social bludgeon on some of the younger members of the corps.

Christine nodded like she actually cared. The

new managers had not been nearly as amenable as the old ones, but she had too much on her mind to worry about them right now. Erik seemed not to care since she was not performing, and as long as the managers paid their stipend, Christine was inclined to forget about Box Five.

Erik hadn't spoken to her since Perros anyway. The trip back to Paris had been painful in its silence. Erik had curled up and slept most of the way, and when he was awake he kept what counted as his nose buried in a book to avoid having to speak with her. Christine played solitaire and plotted out her next move in getting Raoul to marry her, doing her best to ignore Erik's brooding sulk. It hadn't worked; she just sat in the silence and stewed.

In her frustration, she'd lashed out at him toward the end of the train trip. "Are you planning to spend your entire life pretending I no longer exist?" she'd snarled, snapping the cards together in an angry shuffle.

He'd simply gazed up at her reprovingly from the pages of his book, gave a sigh, and said, "Stop acting like a child." Then he went back to his reading.

She'd thought about reaching over and yanking off his mask and throwing it from the train car's window. Let him walk the corridors of the train—or better yet, the streets of Paris!—without it. That would show him. With a final glare, she settled in her seat and eventually dozed off a few minutes before they had to disembark.

"What about you, Christine?" Meg asked, loud enough for everyone around them to hear. "Aren't you worried about what the Opera Ghost will think? He kept you in his lair!"

She found herself the center of attention as all eyes of the chorus stared at her. She gave a nervous laugh, wishing that she could sew Meg's mouth shut. "Why look at me? I have no idea what he'll do!"

Meg gave her an arch look, then flounced down the wide hallway so that her skirts bounced in time with her steps. "They are playing with fire. If someone else turns up dead, no one is going to want to come to the theatre!"

"Do you really think the ghost will kill someone?" one of the newer girls whispered.

"He's done it once," Meg declared, a bit too loud. "I can't imagine why he wouldn't do it again."

Christine was surrounded by an ocean of murmurs and whispers as the chorus girls speculated on O.G.'s next course of action. She was grateful to see her dressing room door; less so when Meg followed her into it.

Christine quickly changed from her rehearsal clothes and belted on her robe. She cast about for something to say as Meg tripped about the room, finally landing on, "How is your mother taking it?" She couldn't fathom why the dancer had followed her

"Hmmmm?" Meg hummed distractedly. "Oh, you mean the boxkeeper thing?" She danced over to the dressing table where Erik's music box sat. "She's very upset, though she's hiding it well. Says they impugned her honor, whatever that means."

"They didn't fire her though." Christine tensed as Meg gently touched the composer figure with a fingertip.

Meg laughed, her dark face alight with humor. "And find someone else to wrangle these girls while a crazed murderer is on the loose? Unlikely."

"I wouldn't call him a crazed murderer," Christine protested. She dug her fingernails into her palms as Meg continued to play with the music box.

"*You* wouldn't," Meg said. "But then you're more than a little biased."

Christine blinked, frozen in shock for the barest of moments. Then she reached out and jerked the girl around by her arm so they were face-to-face. "Meaning?"

Meg grabbed at Christine's hand, but Christine dug her fingers in harder. "Ow," the dancer complained, locking gazes with her. "You're hurting me."

Christine ignored her struggles, still holding tight. People were always surprised by her strength. "What did you mean by that, Meg?"

"Just that this ghost mysteriously appears and you end up singing like a siren. And you go missing right in the middle of it all." She scowled when Christine made no move to let her go. "Seems a bit of a coincidence is all."

Christine pulled Meg closer, words slipping between tightly clenched teeth. "And who else have you told?"

Meg seemed to finally realize the precariousness of her situation. Christine thought she recognized the fear blossoming in her dark eyes as Meg's gaze slipped to the door. "Nobody," she dancer whispered.

"It will stay that way, yes?" Christine prompted with a hard shake of the dancer's arm. "We wouldn't want another accident like what happened to Joseph Buquet, right?"

Swallowing, Meg nodded quickly. Christine released her and stepped back. Meg rubbed at her arm absently, brown eyes wide and scared.

"The Opera Ghost is real. And he has been giving you music lessons, hasn't he?" Meg asked softly.

"That's really not your business, Meg." Christine took refuge in that cold place inside of her. She'd liked Meg—as much as she liked any of the dancers in the company—but Christine couldn't afford to be sentimental. "It will be over soon."

"Does the Opera Ghost know about the Vicomte?" Meg tilted her head to the side, observing Christine with far too much intelligence for her liking.

Turning to her dressing table, Christine began to unpin her hair. "The Vicomte de Chagny is a no one you need to worry about."

Meg met her gaze in the mirror. The fear on

her face had been replaced by something more cunning. "You think you've got it all figured out."

Christine settled on the chair in front of the mirror that opened into the network of tunnels that riddled the opera house. Was Erik watching right now? Could he hear what was being said? She put those thoughts from her mind, remembering her anger with him.

Meg paused, waiting for Christine to say something. Christine had no intention of giving the girl more ammunition to work with. When it became clear Christine was not going to respond, Meg continued. "He was frantic when he couldn't find you after your performance, you know. He went and got the managers and everything."

"Why are you telling me this?" Christine asked, arching her eyebrows with her question.

Meg opened her mouth to respond but was interrupted by a knock on the dressing room door. Christine was just as surprised—she hadn't expected any visitors to her dressing room this afternoon before the performance. Raoul usually saved his visits for after the show.

The knock came again as she and Meg shared a confused look. "One moment!" Christine called, making her way to the door. "Remember my warning," Christine whispered darkly as she passed Meg.

Upon opening it, she froze, stunned. Philippe, the Comte de Chagny and Raoul's older brother, stood in the hallway in dour face and day dress, looking as out of place as a wolf among a flock of sheep. Christine couldn't fathom what might bring him there, though there was the persistent talk of his longstanding affair with the opera's premiere dancer.

"Excuse me," Meg said, slipping out of the doorway. She glared at Christine where the Comte wouldn't see before hurrying down the hall to another dressing room.

"Good day, Monsieur," Christine said, offering him a shaky bow. She didn't know why the Comte would be here and it made her nervous. "If you are looking for La Sorelli, I'm afraid she has changed dressing rooms."

His expression turned even more sour, something Christine hadn't thought possible. He brushed past her and spun around in the center of *her* dressing room as if he belonged there more than she did. Christine clenched her teeth and did her best to keep a benign smile on her lips.

"I am well aware of where Madame Sorelli now resides," he said in a smug voice that made her want to dig her nails into his cheek and yank. "It is not her I wish to speak with at present. It is you."

"Me? Whyever would you wish to speak with me, my lord?" Damn. She had a very bad feeling she knew what—or rather who—he wished to speak with her about, and she did not want to hear any of it.

He gave her a level look and Christine found it hard to breathe. Her heartbeat echoed in her ears, but she forced her body to remain still rather than run away and hide. "My dear Miss Daaé, let's dispense with pretense, yes? You've designs on my brother, Raoul. I have come to tell you that whatever it is you are playing at, you will cease at once or you will come to regret it."

Christine went with indignation as her first defense. "I have no idea what you are talking about, Monsieur," she began, but stopped when he waved his hand for silence.

"I am not an idiot, child, so do not presume to treat me like one of your little marks." His lip curled with the force of his scorn. "You may not remember me, but I most definitely remember you *and* your late father. And I have come to tell you that if you expect to marry my brother, you will be woefully disappointed."

Christine's feet took root in the floor. She tried to move them, but found she couldn't. She wanted to run, to hide from this man's words, but she couldn't find the strength to move. "I do not recall meeting you," was the best response she could manage.

"You did not. But I'd heard enough of you, Miss Daaé—and of your father—to understand what you had in mind for my brother when you two played on the shore in Perros as youngsters. I took measures then to stop it." He took a step closer to her, staring at her like she was a bug on the bottom of his boot. "But apparently that was not enough to be rid of you, so let me make this plain."

Now he invaded her space, looming over her. She felt suddenly cold in his shadow even as she threw back her shoulders and straightened her spine to counter him. He would not know he made her feel small. She wouldn't let him.

"My brother is trusting in ways that I am not. He sees only the good in people, sometimes to his detriment." He swept Christine with a dismissive glance. "You will come nowhere near my brother Raoul again or I will end your miserable existence. He might be innocent enough to be taken in by your wiles, but I, Mademoiselle Daaé, am not. While I'm sure you would make a perfectly charming mistress, you aspire to more and that is unacceptable. I let Raoul know this several years ago, but he is young and appears to have forgotten the lesson."

He raked her with another assessing look. Christine felt the need to cover up, even though she was decent in her robe. To be dressed down and insulted so was humiliating. She bit back the words that collected on the tip of her tongue, the outrage building in her chest helping her keep her composure. She refused to lose her temper and prove Philippe right.

She remembered one night when Raoul had come to see her. It was summer, and she and her father—along with Madame Valérius—had returned to the house in Perros for a brief respite from Paris. Pappa had been ailing, fighting a persistent cough, and the doctor suggested the sea air might do him some good. She hadn't expected Raoul to knock on the door of their cottage one evening after an absence of three years. But there he stood, and she welcomed him in as if they'd never been apart.

Pappa had perked up upon seeing Raoul and immediately fetched his violin. He played long into the night, well past the time he should have been in bed. When he'd finally exhausted himself, Christine had walked Raoul to the door. He'd been strange and distant all evening, so it surprised her when the Vicomte took her hand and said, "Mademoiselle, I will never forget you!" and raced off as if the very devil himself was after him.

The odd visit made sense now. "You told him to come and tell me goodbye in Perros," she said, looking up to glare at the Comte de Chagny. "That's why he came back after disappearing without a goodbye all those years ago."

Philippe nodded curtly. "I expected that to be the end of it. Imagine my surprise when we saw you performing here."

He finally stepped back and began to walk about the dressing room, only to drag his fingers over the music box that Erik had given her. Christine longed to reach out and snap each of the digits that dared to touch her gift like they had any right to it. But that was the problem with nobility—they always thought they owned everything anyway.

"I wasn't worried—not at first," he continued, and Christine ground her teeth together to keep the angry words from spilling from her lips as he lifted the music box. "Raoul is only to be in Paris for six months, you see." He turned so he could gauge her reaction. "Didn't tell you that, did he?"

Shaking her head, Christine crossed the room and snatched the music box from the Comte's over-curious hands. He slipped his hands behind his back and told her snidely, "Yes, he's due to start an expedition to the Arctic. He'll be gone for who knows how long."

Setting the music box on her dressing room table, Christine placed her body in front of it like a barricade. She watched the thick line of Philippe's back warily. "Why are you bothering to tell me any of this?"

He turned his head, a hint of amusement in his dark blue gaze. "Because, my dear, my brother is unbearably naïve, but you are not. He fancies himself in love with you. If he saw you as you are—a bit of baggage good for a tumble and not much more—I would have no issue with him pursuing you. But he's got it in his head that he wants to marry you, and that I cannot allow."

"I have no say in what your brother chooses to do," Christine snapped. "And neither do you. He's a man grown and able to make his own decisions. You can't control him forever!"

Philippe sighed, and then reached into the pocket on the inside of his jacket. She tensed, kicking up her leg so she could grab the knife sheathed in her boot. But instead of withdrawing a weapon, the Comte de Chagny held a leather checkbook in his hand.

"How much?"

Christine blinked, taken aback by his curt words. "For what?" she asked.

"For you to no longer be a problem." Philippe glanced around the room, then decided to sit on the small couch and use his knee as a writing desk. When she didn't answer immediately, he glowered at her from across the room. "Come, come, don't be shy *now*." He waved the checkbook at her as if she were a pesky fly he was shooing away. "Name your price and I'll gladly pay it."

Christine held herself very still as her inner voices railed. The one that sounded suspiciously like her father urged her to utter an outrageous sum of money. She wouldn't have to sing or con anyone for a good long while. But another part of her adamantly refused to be treated as nothing more than inconvenient trash to be removed as quickly as possible. She had her fair share of pride. As much as she wanted to take the payoff, to do so would be admitting to everything Philippe thought of Christine and her father. She absolutely refused to give the Comte de Chagny that kind of satisfaction. He could choke on his check.

She marched to the door and yanked it open. "You've said quite enough. Good day." She gave a short bow and gestured for him to leave.

Philippe's face turned thunderous, but he seemed to master himself quickly. The man was frightening when angry, making Christine glad to hear the bustling sounds of backstage life. If she screamed, people would come running. As she watched, he scribbled something on one of the checks before rising to his feet. As he approached her, his face darkened, mouth pulling down in a fearsome scowl.

He stopped in front of her and held up the check so she could see it. The amount was reasonable but still more than she'd ever seen at any one time before. "Think about what I've said, Mademoiselle." He opened his fingertips and let the check flutter to the floor.

Christine made no move to pick it up. Philippe stepped out and sauntered away in the direction of La Sorelli's new dressing room. Christine wanted to throw up. Instead she slammed the door, leaning her back against it when her trembling legs threatened to send her to the floor. Slowly she slid down until she could rest her head on her drawn-up knees. Gulping in air as though she'd just dashed up the great staircase in the Grand Foyer, Christine surreptitiously wiped her eyes on the hem of her robe. She wasn't crying, hadn't let a tear fall, but it had been a close thing.

Her head pounded with her reaction to Philippe's words. He wanted her away from his brother? It made her want to press for Raoul more! Let Philippe try to come after her—what could he really do to her? Christine's gaze fell on the check. With his money, Philippe could hire men to take care of her. An accident backstage or when she was walking home one night could easily be bought with the wealth Philippe had at his fingertips. Was her spite worth the risk?

She wanted to say yes more than anything, but she was also her father's pragmatic daughter. Spite wouldn't feed her and if what Philippe said was true about Raoul leaving for an expedition, it was likely nothing would come of their brief dalliance anyway.

Picking up the check, she folded it into a small square and rose. She tucked it into the hidden drawer Erik had built into the music box he'd made for her. The need to scream out her frustration made her practically vibrate, but she held it inside, even if it made the back of her throat ache. With an audible swallow, Christin set the music box down and smoothed her hands down the folds of her skirt.

Deep breaths. Deep breaths. She sucked in one, holding it in her lungs for a count of ten before exhaling. She did this twice more, then reached over and grabbed the hand mirror from her dressing table and flung it as hard as she could at the wall. A spiderweb crack in the paint where the top of the mirror dug into the plaster and the splintering of glass made her feel only marginally better.

Philippe would never allow Raoul to see her alone after this. Even if Raoul sought her out, Christine was certain Philippe—or his lackeys—wouldn't be too far behind him, ready to drag him away from her. And if Philippe was telling the truth about Raoul's arctic voyage, the young man didn't have long in Paris anyway. So that left her with only one option.

Leaving the shards of the broken mirror and its frame where they were, Christine pulled on her traveling cape and pressed the mechanism that opened the mirror. She needed to speak with Erik whether he was still angry with her or not. He had to help her.

La Carlotta was going to have to be persuaded to retire.

CHAPTER *17*

ERIK WAS SINGING WHEN she entered the house on the lake. Christine stopped to listen, not recognizing the tune or the lyrics, but entranced by their beauty nonetheless. Abruptly, Erik stopped and walked to the table. She watched his rounded shoulders as he bent to notate his sheet music, feeling the loss of his voice keenly.

Shaking out her skirt, she asked, "What was that?"

He jumped, nearly upending the ink pot. Seeing her in his doorway, he frowned. "I would have thought you would have been with *Raoul*."

Christine entered, matching his frown with a scowl of her own. "Don't be like that."

"Like what? I am being perfectly reasonable."

He blew on the sheet music to help the ink dry.

His emphasis on the *I* made it clear who he thought was being unreasonable, but Christine managed to keep her temper. Swallowing it down, she managed a smile that was all teeth and no feeling. "Of course, you are. You are the very picture of good manners and conversational restraint."

He closed his eyes wearily. "What do you want?"

Christine did her best to look contrite, though it did not come naturally to her. She needed his help with the next stage of her plan, and if she had to pretend a bit to get it, it cost her nothing. "I wanted to apologize," she told him in a voice barely above a whisper.

He leaned closer. Erik didn't wear his mask, instead using his longer hair to obscure that part of his face.

"You want to apologize? To me?" His good eye was round with shock. He looked around as if expecting to see someone hiding behind him.

She glared at him. "You don't have to act so surprised," she groused.

"Forgive me, I just never expected it of you." Erik stood up straighter and crossed his arms over his chest. "Do go on," he prompted.

Giving him a poisonous smile at his high-handedness, she said, "I am sorry for any unkindness to you in Perros, Erik."

Cocking his head, Erik stared at her thoughtfully, almost as if making a decision. After a few moments, he dropped his hands and said, "That will do, I suppose." He picked up his sheet music once more. "Apology accepted."

"Excellent," Christine answered, clapping her hands together. "Now, I need your help."

"Of course, you do," Erik said with a groan and tucked the pages of music away in a drawer.

♪♪♪

"How does this sound?" Christine shoved the note she had drafted into Erik's hands. When he gave her a skeptical look, she flapped her hands at him. "Well? Go on and read it!"

Scowling, he glanced down at the piece of paper. Christine watched his gaze slide along the page and threw up her hands. "No. Read it out loud! You know, in an opera ghost kind of voice."

"Must I?" He sounded so put-upon Christine wanted to laugh.

"Yes."

"Fine." Erik cleared his throat, then read out in a booming voice, "*My dear managers. So it is to be war between us? If you still care for peace, here is my ultimatum. One—you must give me back my private box. Two—the part of Maguerite in Faust shall be sung this evening by Christine Daaé. Three—you will reinstate Madame Giry as my boxkeeper forthwith. Should you refuse, I will not be held responsible for the curse you bring down upon your heads.*"

He dropped his hands back to his sides, the letter still held in his fingers. "This is ridiculous.

Christine, we can't make them do anything!"

She'd already thought of that. Taking the page from Erik, she began to set up the paper and red ink he would need to make his own copy to send to the managers. "We can if we play this smart." At his doubting look, Christine turned fully to face him, hands planted on her hips. She tossed her heavy mane of hair off her shoulders and said, "Look, Carlotta will never willingly concede her spot to me so we have to get creative if I'm ever to take her place as Diva."

"This," Erik said, picking up the letter and waving it at her, "is not creative. It's a threat."

Christine nodded. "Of course it is! Do you really think they're going to hand over a box and two hundred forty thousand francs to a couple of orphans?" When Erik refused to say anything, she rushed on. "We're going to send Carlotta a note, warning her not to sing tonight because if she does something terrible will happen."

He made a scoffing noise. "Carlotta will never pass up another performance for you. She'd ask the managers to wheel her corpse onstage before she'd give you a chance to out-sing her again."

"I know," Christine assured him. "That's why I'm counting on her to go on." At his raised eyebrow, she continued. "That's where you come in."

"I come in?" he asked incredulously.

"What's the worst thing that could happen to someone like Carlotta?" Christine asked.

Erik shrugged. "The pox, losing her voice, a

horde of rabid weasels descending on her? I have no idea."

"Embarrassment. Public. Brutal." Christine folded her arms across her chest and smiled smugly. "Total humiliation."

"Dropping a banana peel for a pratfall seems far too chancy to risk." He moved over to a shelf where his figures sat and began to adjust their placement. She noticed he'd added some new ones: a turtle and a scorpion.

"Be serious, will you?" Christine joined him, shoving lightly at his shoulder. "That thing you do with your voice—when you make it sound like it's coming from somewhere else?" At his nod, she grinned up at him. "You are going to do that to her during one of her songs. Make her sound like she's quacking like a duck or croaking like a frog in front of the entire audience. She'll never be able to show her face in Paris again!"

"That's it? That's all you want me to do?" Erik sounded like he didn't believe she'd want something so relatively benign.

Christine nodded. She had other ideas, brought on by her conversation with Meg earlier, but she didn't need his approval for those. "Oh, and maybe say her singing will bring down the house or something like that too." She tapped a finger to her chin. "Yes, that's good. Something to scare the managers."

"But nothing is going to happen, right, Christine?" Erik took hold of her arm and pulled her closer to him. She let him, knowing that she walked a fine line with him. He'd just gotten over his upset at being used in Perros to advance her relationship with Raoul. She didn't want to alienate him further. Besides, if she worked it out correctly, no one would even be hurt. Only Carlotta's pride would suffer and the Lord above knew the woman had a surplus of that.

"Of course, Erik." She placed one small hand atop his large one. "It's a performance, that's all it is. Carlotta will go home and sulk for a few weeks and I'll have the time to astonish all of Paris and then I can go anywhere I like."

The thought of a flat of her own, with her own furnishings and clothes and art—everything chosen for and by her—was a giddy fantasy she'd dreamed of for years. She would have admirers showering her with gifts, offers to dine, private performances for small, exclusive groups of people in the highest circles of society. This was far preferable to being someone's wife.

"What about Raoul?"

Christine jerked out of her pleasant daydream at Erik's question. Fluffing her hair, she returned, "What about him?"

He touched his mask with two fingers, then began to painstakingly copy Christine's note in his cribbed, shaky handwriting. "You have been doing your best to ensure he follows you around like a lost sheep without a thought to your vocal training or next performance." His words were labored as he worked to make his handwriting legible. His writing only flowed when he was writing musical notes.

"And?" She hadn't told Erik of Philippe's visit. She wandered around the room, absently touching the draperies and strange things he chose to surround himself with. His taste was haphazard at best.

"Why the sudden change in direction? You seemed intent on pursuing the young man in Perros. You said as much." He glanced up to eye with speculation.

Hands fluttering, she waved away his words. If only her concerns could be so easily dispatched. "It is always a good idea to have a plan in case things do not work out," she conceded. "Besides, I've grown bored with him."

Erik pinned her with a disbelieving look. "You've grown bored with him," he deadpanned.

Plucking up a fan, she waved it at her neck before snapping it closed. "Yes, such things can happen."

His eyes narrowed as he watched her. "Not to you."

Dropping the fan, she put a hand on her hip. "Whatever is going on with Raoul is not important. Are you going to help me or not?" She tossed her heavy hair over her shoulder with a jerk of her head.

"Will this make you happy?" he asked, his expression weary and a little sad.

"Exceedingly." She twirled in mock delight. "Ecstatically."

He blew out a heavy, long-suffering breath.

"Fine. I'll do it."

CHAPTER 18

CHRISTINE WAITED IN THE WINGS for her cue. She was in the chorus, again, just as she expected to be. Carlotta strutted around the stage as Marguerite, even after Christine had the Opera Ghost deliver several notes to the woman warning her not to sing. The Spanish diva had filled the seats with a number of admirers if the cheering each time Carlotta hit a note successfully was any indication.

Perfect.

Carlotta had been grandstanding her way through *Faust* even more than usual. Christine had left it to Erik to know when to do his voice trick, but if he didn't do it soon, she wouldn't have any teeth left from the way she was grinding them together. She hadn't though Carlotta could get more insufferable.

She was so so wrong.

Christine fidgeted in her boy's clothes, awaiting her line. Her gaze strayed to the audience and she unconsciously searched for Raoul's face. He sat in his brother's box, his face wan and drawn with exhaustion and illness. Philippe sat beside him, staring daggers at her. Raoul covered his face with his hands and slumped down in his chair. Philippe's look of hatred intensified.

Christine was so surprised by Raoul's wretched appearance that she nearly missed her part. Her voice came out tremulous, with none of the power or presence she had in previous performances or when she practiced with Erik. She was relieved when her few lines were over.

Carlotta made it through the ballad of the king of Thule and the jewel song without incident, her fans growing louder and more effusive in their applause. Christine whispered, "Come on, Erik," under her breath as Marguerite and Faust began their duet.

"I feel without alarm," Carlotta sang, her voice filling the space with delicate thunder, "With its melody enwind CRO-ACK!"

Carlotta's hand flew to her mouth. The entire opera house went still. Christine put her fingers to her lips, hiding her smile. "Perfect timing, Erik," she murmured, her heart pounding in her chest with excitement. She should never have doubted him. He had an uncanny flair for the dramatic.

She heard someone whisper for Carlotta to continue. The woman nodded and instead of continuing the song, began the line again. "I feel . . . feel without alarm—CRO-ACK!"

Whispers. Still Carlotta tried to power through the performance. "With its melody enwind—CRO-ACK!"

Shouts of disbelief from the audience. "And all my heart sub—CRO-ACK!"

The croaking continued every time Carlotta opened her mouth. Her fans in the audience stood, demanding to know what was going on. The music master signaled for the orchestra to play. Chaos erupted onstage. Carlotta appeared caught between hysterics and fainting.

This was it. She wasn't going to get a better chance. Christine sprinted off, ducking behind props and skidding offstage as she made for the stairs that led to the upper portions of the opera house. Stagehands were all rushing about searching for the origin of the croaking sound as Christine ran as fast as she could to a tangled set of ropes.

She hadn't had a chance to go earlier to prepare the rope, though she had checked the location from the ground. Christine had done her best to trace the rope she wanted back to where it was anchored and felt confident she could find the right one. All it would take was a bit of help from her knife to fray the rope enough to send the counterweight down. She'd done it before with the body of Joseph Buquet; this wasn't so different. With this, no one would ever doubt the seriousness of the Opera Ghost's threats ever again.

Erik's mad laughter rang out now, seeming to come from everywhere. The managers, Moncharmin and Richard, had been sitting in Box Five for the performance, hoping to catch the elusive ghost, but they ran out when the booming laughter seemed to issue from where they sat. People began screaming; a few ran toward the exit.

Carlotta collapsed in a hysterical heap in the center of the stage, even as the croaking continued. Dancers surrounded her and Christine knew she needed to get back onstage quickly. After a quick check to make sure no one was nearby, she swiped her blade through the rope of the counterweight. Then she turned and pelted back toward the stage.

Erik's laughter rose to a crescendo, growing more unhinged. "She's singing to bring down the chandelier!" his disembodied voice shouted before dissolving into cackles once more.

"Don't oversell it, Erik," Christine whispered as she galloped down a series of stairs that would let her down near the dressing rooms.

She could hear more screaming from the front of the opera house and ran faster. She'd just made it to the wings when one of the dancers pointed up toward the ceiling and shrieked. One of the counterweights to the massive crystal chandelier plummeted toward the ground.

"No. Oh no," Christine whispered as the bag fell. She watched in horror, realizing that she'd cut the wrong rope. The bag she'd targeted should have landed at the edge of the stage, taking out the footlights on one side.

Instead, this bag crashed into the middle of the audience. Christine screamed along with everyone else as the counterweight crushed a woman standing in front of her seat.

The screams of the fleeing audience and their panicked footfalls would have drowned out Erik's voice if he were still speaking, but he'd fallen silent before the bag landed. Christine hoped he was far away from the stage and couldn't see what she'd done.

The new managers stumbled onto the stage, as their audience fled in fear. "We're ruined, Armand!" Monsieur Richard shouted, looking like a man possessed.

"Fetch the gendarme!" Moncharmin yelled to anyone who would listen.

The stage was pandemonium. Carlotta had fainted from her ordeal and was being carried off the stage by Monsieur Gaspard. Ushers and stagehands helped lead people safely from the Palais Garnier, funneling them out of the Grand Foyer and into the street where they could take carriages home. Meg and a few of the older chorus girls began to round up the hysterical girls and shepherd them to a dressing room.

Christine fell to her knees, head bowed. She

didn't want to look into the audience, didn't want to see that woman's body. She'd done that. She'd killed an innocent woman.

She expected it to feel different. She waited for the debilitating guilt to consume her; instead, all she felt was a passing shame that she'd cut the wrong rope, coupled with an overwhelming relief that her plan had worked at all. That sense of horror that she'd killed a person was absent.

Dear God, what was the matter with her? Why didn't she feel worse? Because that was what truly bothered Christine, both about Buquet and now this woman—she barely cared. She felt sorry in a vague way that they were dead, she felt slightly worse that she'd been the cause, but she hadn't known them, and didn't wish to now. They were nothing to her. How could she feel bad about people she didn't know enough to like or dislike?

"Mon Dieu! Christine!" Meg hauled her up by her arm, dragging her away from the chaos that threatened to overtake the stage at any moment. "What did he do? Is he still here?"

Christine allowed herself to be dragged along behind Meg. At some point, Madame Giry also joined them, her gaze trained on the catwalks above them. She kept her hand up at her face for some reason Christine couldn't fathom. Christine had never been more grateful for her over-exaggerated performance when she'd reappeared after her disastrous night with le Fure—people assumed she was in shock and didn't expect coherent answers from her whenever the OG made an appearance.

Meg and her mother spoke quickly to each other as they walked. To Christine, everything happened in slow-motion, as if people were moving through water. Even their voices were muffled. She didn't even register Meg sitting her down in the chair of Christine's dressing room until she felt a sharp slap across her face.

"Ow!" she shouted as Meg shook her hand out. "Why did you do that?"

"Because you were staring at the wall like a disgusting dead fish!" the dancer snapped, her dark face glistening with perspiration. "You needed to wake up. The inspectors are questioning everyone in the company."

Christine shook her head groggily, not knowing how much time had passed. She swayed, suddenly exhausted. She felt like a bucket with a hole in the bottom, all of the water draining out at an alarming rate. Her head didn't feel tethered to her body anymore.

"About what?" Christine asked, putting her hand on the bed for support.

Meg gave her a look of disbelief. "Probably something about that damned sandbag that fell from the ceiling and killed somebody." She threw her hands in the air. "Did you know that was going to happen? Carlotta's been getting threatening notes all day."

"No," Christine lied, her voice sounding cold and dead. "I just knew he wanted me to sing tonight."

Meg eyed her dubiously and Christine didn't blame the girl for not believing her. Pleadingly, Christine looked up at. "I mean it, Meg. I never expected this to happen." That much was true. If everything had gone according to her plan, the correct sandbag would have fallen.

"I don't feel well," Christine whispered, slipping her hand down so she could lie on the bed. "I'm sorry, Meg." Maybe that would help get the young dancer back on her side.

"Yes, well, I don't think anyone is feeling particularly joyful at the moment." Meg paused and peered into Christine's face. "You really don't look good." With a sigh, she turned toward the door. "I'll see if I can find someone to help."

Christine didn't say anything, she simply huddled on the bed with her head in her hands. Meg made a *tsk*ing noise. Waves of disapproval spread out from the other girl like the ripples in still water from a stone's passing. The dressing room door opened, hinges squeaking thinly.

As soon as she heard the door click closed behind Meg, Christine bounded up and raced to the mirror. She was not up to speaking with the police and had no intention of doing so. Her heart rattled in her chest like an old railroad car on shaky tracks. Her palms were clammy with sweat and her body alternated between too hot and too cold. The need to run overwhelmed her, and this time, Christine wasn't interested in fighting it.

She pressed on the hidden catch that triggered the mirror and the pane of glass swung inward.

Christine stepped through it, closing the hidden door behind her. She stood in the dark for several minutes, allowing her eyes to adjust. She should have lit a candle, but hadn't thought of it and didn't want to go back for one now. She knew the way to the house on the lake blindfolded. She could make her way with what little light there was.

Moving slowly, Christine made sure to keep one hand on the wall at any given point. The connection with something solid helped ground her and kept her from descending into panic. As she stepped, she counted. What had started as a way to pass the time during her journey had turned into a useful tool.

It took her longer than usual to reach Erik's house. Christine staggered inside, not bothering to knock. She'd kicked her uncomfortable shoes off halfway through the journey, not caring if she ever saw them again. The managers had more to worry about than missing costumes right now.

"You said no one was going to get hurt!" Erik bellowed as soon as he saw her. He'd stopped mid-pace and glared at her. He still wore his mask, but his hair was in disarray, and he'd removed his dress jacket to stand in shirt and vest. "You lied to me!"

"I didn't mean to. It was an accident!" she yelled back, surprised at his ferocity. What did he care for some no-named woman in the audience?

"Like Joseph Buquet was?" He stalked over to her, putting his face close to hers. "A lot of accidents seem to occur whenever you are near," he spat.

She smacked him across the cheek, surprising them both. "How dare you?" she breathed, angry beyond all measure.

Erik gaped at her in shock, his hand pressing against his cheek. Beneath his fingers, Christine noticed the skin of his face turning red from the blow. He reeled back, stunned to silence.

Christine waded in, knowing that she had to reach him before he regrouped. "If you would just listen to me instead of jumping to conclusions—I didn't mean for that to happen!" She moved forward, pressing her index finger into his chest.

Erik stared down at her hand, dumbfounded. She continued. "I cut the wrong rope! The bag I meant to drop was supposed to hit the edge of the stage and it wouldn't have killed anyone."

"You couldn't know that." Erik had found his voice again. It held an edge of panic. "What on earth could possess you to do something so dangerous?"

She wanted to pull her hair out by the roots. Why did he always ask her questions she thought the answers were obvious to? She placed her hand flat on his chest and shoved him backwards. Christine realized she was ridiculous—with their height difference, it probably looked like a mouse trying to bully a cat—but the physical push coming from someone her size helped her dominate the conversation. That movement put her back in control.

"I didn't have a choice, Erik!" she countered, voice dropping with the force of her rage. "Carlotta wasn't listening to the notes. Neither were the managers. I had to do something or else I'm never going to get away from this place!"

She didn't mean the Palais Garnier, not anymore. Christine had to break free of her father and the legacy he'd left her, of his expectations and hopes for her and find her own. She'd learned music from him, but she'd learned other things too, and they were all tangled in a messy web she wasn't sure how to extricate herself from without killing herself. She needed to find a way out, and if that meant some people had to get hurt, well, she'd make her peace with that.

Christine didn't realize she'd grown short of breath until she felt light-headed and stumbled. Her breathing was shallow and all over the place, and she couldn't get enough air into her lungs. The room wavered before her eyes like a heat mirage, the edges of everything becoming fluid. Erik's hands on her upper arms felt frighteningly cold, despite the costume she wore.

His voice sounded like he was calling her from a tunnel. "Christine!"

Nodding so he knew she heard him, she sank to her knees. His strong, graceful hands guided her down. How had she never noticed how nice his hands looked? Long fingers made for playing a piano, gentle but powerful. She wondered if Erik knew how. If he did, she'd love to hear him play.

"I'm fine," she gritted out around teeth that

chattered. Her body trembled and Erik hauled her close, wrapping his arms around her. The top of her head sat tucked beneath his chin, her hair serving as a cushion. "Really."

"You're not," Erik said, but he sounded worried and fond. "You are so very not fine, Christine."

She didn't realize he'd pulled her into his lap as she cuddled against his chest. He was solid, present, and that's all that mattered to her in the moment. Erik grounded her, rooted her somewhere solid and safe while she fell apart. "I didn't mean to," she whispered into his chest, unable to make sense of the guilt that assailed her. "I didn't mean to."

"Shhhh." Christine felt Erik run careful hands through her wild hair. "I know you didn't. No one thinks you meant it on purpose."

Sniffling, she wiped the tears from her face with the back of one hand. Erik said nothing else, just rocked her and hummed, allowing her precious moments to pull herself back together.

"I'm sorry," she said in a small voice after several long minutes of just his quiet humming.

Erik loosened his hold but did not let her go. He seemed to understand that she still needed him to anchor her lest she fly apart again. The desperation to be free gnawed at her incessantly, driving her to make the choices she did.

"I know," he murmured back to her. Tilting up her chin, Erik gazed into her eyes. Christine found she wasn't bothered by the sight of his cloudy blue eye anymore. It was normal for him.

He was just Erik, and this was just the way Erik looked. "But someone died. And you lied to me." He chucked her under the chin. "You need to stop doing that."

She felt horrible enough about dropping the counterweight on that woman; he didn't need to keep reminding her. "I didn't deliberately lie to you," she managed, wishing he would let go of her face. Eye contact made her feel uncomfortable in times like these, like she was too vulnerable, too open, and everyone who looked could see all her soft and damaged places.

Erik never appeared to mind though. "Deliberate or not, you lied. To me."

"You wouldn't have helped," she said. She sounded like a bratty toddler

"You're right. But I could have helped you think of a better way, Christine. A way that didn't involve the death of a woman."

She loved the way he said her name, like it was the most magical form of music he'd ever heard. His reverence was clear in his voice. He said her name like a hymn, a prayer, a paean to pagan gods long forgotten. He breathed it out like air. He said it like her name was something essential.

Her eyes drooped. Exhaustion wrung her out like a wet rag, leaving her limp and weak. "There wasn't a better way," she argued, unwilling to admit defeat. It was too close to admitting she was wrong.

"First Buquet and now this woman. There is always a better way," he chided her.

She shook her head. Buquet had been out of his head drunk and he had hurt and frightened her. She didn't feel guilty for that—she really had thought he was going to kill her. But the woman in the audience.... She shuddered. Maybe Erik was right. Maybe she was going about everything all wrong. She was too tired and worn out to think about it now though.

"Promise me something." When she didn't respond right away, Erik shook her gently. "Christine, I need you to promise me something."

"What is it?" *Merde*, how she hated promises. Sticky things, impossible to keep and just as hard to get rid of. But for Erik, she could at least try.

"Promise me that you will not lie to me again."

She turned in his lap so she could look up at his face and got a fantastic view of his stubborn chin. Erik shifted his head so he could look down at her and she saw his patience reflected in his eyes. She could at least try for him, even though it was like asking a cat to wear a cravat. Christine couldn't remember anyone actually looking at her like that—like they expected her to be better than she was.

"I promise," she said. *I'll try*, she amended to herself.

They sat in comfortable silence for several minutes more. Erik hummed softly, but whether it was for himself or her, Christine didn't know. She didn't much care either; all of the excitement of the evening had exhausted her. She was content to be held and rocked and treated a bit like the child she hadn't been in years.

"Look on the bright side," she muttered after some time. "At least it wasn't the chandelier."

Erik stilled. "Your sense of humor leaves a lot to be desired," he commented drily.

"You like it."

"And what does that say about me, I wonder." But Christine could hear the smile in his voice.

She could try and be better. For him.

CHAPTER *19*

IT WAS LATE THE NEXT morning when Christine returned to Madame Valérius' flat by way of the Rue Scribe exit. The front of the Palais Garnier resembled an ant mound that had been kicked. Investigators and workmen swarmed in and out, while curious onlookers gathered as close as they dared. Christine hurried past, the hood of her cloak pulled up.

As she let herself into the flat, she heard voices. Who would be visiting this early in the day? Christine dropped her cloak to the floor and crept forward to listen.

They were in Madame Valérius' room, not surprising since the woman was bedridden. As she peeked around the doorway, she saw Raoul sitting in a chair beside the bed. A tea tray sat forgotten on a table beside him. What was he doing here? Did Philippe know where he was?

Madame Valérius caught sight of her and her face brightened. "Christine!" she cried, relief in her voice. She set aside her tea cup and opened her arms. "The Vicomte was just telling me of what happened during the opera last night. Are you well?"

Christine slowly approached, accepted the embrace, and moved away, refusing to look at Raoul. Madame Valérius pulled Christine down to sit beside her. "I'm fine, I was at the back of the stage when the bag came down."

"I didn't see you. I lost you in the commotion," Raoul said.

He looked terrible. His eyes were heavily shadowed, the skin below puffy and lined. Christine wondered how long it had been since he slept. His hair looked like he'd been running his hands through it constantly. He was still in his evening dress, rumpled and creased.

"I got caught up with everyone fleeing backstage," she explained. Worry blossomed in her guts—if Raoul had noticed her going missing, had anyone else?

"Ah."

Madame Valérius patted her down anxiously, as if verifying that Christine was unhurt. Christine batted at her hands, irritated at the distraction.

"Raoul has been telling me some disturbing things, Christine," the woman said with a sigh. She fixed Christine with a worried look. "That perhaps your Angel of Music is not as benign as he appears."

It took all of Christine's waning mental strength not to roll her eyes heavenward. Instead, she furrowed her brows in confusion and turned to Raoul. "What do you mean?"

"I fear that you are being taken advantage of," Raoul burst out, his hands clenching into fists. "I think the Angel of Music and the Palais Garnier's Opera Ghost are one and the same, and that the man behind them both is abusing your innocence!"

Interesting. She could work with this. If Raoul was willing to go against the wishes of his elder brother, she might be able to salvage her plans after all.

Erik's disapproving face flashed in her mind's eyes. She felt a brief pain, then put it from her memory. This was her chance. Erik would understand.

Christine gasped and pressed her hand to her chest in mock shock. "Raoul, you must stop," she ordered, glancing around fearfully.

Raoul looked around as well, turning around in his seat to scan the room. "Why?"

Twisting her hands together, she whispered, "If he discovers that you know of him, I don't know what he'll do to you!"

"My dear," Madame Valérius gasped, clutching at Christine's hands to still them, "are you in danger?"

"No." She shook her head emphatically. "He would never hurt me." She met Raoul's frightened gaze. "But others . . .," she trailed off significantly.

"Christine, is that why you left me in P—," Raoul began, but Christine shook her head.

"He took me to his underground lair," she whispered, silently praying that Erik would forgive her. She would somehow make this up to him. "He wants to marry me. Oh Raoul, he's terribly jealous. It took all of my convincing to get him to let me leave the opera house after last night."

"Has he . . . made advances?" Madame Valérius stared at Christine as if she could detect anything odd beneath her clothes. When Christine glanced over at Raoul, she saw he was leaning forward, eyes burning.

Offended, Christine grasped her blouse and drew it even closer to her neck. "No!" she practically shouted. "He's never touched me!" Remembering Raoul's question in Brittany, she added, "I'm a good girl!"

Well, that one might be reaching. But their implications angered her. Her memory of the closeness of Monsieur le Fure's carriage flashed in her mind and her heart began to race. The idea that Erik, of all people, would force himself on her was repulsive—he would never do anything like that. "He's only confessed his love to me. He's told me he's my slave and his whole existence is bent to my happiness!" She suspected that part might be true.

Raoul sat back, appearing by turns relieved and upset. "He sounds like a madman."

Bristling, Christine snapped, "Because it is so unbelievable that someone might want to make me happy?"

Raoul wilted beneath her anger. "That's not what I meant," he stammered, staring at his feet.

"I'm sorry," Christine said, after taking a deep breath. Sometimes dealing with Raoul was exhausting, especially when he responded like a kicked puppy. "I'm very tired."

"You should rest, Christine," Madame Valérius told her, patting her arm. "We can discuss this later." She looked at Raoul, then toward the door.

Taking the hint, Raoul rose. "I'll take my leave then."

"I will see you out." Christine got up and followed him.

She noticed how he bit his lip, as if he were trying to keep silent about something. He walked stiffly, taut with tension. Taking pity on him, she grasped his elbow and pulled him to a stop. His eyebrows flew up in surprise.

"Your brother, Philippe, paid me a visit," she told him in a low voice. When his eyes widened, she continued. "He told me to stay away from you."

Raoul's mouth worked for a few moments before words came. "Philippe? Are you certain?"

Christine pursed her lips and stared at him. He shook his head as if to clear it. "Right. Of course, you're sure. My apologies." He dragged a hand down his face, eyelids drooping tiredly. "Is that why you refused to see me?"

She nodded, lowering her head sadly. "He isn't wrong, Raoul. I'm only a chorus girl."

"He has no right!" Raoul burst out, face darkening angrily. "It's my decision to make. He can't control my whole life!"

"He loves you, Raoul," she placated, "and he is only looking out for your well-being." Her belly warmed with glee. Anything she could do to drive a wedge between the brothers worked in her favor.

"Still, he overstepped." Raoul bristled, pale eyes snapping with his upset. "I can speak for myself!" He caught Christine's hands in his. "Christine, may I see you again?" He raised her hands to his lips.

Her cheeks heated with her blush. This was going better than she expected. "You would still want to? Even with your brother?"

He nodded enthusiastically. "Yes. Very much. It doesn't matter what my brother says."

"The Angel wants me to stay at the opera house from now on, but I think I can arrange something." She squeezed his hand. "I'll send a message."

Raoul's face brightened immeasurably. "Yes?"

"Yes," she said, nodding. She opened the front door.

"I'll await your word." He reluctantly stepped outside.

Christine kept her smile up until she'd closed the door. When the lock clicked, she leaned against it and wondered what she'd just done.

CHAPTER 20

RETURNING TO THE OPERA house, Christine immediately headed down to see Erik. It was habit now, to check in on him, spend time with him. As she walked, she debated with herself the entire time. Did she tell him what she'd told Raoul about him? Or did she just maneuver him carefully without his knowledge? She'd tried that in Perros and it had half-worked.

The twinge of conscience she felt bothered her. She'd never experienced that before. She felt bad about using him, manipulating him. That didn't happen to her. And then there was her promise. Lord, she hated promises.

There was no sign of Erik when she arrived, so she settled in to wait. None of his piles of books had anything that would hold her interest, so she found herself drawn to a stack of pages on a table. The black bars of sheet music looked like some arcane language. She didn't recognize any of the songs. Had Erik written these? She paged through them, amazed at the beauty and complexity of the music she held in her fingers.

Christine sifted through Erik's work, humming the music he'd painstakingly written on the paper she'd brought for him. It was good, she had to admit. But what was it? Why was he bothering with composing at all?

"What do you think?"

She dropped the pages, startled by Erik's voice. He'd entered the house without her knowing, moving as quietly as a spider. Bending down, Christine began to collect the papers, only for Erick to kneel beside her and join in the effort. He didn't seem angry at the invasion to his privacy.

"It's good." She didn't want to get his hopes up. "Interesting, for an opera. But why?"

Hands full of pages, he cocked his head at her. "Why?"

She gestured to him, her own hands likewise full. "Yes, why? It's not like anyone is ever going to hear this no matter how good it is."

Erik sat back on his heels, resembling a lanky-limbed vulture. "I'm not doing it for just anybody," he told her. His voice held that quiet intensity Christine had grown familiar with in their time together, that vibrating quality to his voice that sent a shiver up her spine. "I'm doing it for myself. Because I want to."

He held out his hand for her set of pages. Christine stared at the long fingers, no longer seeing them as bony, but imagining how they'd look stroking the keys of a piano, remembering how they looked as he pressed the strings against a violin's neck. Her mouth felt dry as she handed the paper over to him.

"Only for yourself?" she found herself asking, staring into his mismatched gaze.

A shy smile lifted the unmarred side of his face. Christine found it was no longer a hardship to look at him—she barely noticed his deformity any more. She'd become accustomed to his face; she'd even go so far as to say she liked it. Not that she'd ever tell him.

"I had an idea," he began haltingly, as if unsure of how to phrase his next thought, "but I—" he trailed off, huffing out a frustrated breath. "Never mind. It's stupid."

Christine put her hand on his arm. She could feel the tension in his muscles beneath the fabric of his shirt. Squeezing his forearm, she said, "No, tell me. I'm sure it's not stupid, and I want to hear."

His eyes searched her face. Christine felt her heart beat faster, wondering what he might see when he looked at her. Erik knew her like no one else did. He had seen her vulnerable and weak. And he still seemed to like her. She didn't understand it.

He exhaled slowly as though still making up his mind. Placing his hand atop hers, Erik finally said,

"I was hoping you would sing it with me."

Her body locked up so that all Christine could do for a moment was blink at him. "Me? Why would you want me to sing it?"

Grinning, Erik placed the sheet music aside. He took both her hands in his and stood, raising her to her feet at the same time. "Christine, only you could sing it. I wrote it specifically for your voice and range. There is no one else for it." At the same time that he spoke of music, she thought Erik might be speaking of something else too.

She felt like they stood on the verge of something vast, something greater than the two of them. She so badly wanted to leap into it with him beside her, the great unknown of it, but there was a part of her that held back. The part that spoke with the voice of her father.

"Oh," she breathed, then blushed at her less than erudite response. She swallowed, a shudder rolling through her, bringing her back to reality. "I guess I could sing it." Christine wanted to cringe. What was wrong with her? Nothing was coming out right. It was like she was deliberately trying to insult him!

"Are you feeling all right?" he asked, eyes narrowing. "You sound strange."

High pitched laughter escaped her before she could stop it. "Just tired from all the activity," Christine told him, certain she sounded like a lunatic.

His expression sobered. "We need to be careful, Christine," he told her. "I don't think it's a good idea to draw any more attention to us after that woman's death."

Christine flinched. She hated to be reminded of what she'd done; it was easier to just pretend it never happened, but she agreed with him about the attention. The police were out in force, with inspectors combing the opera house for clues. Box Five had all but been torn apart. Performances had been put on hold for the rest of the week to allow the company time to recover and the police time to investigate, though it was obvious who was behind it. What they planned to do about it was not so easy to determine.

"Have you heard anything?" Christine knew Erik would be listening in to conversations as much as he could to glean information the two of them could use.

"Nothing that makes sense." He put his sack down and dropped into a chair. "The managers are too focused on making amends with that poor woman's family. They don't have time to worry about anything else. Everything I'm hearing is about how to keep the opera house from going under."

"Let me know if anything changes," she told him. It was expected that they would lose money after an event like the one two nights ago. People were scared.

Leaning forward, Erik watched her intently. After a few silent minutes of this, he asked, "Why are you here?"

Christine, who'd been in the middle of telling

him what she had thought was a delightful story that she'd heard from one La Sorelli's hangers-on, paused. His question surprised her, causing her words to dry up. "Do you want me to go?"

He shook his head. "That came out wrong. I apologize." He sighed. "I was wondering why you were here. With me."

"Doe there have to be a reason?"

"Usually? Yes." He stared at her, waiting for an answer.

She didn't have one, not one she wanted to give him anyway. He'd made her promise not to lie to him and she didn't want to break that promise if she could help it.

"It's not a hard question, Christine," he encouraged with a bracing smile.

Maybe for him it wasn't difficult, but for Christine it felt nearly impossible. To tell the truth left her vulnerable, but she couldn't lie either. Keeping quiet was her best option. She felt caught, trapped. She couldn't put into words why she kept a friendship with Erik. He helped her with voice lessons and played a part in her schemes, but she knew those weren't the main reasons. She wasn't willing to examine her feelings any deeper though.

Erik nodded, as though he took her silence as another kind of answer. "Do you still want lessons? Are you going to pursue a career in singing?"

She didn't know. Raoul had fallen into line easily, but there was still his brother to consider.

Despite the growing rift between the two, Raoul could still decide to listen to Philippe. It was unlikely, but family bonds never ceased to surprise her. So it would be prudent to continue as she had been, at least until she knew Raoul was hers.

"Yes," she told him, rubbing her thumb hard against her palm.

"And the Vicomte de Chagny?" his voice had taken on a darker edge. Christine didn't like hearing it.

"His brother told me what he thought of the match."

"I'm not asking after his brother." Erik paced in front of her, exuding frustration with every step.

She cocked her head in confusion. "I don't understand where you're going with these questions?" Christine finally asked him. She realized she knew very little about adult Raoul, but didn't think it important enough to try and fill in the gaps. There'd be time enough later.

"You killed someone to ensure you got a chance at the stage," Erik said, crossing his arms over his chest. He didn't look remotely sorry for what he'd said.

The horrified noise that emerged from her shocked them both. How could he bring that up again? Did he want her to keep reliving the past? She couldn't go back and change what had happened, so what was the point of dwelling on it? She was trying to move forward, to forget the mistakes of the past.

She spun around to leave. "You're not my conscience, Erik!"

"Someone has to be!" he shouted after her.

She ground her teeth together. She didn't know what he was playing at, but she was sick of it. "Not you!" Christine heard his dark laughter echo behind her as she began to make her way back to her dressing room.

"Don't play me against that boy, Christine," he called, his voice carrying with little trouble. "Or you will regret it!"

CHAPTER 21

CHRISTINE HURRIED TO THE house on the lake, excitement making her trip over her own feet in her haste. The managers, Moncharmin and Richard, were throwing a masked ball in celebration of the re-opening of the Palais Garnier after the tragic events during the last performance of Faust. All of the company was expected to be in attendance. Christine knew this was the perfect time to meet with Raoul; the mystery and drama of it appealed to her. But for it to work, she needed Erik's help.

She hadn't gone to see him since their last conversation. She refused to call it an argument—that implied that she might not be in the right. Christine was certain that Erik would have gotten over whatever was bothering him by now and forgiven her for whatever it was that she supposed she'd done this time. She had incredibly good news.

"There's going to be a masquerade!" she crowed as soon as she pushed open the door to the house on the lake.

Violin music cut off as Erik lowered the instrument from his chin. He'd found another one to replace the one Raoul had broken in Perros. Long fingers loosely held the bow at his side as his lanky frame straightened in slow increments. His gaze was abstract, as if he were returning from somewhere very far away. Gently, he placed the violin on the table and said, "A masquerade?" He wore his mask so she could only make out half his face.

And just like that they were friendly again. Erik could never seem to stay mad at her, and Christine never gave Erik's moods much thought. They picked up right where they'd left off as if nothing had happened to put them at odds. It was better that way.

She thought it strange that he wore his mask even when no one else was around to see his face. Was he afraid of catching a glimpse of his reflection? His house had no mirrors, so it was unlikely. Putting it out of her mind, she focused on the task at hand. "A ball—people come in costumes to drink and dance and eat. It's all terribly fancy." It was also a good way to earn sponsors and gain patrons for the opera house.

"That sounds horrible." Erik shuddered.

Pouting, Christine lightly smacked him on the shoulder. "Don't be like that. It will be a grand night."

With the long-suffering sigh of a martyr, he replied, "I am very happy for you then. I'm sure you'll have a lovely time."

"You mean *we'll* have a lovely time. You're coming too."

His mouth dropped open in shock, speech clearly deserting him for a time. "I most certainly am not," he said when he finally found his voice. Christine had to fight a giggle at his offended tone. "I highly doubt I'm invited for one thing."

"You're the Opera Ghost. You don't need an invitation!"

Erik pressed his lips together and stared at her as if she was speaking a foreign tongue. Christine waited, suddenly feeling like a lioness stalking her prey. "I don't want to go," he finally said.

"You must go, Erik! I need you!" She widened her summer-blue eyes as far as they would go to plead with him. "And you can't stay cooped up down here forever. It's not good for you."

"Why do you need me?" His voice was suspicious, but there was something else mixed with it. Was it hope? Longing? Christine wasn't certain.

"Is it too much to expect I might want to spend time with you? Don't you want to go out in public?"

He gestured to his face. "When I go out in

public, things don't end well for me."

"That's why a masked ball is perfect!" she enthused. She could implement her plan without Erik, but he would certainly make it easier. "You can cover your face and no one will think it odd. *Everyone* will be wearing a mask. You could even go without one and people wouldn't even blink."

He shook his head emphatically, a horrified expression crossing his face. "That will not be happening."

Christine huffed and crossed her arms. "Say you'll go. For me."

Erik bit his lip. He stood tense, body strangely still. It was obvious to Christine that he didn't want to do this, but that he was considering it for her. Her stomach twisted with something almost like guilt, but she ignored it. She needed this; if all went well, Erik wouldn't even miss her presence.

"Will it please you?" he asked softly.

"Very much."

He nodded. Christine squealed and clapped her hands. Erik regarded her like she was detailing his execution but said nothing as she said, "I have the perfect costume for you. Leave it all to me."

♫♫♫

"This is a little much, don't you think?" Erik asked, gesturing at himself.

Christine cocked her head and surveyed him with a critical eye. The costume she had chosen for him was resplendent. Erik's height worked for him in it. Modeled after a Musketeer's uniform, the outfit was meant to be seen, and by putting Erik in it, Christine had taken away what anonymity he'd have that night. Everywhere he went, people would notice Red Death.

She couldn't ask for a better distraction.

"It's perfect!" she declared, sliding the skull mask down. It covered Erik's face entirely. "No one will have any idea the Opera Ghost is in attendance. You'll be able to move about freely."

"When you said you were choosing my costume, I assumed you'd select something a bit more . . . subdued?" He pushed the mask up.

"Oh Erik, live a little!" She handed him the gloriously feathered monstrosity of a hat. "Don't forget this."

"This hat is the size of a small country," he said sourly. "It has its own ambassadors."

"Stop being a baby," Christine said and pulled his mask down again. Then she turned him around to face the mirror. "Just look."

She could feel his body stiffen beneath her hands as he reluctantly brought his eyes up to see his reflection. When his eyes met those of his reflection, he froze, staring into the mirror intently. Christine was close enough to note the change in his breathing; Erik sucked in shallow draughts of air. She feared he might pass out.

"You look magnificent," she whispered in his ear, hoping to calm him down.

The costume was a miracle. Draped in red velvet and white silk, Erik would be the center of attention. The frock coat was remarkably detailed, the fabric rich and sumptuous. The cape was an arterial red, draped over Erik's thin shoulders to cascade in a bloody river to the floor.

"Your mask is terribly plain," he said absently. He ducked his head so he didn't have to look at the mirror, twisting his body so he wouldn't be reflected in it anymore.

Christine nodded, checking her appearance in the mirror one last time. She'd gone with a simple white ballet dress and a black domino mask. She wanted to blend in, to not be noticed. Erik would attract all of the attention, leaving her free to reel in Raoul. Erik would look quite threatening as Red Death stalking the opera house. She allowed herself a congratulatory moment to bask in her own cunning.

She heard Erik swallow nervously. "I don't think this is a good idea," he said.

Frowning, Christine fluffed her hair in the mirror. She didn't have time for Erik's crisis. "No no no. No getting cold feet now."

"Christine, I don't do well in crowds."

"You'll be fine," she assured him, ignoring the faint note of panic in his voice. "Besides, I'll be with you. There's nothing to worry about."

"You'll stay with me the whole evening?"

"Of course," she said, the lie coming easily. Erik was worrying over nothing. There would be so many people to watch at the ball that he wouldn't even notice she was gone. "I'm going to go out first," she told him. She wanted to get a good spot where she could see Raoul when he arrived. "You can follow a few minutes later."

Erik held out his hand as if to grab hers, but Christine moved away quickly. She threw him a wave as she closed her dressing room door behind her.

As she made her way toward the grand staircase and the front of the Palais Garnier, Christine's stomach clenched with guilt. The feeling was strange and unwelcome. Erik would be fine. She couldn't understand why she might feel bad for leaving him. It was a party! Nothing terrible could happen to him so long as he kept his mask on—and even then, he'd be fine. She'd thought of everything. This tightness in her chest was unnecessary.

Her body didn't listen to her, much to her frustration. The feeling of wrongness twisting in her stomach grew *worse*.

Christine did her best to ignore it. The flurry of color and sound in the public portion of the opera house made it easier to put her concerns out of her mind. People dressed in stunningly ornate costumes clustered in groups or milled about the large space. The noise of conversations filled her ears with the dull roaring of many voices trying to be heard over the din. Wine and laughter flowed generously.

She took up a spot with an excellent view of the door and waited, tapping her heel impatiently. She spied Meg, fully done up in her ballet corps outfit from *Romeo and Juliet*, a golden bird's mask covering the top half of her face. She flitted between several older patrons, impeccably dressed in the finest evening wear. Their only concession to the night's theme were simple white masks.

Raoul entered with his brother, Philippe. The Comte wore the costume of an Egyptian pharaoh, the heavy headdress and mask obscuring much of his features, though La Sorelli recognized him immediately. The principal dancer joined the Comte in a matching Cleopatra costume, and the two began to thread their way through the other guests.

Raoul wore his sharpest evening dress and a white domino mask that was twin to Christine's. She switched her black one for a white one, thinking to throw Erik off should he look for her. She pulled her distinctive hair back into a bun, like all the other dancers in the company. Hopefully this would be enough to keep him from recognizing her from a distance.

Slipping into the crowd, she approached Raoul where he stood awkwardly near the door. He searched the crowd expectantly, ignoring greetings and offers of refreshment. Christine slid beside him and tugged at his sleeve. He looked down, a scowl on his face which disappeared the moment she raised her mask.

"Follow," she whispered, lowering the mask once more. He nodded.

She turned and made her way through the crowd of wealthy people, Raoul walking in her wake. There were plenty of abandoned storage rooms and dressing rooms in the opera house, not to mention the various floors and catwalks. Finding a private space was easy; finding it unoccupied would be another matter. Christine suspected a number of rich men would be spending time with their mistresses at the masquerade.

Gasps spread through the crowd like fire through a dry field. Christine couldn't see over the heads of the assembly, but then the crowd shifted and she was able to catch a glimpse through a break in the bodies.

Red Death had joined the party.

Erik stood frozen, the center of attention. His red soldier's tabard glimmered, the giant plumed hat he wore throwing the skull mask in deep shadow. He turned his head this way and that, obviously looking for her.

Raoul grabbed her hand in a tight grip. She squeezed back and urged him in the opposite direction.

"Christine, is that the man? From Perros? The one dressed as Red Death?" Rage contorted his voice, making him sound strained. "Your Opera Ghost!"

She nodded, unable to be heard over the talking of the crowd as they broke their stunned silence to converge on Erik. Raoul pulled hard on her hand, digging in his heels and refusing to follow her further.

"What are you doing?" she whispered, putting

her masked face next to his.

"I'm going to have it out with him." Raoul's voice shook with his anger. "He's here, in public! He won't escape me this time!"

Christine bit back a mocking sigh. Of course, he would have to make things complicated. She couldn't imagine how Erik would react to Raoul confronting him, but it wouldn't be good for her plan. She needed to distract Raoul.

"You can't do that!" she exclaimed, thinking quickly for something to say that might pull Raoul from this course. "He'll kill you!"

He blanched, but rallied. "I'm not afraid of him!" he rallied.

"Oh, Raoul, don't be foolish." When he moved to pull away, Christine played her trump card. "You can't, Raoul. I couldn't bear it if something happened to you. I love you!"

She clapped her hands over her mouth as if she'd just revealed a horrible secret. Raoul stared at her as if she'd just pronounced him the King of Spain, his blue eyes glistening. "Christine—," he began, but she put a hand over his mouth.

Putting her finger over her lips, she tugged him on. She glanced in Erik's direction and saw a man reach out to try to take off his mask. As Christine watched, Erik slapped the man's hand away and grabbed him by the throat. He flung the offender into the crowd and stalked off.

Guilt welled up inside her once more, but she stuffed it down with all her other unwanted emotions. She needed to pay attention to Raoul now. She would make things right with Erik after the masquerade.

When they were deeper in the guts of the Palais Garnier, Christine let go of Raoul's hand. He could follow her easily as she led him through the lesser used spaces of the opera house, always on the lookout for Red Death. If Erik was looking for her, she didn't want to risk running into him and having to explain herself. At one point, she thought she saw a glimpse of vibrant red off to the side, down one of the many corridors that wound through the backstage areas.

"This way," she whispered, hauling on Raoul's hand and nearly throwing him through a doorway. She closed the door quietly behind her and pressed her ear against the wood, listening carefully for footfalls.

"Chri—," he began, but she slashed her arm down violently. They stood in silence for several minutes before she signaled they were safe.

Before she could say anything, Raoul grabbed her in a bone-crushing hug. She let out a distressed squeak. "Oh Christine, you love me? You love me!"

"Yes, Raoul," she choked, bringing her arms up to hold him. Not that he needed encouragement; she was fairly certain he'd bruised her ribs at least with the force of his affection. "I love you."

"Darling," he whispered, pressing a chaste kiss to her temple. "I'm so happy."

I never would have guessed. Christine allowed the closeness for another moment more before wriggling free of his grasp. She signaled for him to keep his voice down.

"Is he still out there?" Raoul asked, rage and worry battling with joy on his face.

She nodded. "He expected me by his side tonight," Christine told him, pleased that it wasn't actually a lie for once. "He's going to be very angry when he can't find me."

"What will you say?"

She smiled bravely, but she made sure her lower lip quivered. "I'll think of something."

"We should leave!" Raoul announced, as if it were the most logical thing in the world.

"Where would we go?" she asked, warmth seeping through her chest. Yes, this how it was meant to go. Raoul in the role of her protector and provider, and she, the delicate orphaned waif needing his help. Men liked to feel necessary. "And what of your brother?"

"Don't worry about Philippe. He can't tell me what to do any longer," Raoul assured her, and Christine had to grit her teeth together tightly to keep from spewing sharp words at him. She hated being told not to worry about something that affected her life, as if she was no longer an active participant in it. Still, Raoul wanted to feel like her knight in shining armor—she could let him.

"He said you were leaving—and that he was going to try to move the expedition's departure date forward," she told him, working a quaver into her voice.

Clutching both her hands in his, Raoul pressed

a kiss to her knuckles. "The preparations for an arctic expedition can't be rushed, Christine. Philippe can push all he likes, but we won't leave until the captain deems us ready." He smiled shyly. "And now, I may not even want to go at all."

"Ah," she said, relaxing her shoulders consciously. "Were you serious about attacking Erik?"

"Erik? Is that his name?" He nodded, a fierce scowl twisting his normally pleasant face. "Yes, I planned to call the man out for his deception."

Christine threw her arms about Raoul's neck. "Raoul, you must promise me you will not fight him. He'll kill you!"

"I'm not completely incapable of defending myself, Christine," he replied sourly, as if she'd offended him with her warnings.

"I know," Christine quickly agreed, not wanting to put him off by insulting him, though she thought if it came to a fight between Raoul and a croissant, she'd have a difficult time predicting a winner. She apologized silently to Erik for making him sound like a monster. She needed a villain to properly paint herself as a damsel in distress and he was the obvious choice. He would forgive her.

She realized how often she thought that when it came to Erik and it bothered her in a way she didn't feel comfortable exploring at the moment. Better to focus on Raoul.

"I told you before, he's obsessed with me. I've had to convince him that I return his affections for him to let me leave his side for even a moment. It would be horrifying if he weren't so pitiful, so emphatic about being my slave. He strives to make me happy, but he's terribly jealous and violent. You saw what happened the night of *Faust!*"

"How can you stand it? One glimpse of his face was more than I could bear," Raoul said, shuddering. "When I saw him in that church in Perros I thought I had never seen anything so horrible in my life." He clung harder to her hands.

Hiding a wince, it took Christine a moment to realize Raoul spoke of Erik's disfigurement. She'd spent so much time with him that his face had ceased to bother her; now she didn't even register his scars or deformity. He was simply Erik and his appearance was only a small part of what made him who he was. She found herself bristling at Raoul's words and had to remind herself to relax.

"It was why I left Perros so quickly after you were found," Christine explained. "After your confrontation in the church, he was furious. He threatened to kill you. I had to promise to leave with him on the morning train to calm his anger."

Raoul smile put the brightness of the sun breaking over the horizon to shame. "So that's why you weren't there when I woke up." He raised her hand to his lips and pressed a gentle kiss to the back of it. "I was despondent. I thought I'd done something to anger you. Or worse—that you were leading me on." He shook his head and gave her a fond smile. "But I see now you are a good girl,

Christine."

His words struck her harder than a slap to the face. Her face grew hot, but it was nothing to the rage boiling inside of her. Good girl? His words so offended her that she thought she might spit fire. What did he know about what made a person good or bad? He'd had everything handed to him, had lived in comfort and warmth, had parents and a brother who loved and cared for him. When had he even been faced with a difficult choice?

Reminding herself to breathe, Christine leashed her temper. She'd accomplished what she wanted and now it was time to leave while there was still some mystery between them. Creeping toward the door, Christine pressed her ear to it, then opened it a crack. She thought she saw a dancer's costume and a golden mask disappear around a corner, but when she scanned the area, no one was in the corridor. "Come on, I've got to get back before he misses me."

"You can't go back to him!"

Christine turned to him, fixing him with a mournful expression. "What else can I do, Raoul. I have nowhere else to go."

"Then we'll leave." Raoul's eyes went wide as he said it, as if he'd surprised even himself. "We'll run away together!"

Christine nearly shouted in glee, but managed to suppress her joy. This was working out better than even she'd hoped. But she had to sell it; it wouldn't do to look too eager. "It's too dangerous," she told him instead and slipped out the door. "We really need to get back before he notices we're gone."

Catching her hand, Raoul pulled her back. "I don't care! I love you!"

"Shhhh!" she warned, putting a finger to his lips.

"When can I see you again?" he asked, pulling her close to his chest.

She bit her lip, brow furrowed. "In two days," she said, hesitant. "I'll meet you in my dressing room. Knock twice, wait, and then twice more so I know it is you. And tell no one!" She pulled away and glanced around as if they were about to be discovered.

"As you say, Christine." He let her go and followed quietly as she led him back to the main party.

They returned to controlled chaos. Christine slipped away from Raoul before they'd even breached the Grand Foyer, only to hear about the spectacle that was the Red Death. Guests had followed him incessantly, heedless of his orders to be left alone. More than one person had tried to remove his mask only to be physically rebuffed and threatened. No one had seen him since he'd punched a man who'd come close to unmasking him and then run away from the party.

It was all anyone could talk about.

Christine's stomach fell, a horrible swooping sensation. She had to get to Erik. He'd come to this ball for her and she'd left him to his own devices. She could only hope he wasn't too angry with her as she ran back to her dressing room.

The mirror that hid the tunnel's entrance stood ajar. Christine gasped at his carelessness, wondering what this said about his state of mind. How angry would he be with her? Not bothering to change out of her costume, Christine headed down the hidden corridor, making sure to close the mirrored entrance securely behind her.

She had to get to Erik.

CHAPTER 22

CHRISTINE FOUND PIECES OF his costume as she walked. First came the hat, its feathers frayed and crushed by heedless footsteps. Next were the gloves and belts. Then came the doublet. Then the empty scabbard. Until, finally, the skull mask.

Feeling like she was in a strange version of Hansel and Gretel, she collected each piece of his costume until she was awkwardly weighted down and waddling like a sad penguin. She lumbered along until she came to the ladder, at which point she dumped everything on the floor. Erik could come and pick up the rest or leave it there to rot. It made no difference to her.

As she approached the house, the wailing shriek of a violin filled the air. Christine flinched at the caterwauling that assaulted her ears. Erik's playing was usually a beautiful, sublime thing; this was a psychic howl of anger. The notes came furiously, the pace frenetic. Christine had never heard Erik play this way before.

But for all the frantic desperation of the music, there was a glimmer of beauty there too. This was the sound of a soul unmasked, the ugly deep truths that were too unpleasant to give voice to. The music held pain, yes, but power as well. It was breathtaking and terrifying and compelling in its violence and ugliness all at the same time.

Stopping just inside the door, Christine watched while Erik lashed at the violin with the bow. He swayed back and forth as the music poured out of him, the bowstrings fraying quickly with the force of his playing. He still wore the pants, boots, and flowing undershirt of his costume, though everything looked rumpled and stained. His black hair hung loose about his head, falling into his sweaty face. He did not wear his normal mask. She could see that his eyes were squeezed tightly shut. He'd gone inside himself to someplace dark and angry.

His fingers flew over the strings, the bones in his hands standing out in stark relief as he pressed them into the instrument's neck. His back bowed as he ripped even higher notes from the violin, the violent screeching causing Christine to cover her ears. Sound exploded out in an extended scream from the strings, until, slowly, it faded away.

Erik dropped his arms, thin chest heaving. He

dragged his sleeve across his eyes as he panted. He staggered over to the table and placed the violin and bow down, then braced his hands to lean on it. His head hung between his arms and he looked a hairsbreadth away from toppling over in exhaustion.

She stepped forward cautiously. He was angry with her. How angry remained to be seen. "Erik, I—," she began.

"Get out!" he roared, his head snapping up. Rage twisted his face into something frightening and ugly. His good eye blazed.

Christine recoiled but didn't flee. His brown eye was red, as if he'd been crying. Had he? Had she done that to him? She couldn't leave until she was certain he would be all right. "No," was all she said.

He took a step away from the table and nearly fell, but he managed to right himself quickly. "That's right," he snarled. "It's not like you listen to my requests anyway!"

Christine opened her mouth to respond and then closed it with a sharp intake of breath. He wasn't wrong, at least on this occasion. He'd asked her to stay with him and she hadn't. She'd promised him she would, already knowing that she'd break it.

"It wasn't like that," she finally countered, knowing that it was exactly like that.

"Stop lying to me! I saw you with him, Christine!"

As Christine watched, Erik slowly straightened,

drawing the shattered remains of his composure around him. His hands trembled at his sides, but otherwise held himself still. She could see the muscles in his jaw work as he clenched and unclenched his teeth. "I was an idiot to think you might have wanted me there simply for my company."

She hung her head, the guilt from earlier flaring inside of her like a wildfire. He was right, not that she wanted to admit it.

He clicked his tongue against his teeth and briskly said, "Well, I hope you got whatever it is you wanted from your Vicomte." Erik turned so she saw the long line of his back. The shirt billowed around him, nearly swallowing him. "I hope he was *worth* it."

"Don't be like that, Erik," she pleaded, moving forward to place her hand on his shoulder.

He swung around, nostril flaring in anger as he shook off her hold. "Do not *touch* me!" he snarled.

For the first since they met, Christine felt afraid. Not of what he might do, but afraid that she'd crossed a line, that she'd done something she couldn't come back from. She snatched her hand back as if he'd tried to bite it. "I didn't me—,"

"I thought you were my friend!"

Christine's eyes widened in shock. How could he doubt her? "I am!"

His lip curled. "Friends don't treat each other this way." Erik swallowed, glancing away from her. "I asked you to stay with me. Do you know what it was like to be gawked at again?" He shook his head, hair falling about his face in disarray. "Do you understand what that felt like?" Erik tossed his head in dismissal. "Of course, you don't. You don't think of anyone but yourself."

Christine's guilt turned to anger. She knew she'd made a mistake, but she didn't need him railing at her about it, making her feel worse than she already did. "If that is the case, then who let you out of that cage?"

Erik's mocking laugh boomed out, filling the house and making Christine flinch. "If that's you're only basis for a friendship, I think you're lacking something. I don't owe you because you suddenly had a moment of human decency!"

How dare he? Fury ignited white-hot inside her, demanding she hurt him in kind. "At least I look human and not like someone's nightmare! Even your own father couldn't stand the sight of you!"

Erik gasped and went pale, eyes very wide. He looked like he couldn't believe she'd just said that. Christine's breath sawed in and out of her lungs, as if she'd just run a race. They glared at each other in silence.

When Erik finally spoke though, his voice was calm. "I wonder what Raoul would say if he saw you like this."

"Why?" she snapped, anger still burning at her core. "Are you jealous?"

Erik's eyes seemed to blaze as if lit by Hell itself. "Why would I be jealous of him?" His lip curled in derision, a horrible sight. He stepped closer, seeming to loom over Christine. "He doesn't know you—he hasn't seen who you really are. Tell me, Christine, what do you think your fine Vicomte would do if he knew what you are willing to do to get what you want?"

"Shut up, Erik," she shouted, her face flushed and hot with the force of her rage. "Raoul loves me! He's always loved me!"

"He loves a fairy tale!" he shouted back with a snarl. "Don't lie to yourself like you lie to everyone else—I expect better from you." He leaned back when she flailed at him, trying to strike him. "He fell in love with the only part you let him see—the part your father cultivated! But if he saw the real you—the one you keep hidden away because you're afraid no one could ever love her? What would he say, Christine? Would he vow to run away with *that* girl? The one who humiliated Carlotta? The one who cut the rope on the counterweight? The one who killed that woman!"

Christine flung herself at him, fury making her reckless. She didn't care if she hurt him—she wanted to hurt him. Hurt him the way he'd hurt her by speaking things she didn't want to hear, remind her of things best forgotten. She wanted to do more than hurt him: in that moment, Christine wanted to end him.

"I'll tell everyone it was you," she threatened, lashing out with her fists. He simply moved his head out of the way. "Do you think they'll believe someone who looks the way you do?"

He held her at arm's length, so Christine slapped at the parts of him she could reach. "They'll find you down here and they'll drag you out into the light and everyone will stare at you. They'll mock you and jeer at you. It will be worse than that cage by a thousand times. Is that what you want?"

He stared down at her, his good eye wide with horror. "You wouldn't."

She smacked his forearm and backed away from him, panting with exertion. "Don't think I won't, Erik. You think you can destroy me? I'll destroy you first!"

He threw back his head and laughed. The sound of it made her flinch as it crashed over her in a dark wave. His brown eye fixed on her, lit with some kind of unholy glee. He took a step closer to her and then another. Christine matched him step for step until she had backed herself into a wall.

He stopped an arm's length away and watched her, head cocked like she was a fascinating contradiction. "Tell them," he whispered in a voice like winter. "I'm used to cages, my dear. I've been living in them my entire life and I've made my peace with them." He smiled, but it held no joy, only strange dark delight that made Christine's stomach turn over with dread. "I doubt you would fare so well. You, who can't even recognize one of her own making."

With a sneer, he bowed low, mocking her. "I

wish you and your Vicomte much happiness. Though I suspect that is too much to hope considering it's you."

Without another word, Erik spun on his heel and left the house by the front door.

"Bastard," Christine breathed as she slid down the wall. She heard the drag of the boat over the rough sand. Erik was gone.

CHAPTER 23

CHRISTINE RETURNED TO MADAME Valérius' flat very late and fell into bed without a second thought. She was exhausted after her confrontation with Erik, wrung out from the emotion of it. She'd stripped out of her dancer's costume and crawled beneath the covers, vowing to burn the clothes tomorrow.

She woke to the early afternoon sunlight streaming through her windows. Her costume had been picked up sometime earlier by the housemaid and a tray of cold breakfast had been on her bedside table. She knew she should be hungry, but had no desire for food. Instead, she washed and dressed before returning the untouched tray to the kitchen.

"Christine?" she heard Madame Valérius call from her bedroom.

"Coming," Christine called.

The older woman looked worse than she usually did, her skin almost grey. "How was the party?" she asked as Christine settled herself in the chair next to her bed.

She shrugged, not wanting to talk about it. Her argument with Erik had left her raw in places she didn't want to think about. "It was lovely," she answered without much expression.

Madame Valérius frowned and leaned forward to peer into Christine's face. "What is wrong, Christine?"

Shaking her head, Christine didn't answer right away. She didn't know what was wrong with her; she just felt odd. Her conversation with Erik had revealed things about herself she didn't necessary want to revisit. "Tired, I suppose. I'm fine."

Madame Valérius captured one of Christine's hands in her dry, cold ones. "Did you see the Angel of Music—or the Opera Ghost? Whatever he calls himself these days?"

Christine blinked back sudden tears at the thought of Erik. "No."

The older woman lowered her voice to nearly a whisper, like she was imparting a secret. "Was the Vicomte there?" She smiled slyly.

"Yes." Christine took her hand back, surreptitiously rubbing it on her skirt.

"He seems very enamored of you, my dear,"

Madam Valérius told her.

"Yes." Erik's words haunted her. If he knew what she was really like, would he still be?

The woman sighed. "You could do significantly worse, Christine. Do you not like him?"

Christine rubbed at irritated eyes. "He's very nice," she told Madame Valérius defensively.

Raoul was fine. He was a nice boy who'd grown into a nice young man. Christine knew he adored her. He had a title and the money that went with it, unlike some other nobles she could name who had squandered their family's fortune. She could build a life with him.

Was it a life that she really wanted though?

Erik was right. Raoul didn't know the real her. And if she married him, she'd have to go on pretending to be this person. Insipid, mousy Christine, too afraid of her own shadow to do anything without Raoul beside her. Naïve Christine who relied on Raoul to guide her through life—even though he had less life experience than she did.

It wouldn't be all bad, she had to admit. Comfort and security went a long way, especially for someone who'd grown up without much of either. Her father had kept them on the road for much of the years after her mother died. It wasn't until he conned Monsieur Valérius that Christine remembered what it was like to settle down. Even after acquiring their patronage, Pappa still took her on trips to local fairs during the summer months. Weeks of walking and sleeping in hay lofts and singing for their supper. She'd hated it.

Madame Valérius' next words chilled Christine's blood. "I want to make sure you're taken care of after I die." She patted the spot above her heart.

"You've got some years left in you yet," Christine assured her.

Madame Valérius pressed a handkerchief to her lips. "How I would like to believe that!" Her smile was sad. "But we both know that isn't true at all." She locked gazes with Christine. "We both know I'm dying."

"I—,"

"Shhhh," Madame Valérius hushed her. "This time with you has been a joy to me. You are the daughter I never had." Christine let her take her hand as she continued. "I have not regretted one franc spent on your musical education. But it won't last much longer and I fear that I have nothing to leave you when I go."

"It's not important," Christine told her, wishing the woman would just stop talking. She needed to think.

"It is," Madame Valérius insisted. "I want to see you settled." She sighed and collapsed back against the pillows. "I had hoped the Angel of Music would bring you to the heights of success, but if what the Vicomte says is true, it seems that is not possible. So you must be smart."

Christine was surprised by the shrewd stare Madame Valérius leveled at her. "Do you understand what I'm telling you, Christine?"

She nodded. She was afraid she did. She was running out of time and options. Madame Valérius was right. Christine couldn't wait any longer, not if she wanted a way out.

Her father would approve.

♪♪♪

Raoul did just as she asked, knocking twice and then again on her dressing room door the following day. Christine felt each rap on the door hit her like a gunshot to her chest. She rose from her seat with all the enthusiasm of someone facing their execution.

Still, she had to do this. Madame Valérius was right. This was the best option.

With Erik on the loose, Christine didn't know how much time she had left. She wished she could talk to him when they both weren't so angry. She knew she'd been kinder to him, had been less selfish. She should never have left him alone during the masquerade.

If everything went as she hoped, she'd be long gone from the Palais Garnier before he realized what she was up to.

When she opened the door, Raoul greeted her with a radiant smile. It lit his face like the sun emerging from storm clouds. There was an inherent brightness to him that could never be dimmed. Where Erik seemed to exist in perpetual night and darkness, Raoul was a creature of the light. He belonged to the day.

Christine didn't know where she belonged, but she suspected the shadows suited her best. Though when Raoul held out his hand to her, she allowed him to drag her into the light.

"We should talk," she said, before he could speak. She glanced around before tugging at his hand. "But not here."

"Is he watching? Listening?" Raoul whispered, his gaze searching the area for signs of the Opera Ghost.

"Higher," Christine told him. "I'll tell you everything, but we must go higher."

"I'll follow you, Christine," he told her and allowed her to lead him to the heights of the Palais Garnier. "Anywhere."

Yes, she supposed he would. That was the problem.

She led him further backstage. Meg Giry called out to them as they passed, but Christine waved her away. She didn't have time for Meg's nonsense right now.

As they wended their way up staircases and floors and still more staircases, Christine ran over the story she'd prepared after speaking to Madame Valérius. She was frightened at how easy it was for her to paint Erik as a villain, and even more frightened because she knew Raoul would take to it like a cat to cream. Christine imagined Pappa watching from wherever he was and beaming with pride. The thought made her stomach churn and a greasy taste rise in the back of her throat.

They reached the roof and Christine settled them beneath the statue of Apollo with his lyre. She pulled him down to sit beside with a breathless, "We should be safe up here."

"Safe?"

She bit her lip, shoring up her courage. The wrongness of what she was about to do made her tremble, but Christine put it aside. Erik would not forgive her, and she didn't expect him to. But she wouldn't be staying at the Palais Garnier for much longer if everything went according to plan.

"He stays close to the trap doors," she lied. "He doesn't care for heights. Plus, he's working on his masterpiece—that means he won't be wandering about the theatre."

"Good for us then," Raoul murmured, relaxing next to Christine. He covered her hand with his.

"Yes." She took a deep breath before beginning and prayed silently for forgiveness. "Do you love me, Raoul?"

He blinked, blue eyes sharp with surprise at her question. "I thought I made it obvious how much I love you."

She squeezed his hand gently. "I need to hear you say it."

"I love you. With all of my heart." He smiled indulgently.

She frowned, serious. "And you want to marry me?"

As she watched, Raoul pulled away so he could more easily see her face. "Christine, what is this about? Of course, I want to marry you. More than anything else in this world or the next."

Christine didn't hesitate, knowing she needed to appear convincing. She threw herself into Raoul's arms, wrapping her arms around his neck and hanging on as though her life depended on it. "Then you must take me away from here!"

Raoul made a gurgling noise and Christine loosened her hold slightly so he could speak and breathe. "There, there, my darling," he soothed. She felt his hands rub her back in an attempt to calm her down. "Certainly, we'll go, but why now? Why so suddenly?"

Pretending to wipe away tears, Christine leaned back. "Because I fear Er—*he's* going to take me away from here and I'll never see you again. He said he wants me to be with him—to marry him—and I agreed to it so he would let me go. But he doesn't trust me, and each day his behavior becomes more and more frightening." She pulled her arms from around Raoul and stared at her hands where they rested in her lap.

"I won't let that happen," Raoul declared, eyes hard.

Christine bit back a chuckle. She knew he tried to be fierce, but Raoul simply wasn't built for it. His face was too open, too sunny for anyone to believe he was a dangerously violent individual. "You may not have a choice, Raoul."

He set his jaw stubbornly. Christine couldn't hide her smile, so she threw her arms around his neck once more. "He's threatened to kill you if you interfere!"

Raoul's breathing went shallow and uneven for a moment. Good, now he was taking things seriously. "It won't come to that, Christine," he assured her, though his voice shook. "We'll get away before he even knows we're gone."

"Tonight?" She wanted it to be tonight. She was afraid she'd lose her nerve and the guilt she felt would eat her alive.

His body went tense beneath her hands. "No," he whispered. "I'm g—,"

"Did you hear something?" Christine's head snapped up and her eyes narrowed as she searched the shadows of the roof. As far as she knew, Erik didn't come up this far, but there was a lot of time she wasn't with him.

Raoul shook his head, but Christine could feel his worry beneath her hands in the way his shoulders tensed. "I didn't hear anything."

She continued to glance about them, certain she'd heard that faint clicking noise Erik made with his tongue against his teeth whenever she did something he didn't appreciate. Perhaps it was her conscience, finally putting in an appearance and ready to drive her mad. There was no outward sign of him, but Christine couldn't shake the sensation of being watched.

Raoul brought her back to herself. "I will need at least a day to make arrangements," he said, pulling her closer.

"Very well," she sighed, unable to keep the disappointment from her voice. At least that was real. She'd hoped he'd run away with her tonight, so she could drag him before a holy man and marry him before either of them changed their minds. But that wasn't to be tonight. "Tomorrow night then."

"Tomorrow night," Raoul agreed. He lowered his head to hers for a kiss.

Christine stopped him, moving her head out of the way. "You must promise me, Raoul, that no matter what happens, no matter how I might fight or cajole you not to, you must take me away from this place."

"Why would you fight me?" He pushed her chest away from his so he could look into her eyes. "I don't understand—you want out of here just as badly as I do."

"Yes, Raoul," she began, then paused as if unsure how to continue. "But when I sing, sometimes I feel outside of myself. And when *he* sings, well, I forget myself altogether!" She grabbed the lapels of his coat and shook him a bit. "If I fight, you must take me from the opera house—no matter what I say!"

"Who is this Erik person anyway? How did you come to meet him?"

Now was the time for Christine to spin the tale she'd fabricated the night before. A giant for Raoul to slay, a dragon to rescue her from. Erik had to be all those things and more.

"I'm not sure where he came from," she began, shivering as a cold wind blew along the rooftop to ruffle their hair. "But he's traveled all over the world. He was in carnivals, you see, learning tricks and techniques wherever he went. He can throw his voice, he can seem to disappear from one place and reappear in another. He knows so many ways to kill a man, but he prefers the Punjab lasso—it's the way he killed Joseph Buquet! He told me he met a sultan once and built a palace for him. A torture chamber too," she threw in, embellishing at the last minute.

"How did he wind up here, then?" Raoul held her close, tucked safely in his arms. Christine huddled against him for warmth.

"Eventually the sultan grew suspicious of him. He didn't trust Erik, not when he knew the secrets of the palace that he'd built for him. Erik escaped before he could be executed and made his way here. With his architectural skill, he got hired on to help build the opera house."

"So that's how he knows about all of the tunnels and such!" Raoul's arms tightened about her. "But he didn't look that old when I saw him at the church in Perros."

Christine faltered for a moment. She hadn't thought Raoul remembered much of that night. "How can you be sure of anything?" she countered. "He had on a mask."

"True," Raoul admitted after several moments spent thinking. "I just always took him for young—like our age." Christine felt him shrug.

"He must have heard me at practices—he has an excellent voice and loves to listen to the rehearsals." Christine knew it was more effective to sprinkle in some truth within the warp and weft of lies she wove. "And he sought me out."

"As simple as that?" Raoul sounded dubious.

"I often prayed aloud for the Angel of Music to bless me with a visit, just as my father told me before he died." Christine's throat constricted at the mention of her father. She swallowed hard and kept going. "And one night, he did."

"Oh, Christine," he whispered and held her so tightly she almost couldn't breathe.

"It wasn't like that," she scolded, offended on both her and Erik's behalf at his assumption, despite the string of lies she was telling. "He didn't even let me see him, not at first. He was just a voice. I thought I was the only one who could hear him until you told me you heard him speaking to me when you were outside my dressing room."

"When did you finally see him?"

"There was the time when I handed the managers that first letter, but I don't remember much of it. He left me alone for the most part. I only heard him playing and singing. But it was after the gala—when I sang Margarita for the first time—that I got to see him."

"Without his mask?"

She nodded, burying her face in his chest, knowing that what she said was another terrible, but necessary, lie. "It was horrible. I've never seen anything so hideous."

That clicking sound again, and Christine flinched. Raoul went still. "Did you hear it that time?" she asked him.

"Yes," he whispered. They both turned their heads to peer into the encroaching darkness. Evening was falling and they would need to return to solid ground shortly.

Christine stood and took a few steps in the direction where the shadows pooled deepest against the eaves of the opera house, but she could see nothing. Raoul walked up beside her and took her hand. "He won't let me go," she whispered, but she wasn't talking about Erik. She felt her father's presence looming over her, heard his voice instructing her. She was so close to having everything he'd ever wanted for them!

"Hush, Christine," Raoul said, once more taking her in his arms. She huddled against him, a desperate pain swirling in her chest. "I need a day's time to prepare for a coach and horses and then we'll leave this place and its ghosts behind forever."

"After the performance tomorrow night." She clutched at him blindly, fingers digging into the thick fabric of his jacket. "Do you promise?"

"I do."

When he leaned forward to kiss her mouth, she rose to meet him.

CHAPTER 24

CHRISTINE SAID GOOD-BYE TO Raoul at the bottom of the grand staircase. He had plans to make and transportation to arrange, but he promised to see her immediately after the curtains closed the following evening. She watched him go, promising to return to Madame Valérius' flat right away.

But first she needed to collect something from her dressing room.

Philippe's check. She and Raoul were going to need money if his brother decided to cut Raoul off in anger. That check would make sure they could live for a time while they waited for Philippe's anger to fade. As far as Christine was concerned, that part of the de Chagny money was

Raoul's by right. She was just making sure he got his share.

On her way to her dressing room, she passed the practice room. Meg was holding court with a few of the other dancers. Christine wasn't planning on stopping, but then she heard a familiar clicking noise.

The noise from the Lyre of Apollo.

Turning slowly, Christine watched the gathering of dancers. Giselle laughed loudly, while one lightly pushed Meg in the shoulder. Meg made that tsking sound with her tongue.

Christine gasped softly at the anger that rose inside of her, a heat that seared her from the inside out. Meg had been spying on them. Why though? Scowling, Christine watched Meg laugh and gossip with the others and felt old beyond her years. When had she become so tired?

Drawing back into the shadows of the wings, Christine waited for the girls to go their separate ways. Meg lagged behind, fussing with her shoe.

Christine stepped in front of her. "Bonjour, Meg."

Meg straightened, eyes narrowing as she took in Christine's tense stance. "Christine."

Christine didn't waste time with subtleties. She didn't have the patience for it. In twenty-four hours, she would be long gone. "Why were you following me and Raoul earlier?"

Meg shrugged an elegant shoulder. Christine slapped her.

That gained Christine the proper respect for

the seriousness of this conversation. Meg cradled her cheek, gaping at her. "Answer me plain or I'll do worse than hit you." She watched Meg the way she would a bug crawling along the floor. "What were you doing up there?"

When the dancer hesitated for too long, Christine raised her hand again. Meg flinched and stammered out, "All right, all right." She raised a hand to forestall any further violence. "I was following you. For the Comte de Chagny."

"You were spying for Philippe." At Meg's nod, Christine frowned. "For how long?"

Meg rubbed her eye with the back of her hand. "Only a few days."

Christine thought of the knife sheathed against her calf, right above her boot. Her fingers twitched, but she forced her hand to stay where it was. "Since when?" she snapped instead. How much had Meg heard and how much had she already told Philippe?

Meg's eyes were fierce when she met Christine's. "The masquerade," she bit out, crossing her arms and cocking out a slim hip. "He asked me to follow you, so I did. I saw you and Raoul disappear into that room and I waited until you came out. I heard you make plans to meet, so I told the Comte. He asked me to watch you both."

"And he paid you." Christine's lip curled up in disgust.

"A very hefty sum," Meg agreed, suddenly not at all like the girl Christine once knew. "What can I say, Christine. I've grown fond of eating. The

Comte's money ensures my mother and I can continue to do so for a while longer."

She could just reach out and stab Meg. It wouldn't be hard. Christine had already killed two people, what was a third added to the list? She could hang her from the ropes or leave her body in the orchestra pit to be found during the next rehearsal. Meg would be just another victim of the Opera Ghost.

Erik's face flashed in her memory, his dark eye regarding her with pity. He wouldn't approve of killing Meg. Christine bit her lip to keep the angry words from surging forth. What Erik thought of her didn't matter. He didn't understand anything.

No, another voice, one that sounded a lot like her own, countered. *He understands everything.*

"Are you going to tell him? About what you heard tonight?" Christine kept her tone neutral.

"I don't know," Meg answered. "Is there going to be another accident?" She stressed the last word, gaze darting to the rafters above them.

Christine smiled broadly, but there was little feeling in it. Her body was strangely numb—it was almost like she didn't care what happened to her any longer. "No, Meg. No more accidents. That I can guarantee."

Meg peered into Christine's face, brow wrinkled as she studied Christine's face. She didn't know what Meg might be hoping to find, but Christine didn't flinch away from the scrutiny. After a few interminable moments, Meg said softly, "Good."

Christine didn't know what was so good about whatever it was Meg had seen in her face. But that wasn't important. She just wanted to get out of the opera house before it consumed her like paper thrown onto a fire. She waited for whatever Meg was going to say next.

"I think I can make sure the letter I send to Monsieur de Chagny is suitably delayed," the dancer offered.

Christine exhaled slowly, feeling some of the tension bleed from her limbs. "Thank you, Meg."

"Don't thank me, Christine," Meg said, moving away. "I don't know if I'm doing you a favor or not."

"You don't know how close you came," Christine murmured as she also stepped away. Now that Meg was settled, Christine wanted to get that check and escape the Palais Garnier until warmups tomorrow.

Meg spun easily on the balls of her feet and skittered farther away from Christine. "I knew," she assured her. "You're not as smooth as you think you are."

Before Christine could respond, Meg had slipped gracefully away.

Christine chewed on her lower lip. When had Meg gotten so sharp? Had she always been this way and Christine just hadn't noticed? The thought bothered her more than she liked. If that were the case, how had she missed it? Or had association with Christine tainted her? Shaking her head, she continued on her way backstage.

Her dressing room was dimly lit, but Christine could find her way through it blindfolded. She didn't bother with a light—she wouldn't be there long enough to need one. The music box sat on the left side of her dressing table. She hurried over to it and picked it up, fingers working on the catch that would spring open the hidden compartment.

"Brava!" The voice seemed to issue from all corners of the room. "Brava," echoed and echoed until it faded away to silence.

Christine froze, check clutched in her fist. "Erik?" she called, peering into the dimness. "I thought you'd left."

She couldn't see him. While she didn't think he would ever physically hurt her, she had the same dread everyone did of being stuck in the dark and vulnerable. Her heart beat faster in her chest and sweat pooled at the small of her back beneath her layers of clothes. Had he been up on the roof, watching them along with Meg?

Erik spoke first, answering her unspoken question. "Unable to keep from lying, I see. That was quite the tale you spun for Raoul." He sounded like he was right beside her, whispering in her ear.

She spun, reaching out, but touched nothing but air. "This isn't funny, Erik," she told him, fear and anger warring inside her. She embraced both because they were better than guilt.

"I worked for a sultan, did I?" He gave that unnerving chuckle he was so good at as the Opera

Ghost. "I created a torture chamber? My, my, the way your mind works."

"Stop it, Erik," she seethed.

The rasp of a striking match and the flare of its light made Christine flinch. Carefully Erik lit one of the oil lamps at the far side of the room and sat on the sofa beside it. He blew out the match with a puff of his lips, his face masked in black. He rested his arm across his crossed knees.

"So you heard," she said, squaring off with him. Christine tucked the check into the bodice of her dress.

"Everything," he said with a heavy nod. "I found it rather . . . edifying. I wasn't aware I was so talented. Or so old."

Christine took a step forward, hands outstretched. "Erik, I—," she began to explain, but Erik's exclamation cut her off.

"Stop lying!" He took a deep breath and released it slowly as he fought to control himself. "Tell the truth for once in your life!"

His words hurt, but it was the depth of the pain that caught her off-guard. The scorn with which he spoke made her feel small and worthless. He didn't understand the position she was in, even after she'd told him of her father. She had few options. Raoul was simply the best one. But Erik didn't see any of that. He just saw a broken girl.

The agony of it was breathtaking and in that moment Christine hated him.

Christine lashed out, as she always did. It wasn't in her to retreat when hurt; she needed to know she gave back as good as she got.

"Very well, Erik. I'll give you the truth," she said coldly, straightening her spine so she could look down her nose at him. "I'm not sorry for what I said. In fact, I'd do it all again if I had to." She waited for that barb to hit and was disappointed when it landed to no effect.

"I'm tired of scraping by, of conning my way to my next meal. I'm tired of working to make someone else happy. I want someone who looks at me and doesn't see a partner in crime or an accessory or any of the rest of it." She paused as her throat closed up with the force of what she was feeling.

"I want someone to take care of me for a change."

Erik stood, his height making him loom over her. Christine glared up at him, eyes hot with tears that she would be damned to let fall. He crossed his arms over his chest and stared at her for a long, silent moment.

"And you think marriage to Raoul is you escaping that?" He shook his head, as if he couldn't believe her decision.

Her temper flared. "Why shouldn't I marry him? Don't I deserve to be happy?

"Is living a lie going to make you so?" He regarded her sadly. It made her want to scratch his eyes out. "Does it make you happy now?"

Gritting her teeth, she said, "I deserve an easy life—a comfortable one. And I deserve someone who loves me!"

"Of course you do, Christine, everyone does!" Erik scoffed, as if he couldn't believe he was having to explain something so obvious to her. Her rage soared as he continued. "Which means Raoul does too!" Christine could feel the tension in his body as he stepped closer to her.

"I make him happy!" she yelled back, voice shrill.

"Are you certain of that?" Erik hardly ever raised his voice, but it thundered out of him now like Judgment. "Do you love him?"

Christine flinched. Slowly she raised her eyes to Erik's face. He stared down at her, lips curled in disapproval. Balling her hands into fists at her side, she said quietly, "I thought you were my friend. Why must you question me so?"

Giving her a sad smile, he answered, "You don't *have* friends. You have tools." He shook his head. "But you are *my* friend. It's because you are that I question you." He placed two fingers beneath her pointed chin and tilted her head up.

For a moment she thought he might kiss her. Christine wondered how she'd react and found that she was excited to know what his lips would feel like against hers. But when he spoke, his voice seemed to hold all of the sadness in the world. "People aren't things, Christine. You can't move them about and play with them like they are pieces on a chessboard." He dropped his hand. "I would have thought that someone in your life would have taught you that."

"My father taught me that you take all you can

274

get because you never know if you're going to get it again." She stepped back. "That's what he taught me."

"That's no way to live, Christine."

"Like you have any basis for comparison, Erik! Your father abandoned you." It was a low blow, but she was good at those. "You're just jealous because no one will ever love you!"

He didn't even flinch. Erik stood before her, serene, unaffected by her temper. "Say all the hurtful things you like. I *know* what love is."

Lip curled in disgust, she bit out, "Oh really?" Her voice dripped sarcasm. "Then do tell me all about it."

He gave her a long, pitying look. It made her want to strike him. She hated pity more than nearly anything else. She wasn't someone to be pitied. She wasn't *lacking*. A scream, deep and primal, built inside of her until she thought she might burst with it.

But Erik didn't speak; he sang. His celestial voice rose up like an angel ascending to Heaven, taking Christine along with it. He sang something she'd never heard before, but the song was compelling and sublime and it broke her heart. At the rising fall of the notes, she nearly did crash to her knees, commanded to do so just from the sheer power of his voice. It was unfair for any human to sound like this. He stared at her face the entire time he sang, his hand outstretched. Her own hand rose to meet his, almost against her will.

She reached out, her fingers closing over a

tarnished silver-backed hairbrush she kept on her dressing table. She hurled it as hard as she could at Erik, striking him in the shoulder. He broke off, rubbing his arm. "Ow!"

"Love is only worth what you can get with it," she snarled, hands hooking into claws. "Raoul needs to believe he's saving me from a nightmare, so that's what I gave him. I'm letting him spirit me away in his coach after tomorrow night's performance. We're going to have a good life together, one where I won't have to lie or cheat or steal anymore! And I won't ever have to come back here again!" She would not miss the Palais Garnier at all or any of the people in it.

Erik flinched, holding his upper arm where the brush had hit. His voice was subdued when he asked, "And what of Philippe? He's the Comte. He controls all of Raoul's money. He's not just going to let him go."

Why must he constantly question her? She was glad Raoul was so biddable, so easy to manage. Erik took too much effort. "Philippe loves his brother. He won't want to see him suffer." Besides, she still had the check that Philippe had written her, hidden safely now in her dress. "I'm sure they'll work it out."

Erik turned his disappointed gaze to her. "Please, think about what you are doing, Christine. Do you think you can keep up a lie for the rest of your life? Do you really think that's fair to either of you?"

"I've done nothing but think about it," she

snapped, having had enough of the conversation. "Raoul and I are leaving after tomorrow night's performance. There is nothing you can do or say to change that fact." Christine turned to leave and said without looking behind her, "Good-bye, Erik."

CHAPTER 25

CHRISTINE WAITED IN THE wings, pacing nervously. She didn't know why she was nervous—she'd sung Marguerite plenty of times. With Carlotta refusing to leave her apartments after the croaking debacle, Christine had taken the lead. She'd experienced butterflies of nervousness before performances, but never like this. Her knees wobbled, and the cold sweat trickling down her back made her want to claw her heavy costumes loose so she could get a decent breath of air in her lungs.

Meg passed by her on her way to the stage and gave her wary look. The dancer had given Christine a wide berth since their confrontation yesterday. Christine's stomach clenched, wishing things could be different. With effort, she put all thoughts of regret out of her mind and turned her attention to the audience.

Raoul sat with his brother in their box. Philippe wore a thunderous expression, as if the opera itself had affronted him. Raoul slouched in his chair, wearing a plaintive air of truculence. Things were not right between the brothers. She hoped that didn't mean Raoul had second thoughts about their plan to leave, but she had no choice but to keep going.

There had been no sign of Erik. Christine had even checked Box Five, in the vain hope she might stumble across him, but its empty seats mocked her. She'd decided it was better this way. A clean break between them. She could start her new life with Raoul with no ties to anyone.

Her heart sat flayed inside her chest for reasons she did her best not to think about. Erik was a part of her, as surely as her voice was. To never see him again felt wrong. He infuriated her like no one else could, but she supposed he felt the same about her. Christine knew he loved her, the real her that others never got to see—she wasn't blind, though she'd never questioned him about it. What she felt for him wasn't something she wanted to examine closely. Christine had made up her mind about Raoul. He was the one she wanted to be with. Erik was wrong in thinking that Raoul needed to know the real Christine. He loved the one he saw just fine.

Smoothing her hands down the front of her

skirts, Christine did her best to empty her mind of chaotic thoughts. Just one more performance. That was all that stood between her and her future. She would sing one last time—like she had never sung before—and leave the opera behind to the sound of thunderous applause.

Swallowing the sour bile collecting at the back of her throat, Christine willed her stomach to be quiet as she heard her musical cue. She took her place onstage, the song rising in her throat. It spilled forth like raindrops, bolstered by the power of the orchestra. From the corner of her eye, she made out Raoul, leaning forward in his seat so he could watch her.

During the Jewel song, Christine's gaze lingered on Box Five, her heart sinking when she realized it sat empty. The disappointment stabbed at her heart, the pain of Erik's absence nearly blinding. Why did she feel like she was missing something vital with him not here? Raoul was in the audience, watching her. Why wasn't that enough?

She shook off the strange longing for Erik and poured everything she had into her performance, imagining she and Erik, practicing in his house on the lake. Her voice was good, but she never sounded like she did when she sang with him. Still, it was good enough to get a standing ovation when she was through.

A shriek interrupted the scene between Marguerite and Faust. Christine glanced up, eyes widening as a scenic flat toppled forward onto the stage. She heard Meg's scream. The company scattered to avoid being crushed beneath the backdrop. The audience reacted with shouts and cries of their own, some launching to their feet and making for the exits, probably remembering the falling counterweight.

Christine scrambled away, her heavy costume slowing her down. She tripped, hitting the floor hard as people ran all around her. Someone's foot clipped her head. A passing dancer stepped on her hand as Christine scrabbled away. Christine cried out and curled it against her chest.

Someone swept her up, holding her tightly in their arms. Shouts rang in her ears. Christine squeezed her eyes shut tight as cries of "The Opera Ghost!" filled the theatre. She was held firmly, her body swaying with her savior's running steps.

Whoever was holding her smelled of dust—the kind that came from old, disused books—ink, and some kind of dry, woodsy smell. She recognized who held her.

"Erik," she breathed, the knot in her guts suddenly loosening before she remembered she their last meeting.

"What in the hell do you think you're doing?" Christine shoved against his chest as he carried her toward the trap door that led to the underground tunnels. He wore a stagehand's rough clothes, a slouching hat hiding his hair and part of his face. She struggled, but Erik's arms were like bars, caging her against his body. He was stronger than he first appeared. "I need to get to Raoul!"

"We are going to talk," Erik ground out as her elbow dug into his ribs. Christine hoped it was at least uncomfortable.

"I don't have anything else to say to you."

"I have plenty to say to you."

"Well, I don't want to hear it!" She twisted around so she could smack his upper arm as hard as she could.

He cried out in pain and nearly dropped her. Christine shrieked, tumbling from his arms as he crashed to his knees. His face was white and sweating beneath his mask and hat. As she watched, Erik clutched at his upper arm, shoulders hunched in pain.

The iron scent of blood reached her nose and she raised her forearm to her face to cover the smell. "Are you bleeding?"

"A little," he gritted out between clenched teeth.

"There's no such thing as a little when it comes to blood," Christine told him, swallowing weakly. Her upset stomach was back at the thought of it. "How?" She knelt in front of him.

"It's not important right now." Erik planted his hand on the floor of the corridor and used it to push himself upright.

When he staggered, Christine reached out and steadied him. "Just tell me," she ordered.

"Your fiancé took a shot at me when I went to talk to him last night."

Christine dropped her hands and regarded Erik with her mouth agape. "You went to Raoul's last night? Are you mad?"

Propping his hand against the tunnel wall, Erik managed to remain upright. After a few moments of deep breathing, he straightened as best he could in the tight tunnel and began to walk forward. "Not at the moment, no."

"Why would you go to Raoul's?" She had a sinking feeling that she already knew.

They continued to walk for some way in silence. Erik held his hand over his upper arm. Christine thought the sleeve gleamed wetly in the dim light. When he didn't answer, she prompted him again. "Erik?"

"He grazed me, that's all." He sounded offended. "I was on the balcony and I startled him from sleep. I wasn't expecting to be greeted with a firearm."

Christine pushed at his chest to get him to stop moving, which he did, albeit reluctantly. "You went to his flat in the middle of the night, climbed up to his balcony, and then tried to wake him up from sleep after I'd just finished telling him how terrible you are, and you were surprised when he shot you?" She shook her head when he nodded hesitantly. "You're not mad. You're an idiot."

"Idiot or not, you're going to help me back to my house," he told her, pushing her arm out of his way so he could move past her.

"Why would I do that?" Raoul was probably frantic looking for her. She needed to return to the stage area to find him.

Turning his head, Erik fixed her with a flat look, his mouth pressing into a thin line. "Because I have that check you came back for."

"The che—?"

Her hands flew to the neckline of her dress even though she knew it wasn't there. She hadn't noticed it was missing when she'd undressed yesterday. Her face flushed hot with embarrassment. Christine had been so tired after the events of the afternoon and from the trip up to the roof that she had completely forgotten about the check she'd tucked in the bodice of her gown.

Erik hadn't. He'd seen her take it out of its drawer and saw where she'd put it. And then he'd used his sleight of hand to snatch it from her.

"Coming, Christine?" he called and she could only grind her teeth together in frustration and follow.

She fumed in silence all the way to Erik's makeshift home, glaring holes between his shoulder blades. By the time they arrived, Christine was certain that if she opened her mouth, she would breathe actual fire.

Erik shucked off his hat, tossing it into a corner. Pieces of his black hair had escaped its tie and hung haphazardly about his face. He tucked them behind his ears and turned to face her.

"I think we've said everything we need to say to each other," she told him before he could speak. She held out her hand, palm up. "Give me the check."

"You still think this is the right course of action?" he asked. He gazed at her with determined eyes.

She nodded, not trusting herself to speak. It would have been easier to never see him again. She could have lived with that, but now she doubted everything. She bit the inside of her cheek, the physical hurt a welcome respite from her emotional turmoil.

"I don't want you to go," he whispered. "But not for the reason you think."

"You love me," she told him, having figured that out some time ago.

"Yes, but that's not the reason." She blinked in surprise. He stepped closer, resting his hands on her shoulders. "I want you to be happy and do not think you will be."

"With Raoul?"

"With yourself." His smile was sad.

"It's not your decision to make, Erik." She took a deep breath and swayed closer. His brown eye widened, but he did not pull away. She stopped just shy of his lips. "It's mine. And I choose Raoul."

He grinned crookedly, inclining her head as if acknowledging the power of her action. "And he doesn't get a say?"

Christine stared up at Erik, brow furrowed in confusion. Why was he bringing this conversation up again? She wasn't likely to change her mind.

"He had his say, Erik. He's leaving with me tonight."

I know," he murmured. Erik looked up suddenly, smile growing wider. "He's here to collect you."

Christine followed Erik's gaze. Raoul stood in the doorway, his pretty, scowling face pale and sweaty. She glanced back to Erik, eyes narrow with suspicion. He'd counted on Raoul finding his way to them.

As she watched, Erik bowed mockingly to him. "Welcome, Monsieur de Chagny. So good of you to come."

"Let her go, monster!" Raoul strode in, looking nothing like the callow young man she knew. He held his hand up in front of his face.

"Raoul, get away from here," she pleaded. What was to be discussed was between her and Erik. Raoul had no place in it. She didn't want him anywhere near them. Erik held too many of her secrets; if Raoul knew some of the things she'd done, he'd never want to be with her.

"Not without you, Christine," he answered, never taking his gaze away from Erik. Christine rolled her eyes at his obstinance. Now was the time he decided to dig his heels in. Of course.

"Welcome to my humble home," Erik said, his voice booming in the stillness. He was using what Christine referred to as his "performance" voice. It seemed to amplify strangely and carried to all corners of the room. "Though I must ask, why are you doing that?" He raised his arm to mimic Raoul's posture.

Raoul looked confused for a brief moment

before his expression hardened. Christine saw the dark skin of his face grow slightly darker with a flush. "The Punjab lasso!" he cried as if that explained everything.

"Excuse me?" Erik crossed his arms over his chest and cocked his head. "What kind of lasso is this?" He turned to Christine. "Is this more of your drivel?"

"The Punjab lasso?" Raoul's voice cracked on the last word, and he turned to Christine for help. "Meg Giry. She led me here."

"Meg? She led you here?" When had Meg found out about the Opera Ghost's house? She turned back to Erik, accusation in her eyes.

"I asked her to show the Vicomte the way," Erik said placidly.

Christine's feeling of utter betrayal stunned her. Erik shared his location with *Meg*? He'd trusted someone else with his safety? Christine was supposed to be the only one who knew about the Opera Ghost!

"When?" she snapped, fingers curving into claws before she could stop herself.

"Mademoiselle Giry and I had a lovely chat last night," he hummed, looking inordinately pleased with himself. Christine bit her tongue to stifle her jealous words. Erik didn't need to know this information stung her.

Raoul glanced at Erik before turning back to Christine. "She said that's how you kill people and that I should hold my hand up at the level of my eyes to prevent you from killing me."

"Oh, well then if *Meg* said it, it must be true," Christine said, unable to keep from shooting a sarcastic glance in Erik's direction despite still being angry with him. This must be Meg's way of getting back at her. Christine would have to compliment her on her creativity.

"I might have embellished some things after hearing your tale on the roof," Erik told her, expression slightly sheepish. He patted himself down to show he was lasso-free. "You can put your arm down."

Raoul glared, hand still hovering in front at eye level. "Like I would believe anything you say, villain!"

"Put your arm down, Raoul, you look ridiculous," Christine snapped, her patience with the whole enterprise wearing thin. Raoul did so immediately, looking chastised.

"I'm not leaving without Christine," Raoul demanded, turning back to Erik.

"And she's free to go with you once she answers one question," Erik replied smoothly.

Raoul stepped closer to Erik, shoulders thrown back. "She doesn't love you!"

"That isn't what I want to know. And also, technically, not a question."

Christine watched Erik step to a small chest of drawers, intricately carved and gilded. Another prop from a long-forgotten performance, lost to time. Nobody missed the things Erik took and the thought saddened her. So much disappeared when people didn't look.

No. So much disappeared when people didn't *see*. Christine was beginning to understand the difference.

He took something out of the drawer and returned to her, his hands held out before him, closed-fisted. "Do you want me to guess which hand the coin is in?" she asked, glancing at Raoul. The Vicomte stood silently, blue eyes staring holes in the back of Erik's skull. "Neither. Because there's never a coin there." It was an old sleight of hand con, and one she was deeply familiar with, even though she and father hadn't run it often.

Erik shook his head, a piece of dark hair falling across his forehead. He opened his hands to reveal two small figurines, one in each palm. They were carved of some black, gleaming stone. In his left palm sat a turtle; in his right, a scorpion.

"A question for you," he intoned quietly, and a shiver of dread shook her. She waited, shifting uneasily. What was he about to do?

He set the figures down on top of a low table. "You have a choice, Christine. The turtle—you tell the authorities about the Opera Ghost and your part in it. The scorpion—you're free to go but I kill the man you claim to love." Erik smiled grimly. Then he reached into the drawer once again to pull out a gun. He pointed the barrel at Raoul.

"Stop it, Erik," she whispered. He wouldn't kill Raoul. He wouldn't.

But uncertainty gripped her. She'd been blindsided by Meg. What if she had pushed Erik too far?

"Christine!" Raoul froze as the barrel swung up from his chest to his forehead. "Wh-what is he talking about?"

Christine narrowed her eyes, searching Erik's face and body for tells. There weren't any. Erik stood, as indecipherable as a specter, his body still, his face expressionless, his blankness only helped by his mask. His hands didn't even shake. "You want to expose me, go ahead," Erik told her. "I don't have much of a life to lose anyway, as you keep telling me." He grinned, a feral showing of teeth. "But I'm used to life in cage. What about you, Christine? Ready to face the music for what you've done?"

Her body shuddered like she'd been doused in ice water. A confession, that's what he wanted from her. A confession of all of her many sins. In front of Raoul. She swallowed the sour taste that filled her mouth at the thought.

"All she's done is sing for you," Raoul countered, but he stared at Christine, confused.

She raised her hand, hoping he'd be quiet. She needed to think. There had to be another way out of this. If only her thoughts wouldn't keep spinning off in a thousand differing directions.

Erik's dark gaze locked with hers. "Tell him, Christine. Or make your choice."

"You're mad," Raoul breathed.

Erik swung around, baring his teeth at the other man. "Be silent!"

Raoul turned to Christine, eyes pleading for

someone to explain the situation to him. "Tell me what, Christine? What is he talking about?"

Christine opened her mouth to speak, but the words just wouldn't come. If she told Raoul what she'd done, how would he ever look at her again? He'd never marry her and she'd be stuck back at the opera. Or in prison. Or worse.

She heard ragged breathing and realized it was hers.

It was the fable of the turtle and the scorpion. Erik hadn't chosen these figurines lightly, oh no, he had to make a *point*. The scorpion needed to cross a river and asked a turtle for a ride on his back. The turtle protested, saying that the scorpion would sting the turtle before they reached the other bank. When the scorpion swore he would not, the turtle agreed. But before they were even hallway across the river, the scorpion's tail arced down and stung the turtle. When the turtle asked why, the scorpion could only respond that it was in his nature.

"Can't you see what you're doing to her? She can't make a decision like this!"

"You don't know her at all then." Erik's aim didn't waver.

Raoul slashed his hand through the air. "No! Don't try and paint her to be someone like you. You're the monster, no matter what mask you wear! You can't force someone to love you. That's what this is about, isn't it?"

"I am well aware of that fact!" Erik shouted, ripping off his mask and turning to face Raoul with his scarring and deformity fully exposed.

Christine held her breath, hoping that Raoul would surprise her. But he didn't. He recoiled with a shout of horror, his hands coming up to block out the sight of Erik's face. Erik adjusted his aim as Raoul stumbled backwards a few paces.

"I know what people see when they look at me!" Erik roared. "My own father was so horrified by my face that he couldn't wait to be rid of me. Now. Shut. Up." He spun to face Christine, fist clenched around the handle of the gun. But his voice was unbelievably gentle when he prompted, "The scorpion or the turtle, Christine. Choose."

Her stomach sank, the familiar feeling of being caught in a trap settling over her. She never thought Erik would be one who would make her feel that way. She felt her whole body shaking.

Christine glanced at Raoul, who watched them with fascinated horror. She thought she might finally understand what Erik was forcing her to do. "You're a bastard."

"I know." He placed the figurines in her hands. "Choose, Christine."

She weighed both statuettes, before looking over at Raoul. "I'm sorry."

"Chris—," Raoul's voice broke as she set the scorpion on the table.

Like called to like after all. It was in her nature.

Raoul's face paled and his gaze jumped from to the gun in Erik's hand before moving to Christine's face. She stared back at him, tears in her eyes, expecting him to rail at her. She watched his throat bob as he swallowed and shut his eyes for a brief moment.

When he opened them again, she saw the sadness in them. There was no accusation, no blame. Christine shook her head, but Raoul only smiled. "Goodbye then, Christine."

She didn't beg for his life; she couldn't. She'd made her choice. But she didn't look away either. She owed Raoul that much at least.

Erik's finger tightened on the trigger. There was a puff of smoke, a loud bang, and then silence. Christine coughed, waving a hand in front of her face.

Raoul stood in place, blue eyes huge in a face gone ashen grey. Erik dropped his arm, gun hanging loosely from his fingertips. Understanding struck her suddenly.

"It was a prop gun," she whispered incredulously. "You absolute bastard!"

Realization dawned on Raoul's face, but before he could say anything, Christine bolted away from both of them.

CHAPTER 26

CHRISTINE WANDERED AROUND THE streets immediately surrounding the opera house in a daze. She ended up at L'église de la Madeleine, sitting in a pew and staring at the altar dumbly. Ordinarily Christine would have avoided churches like she'd spontaneously combust upon entry, but it seemed appropriate after the events of the evening. She wasn't praying, wasn't even sure she knew what to pray for. Forgiveness? Absolution? For God to strike her dead on the spot?

Ripping the wig from her head, Christine threaded her fingers through her bound hair. Mocking laughter ripped out of her, and she squeezed her eyes shut. Everything was ruined.

All of her plans, her work—wasted. Raoul had seen who the real monster that dwelt in the tunnels beneath the opera house was and it wasn't Erik. She laughed harder, shoulders shaking until she thought the whole pew might be shuddering with the movements of her body.

She felt a light hand rest on her shoulder and looked up. An older man in priest's garb stared at her in concern. "Are you well, Mademoiselle? Do you need help?"

Christine straightened, shifting so the man's grasp slipped from her shoulder. "I am fine, Father," she said. Pushing herself to her feet, she moved around the priest.

"If you would like to unburden yourself, I am always pleased to listen." He smiled down at her, eyes shining benevolently. He moved with her as she walked toward the large doors of the Grecian-inspired church.

"Father," she said as she crested the threshold, "I wouldn't even know where to start."

♪♪♪

The Palais Garnier gleamed like the centerpiece jewel in a crown amidst the glittering assemblage still streaming from the building. Gendarmes gathered outside, swarming like ants on a mound as people milled about. Christine didn't see anyone panicking, just a general exodus a bit earlier than usual. She wondered if a member of the audience had thought to call the authorities fearing another sandbag or if management had just called an end to the performance after the disappearance of their principal singer. She suspected the latter from the lack of panic. The crowd held the air of people waiting around for gossip rather than any real danger.

Christine made her way through the Rue Scribe gates, following the path down and around to the lake. She shuddered at the thought of poling the boat to Erik's house, risking overturning and drowning due to the heavy weight of her costume. Her body throbbed with exhaustion. She longed to tear off the dress, but doing so would require her dresser and the trouble she would be in should she ever show her face in the opera house made that impossible.

A longing for home overtook her, so profound she gasped at the sudden ache in her chest. Not for Paris or Perros, but home—Sweden. Upsala. Even if it had meant poverty and hunger and cold, it was the last time she remembered being happy, truly, unabashedly happy. Pappa had sold their farm after her mother's death when Christine couldn't have been more than six years old. They'd gone on the road, playing and singing and dancing at fairs and carnivals and celebrations. They'd slept in barns, in stables, in haybales. It had been a strange adventure in the beginning, everything new and fresh and exciting, and all of it because her home had been a person and not a place.

She missed it. She missed her father. She wanted, more than anything in that moment, to just go home. To feel her father's arms wrap around her, to hear his violin sing out one more tune. She'd spent so much time hating him, resenting what he'd left her, that she'd forgotten what it felt like to love him. It had been easier to hate him than to miss him.

Shaking her head to clear it, Christine pushed aside her feelings. She could look at them later, at Madame Valérius' flat. It would help her pass the long, useless days spent taking care of the woman as she withered away in bed, because Christine certainly wasn't going to be welcomed at the opera any longer. Meg would tell everything she knew. She'd be lucky if she wasn't arrested.

She'd chewed her lower lip raw by the time she reached the trapdoor and ladder that led to Erik's house on the lake. It was difficult to manage in her dress, but she did so, and soon found herself pushing into his inner sanctum.

He sat with his back to her, shirtless. Numerous candles sat on the table he worked at, provided him light. Blood streaked down his arm from a wound in the fleshy upper part. He poured something over it, making a choked howling sound from deep in his throat as whatever it was entered the wound. He stopped, panting heavily. His hands shook when he put down the bottle.

Christine took a step inside this house where she'd spent so much time of late, her stomach clenching and unclenching like she was going to be sick. Erik turned his head, mask back on. His jaw was locked tight with pain, his pale skin glistening with sweat.

"Are you all right?" she asked, pointing to his arm.

He stared her, eventually turning his body a bit so she could see the messy bullet hole in his upper arm; from the looks of it, the bullet had passed clean through the flesh. It appeared angry red and inflamed beneath the streaks of blood. "I was shot. I'm not sure if that classifies me as all right."

Christine watched him wrap a clean cloth around the wound. Red began staining the white fabric almost immediately. Erik grimaced as he tried to tie it off using one hand and his teeth.

"Let me do it before you ruin it," she told him as she crossed to him and batted his hands away.

His gaze was hot on her as she worked on rewrapping it properly. "You should get this looked at by someone."

This close, she heard Erik swallow. "I could never kill anyone," he said, gaze shifting to watch her hands. His usually smooth voice came out jagged with pain.

"I know," Christine whispered. She had known it all along. Of the two of them, only she was a murderer. "I think I knew from the moment you started talking. Those things you said—it was all a performance for Raoul."

Erik tried to shrug, then hissed when it caused him pain. "He wanted a monster. I gave him one."

"You were never the monster, Erik," she

whispered, throat tight.

"Tell that to my father," he said with a sigh. "Or to anyone who saw me at the carnival. Or anyone with eyes." He laughed softly, mockingly. "What are you doing back here? I didn't expect I'd ever see you again."

Christine gently tugged on his hand to get Erik to sit down. When he did, she didn't let go of his hand. "You were right."

"You're going to have to be more specific, Christine. I'm right about an awful lot of things." He squeezed her hand weakly.

She rolled her eyes skyward and brushed the hair from his forehead. When she did so, she could feel the fever burning in Erik's body. It wasn't a conflagration, not yet, but if he didn't get someone to look at his arm, it would become so quickly. "Can you help me get this costume off?"

She saw him grin tiredly and flex the fingers on his uninjured arm. He knew she was avoiding answering, but she needed a space of time to figure out how to put what she wanted to say into words. "I'll do my best."

It took far too long to divest herself of the heavy overskirts, and as they worked, Christine told him, "About Raoul. And me." She stopped, unsure she wanted to ask the next question. "How did you know?" She dumped the pile of fabrics beside the table where they worked, breathing a bit easier. She still wore the corset and blouse, but they weren't nearly as bothersome as the skirts.

"I think you know."

"Tell me anyway."

Erik reached out and caught her chin between his thumb and forefinger. His touch was gentle and warm due to his fever. His eyes burned as they studied her face. "Because you never let Raoul see the real you. I kept telling you that, hoping you would listen. You were so sure that this...," he gestured with his bad arm at her, wincing when it pulled, "fabrication was what he wanted that you never gave him a chance to find out if he'd ever even *like* the real Christine." He shook his head and dropped her chin. "How could he love you like I do when he doesn't even know you?"

He stood and only managed a few steps before she grabbed his uninjured arm. Erik stopped, but refused to look at her, so Christine stepped around him and blocked his way. She stared at him until he finally met her gaze.

"You love me?" Her words came out awed and wondering, like she'd just witnessed a miracle.

"Yes." He touched two fingers to his mask and tried to turn away. "You knew that."

She didn't let him; she moved with him. She wanted answers that made sense. "That doesn't explain how you knew it wouldn't work," Christine said, trying to understand and feeling the frustration grow inside of her. How could Erik love her and Raoul not? She wasn't at her best around Erik, she wasn't putting forth all of her considerable wiles and talents to making him want her.

"You shouldn't have to hide who you are to have someone love you," Erik told her, as if it were the simplest thing in the entire world.

"I don't understand," she said, voice rising in frustration. This wasn't what she was taught, wasn't what she knew. You adjusted who you were based on what someone wanted to see, not on who you were in reality. Nobody wanted reality. Why should they settle for it when fantasy was so much better?

"I know you don't." He gazed at her sadly.

"Then help me! Tell me—why do you love me?" The need to run rose inside of her like a wave, threatening to block out rational thought.

He smiled softly and there was such joy in his expression that Christine didn't know whether to weep or scream. "Because you let me," he whispered, like it was biggest secret he'd ever told anyone.

What came from her was a strangled cry as Erik wrapped his good arm around her and pulled her into his body. Christine clung to him, beset by a storm of conflicting emotions. It had never occurred to her to be anything other than herself with Erik; from the first moment they met with him in a cage as they sang opera to each other, she'd always been fundamentally Christine. Not her father's daughter intent on getting the most she could out of every interaction, not the good adopted daughter of Madame Valérius, not a lowly chorus girl or a striving diva-in-training. There was nothing she offered him outside of just herself.

And he'd wanted it. He'd *treasured* it.

She didn't understand it, but maybe she wasn't meant to. Maybe she was meant to accept the love as the gift it was and be grateful for it.

"That's what I said." Her voice was muffled against his chest. She lifted her hand and set it over his ribs where his heart would be and felt the beat of it against her palm. "When you asked me why I helped you."

"I know." She could hear the smile in his voice as he pressed a gentle kiss to the top of her head. "But just because you said it doesn't make it any less true."

She gave a watery chuckle. "How did you get so smart about love?"

"My mother taught me." He tilted her chin up so he could look at her. "Before she died."

Christine reached up and pulled the mask from Erik's face. He tried to stop her, but she shushed him. "Was she the one who told you that you shouldn't have to hide who you are to have someone love you?"

Erik nodded, his face suddenly tight with fear. Christine smiled up at him and flung his mask away. "She was right."

Christine pressed her lips to his, the kiss soft and delicate, as ephemeral as spun sugar and just as sweet. She didn't care about his face because he'd shown her his heart and that was what mattered. It was beautiful. He'd seen her damage and hadn't run, hadn't tried to change her into something he wanted her to be.

All her life Christine thought love was a different kind of cage, just another con. Erik had showed her that love could be freeing. And real. So very, very real.

The sound of clapping broke their kiss. Christine scowled, fury flaring like a small sun inside her chest. Who dared intrude on this moment that should have been between her and Erik?

"I knew you weren't worthy of Raoul." Philippe said, pulling out a small pistol and pointing it at her. She doubted this was a prop. "Just another scheming bit of baggage looking for a meal ticket far above her station." He peered around the room, lip curled in disgust at what he saw. "Where is he?"

"I haven't seen him for hours," Christine told him, bristling at Philippe's words. "And I don't expect to see him ever again. So you can take yourself back to La Sorelli," she emphasized the name of his mistress since he was being such a hypocrite, "because your precious family name is safe."

"I'll be the judge of that, trollop!" He moved closer to them, body stiff with derision. "The carriage he booked for your flight is still here— oh, I knew all about your plan to run away together." Philippe waved the hand not holding the gun in an airy, dismissive gesture. "My brother was naïve to think I wouldn't be watching for something like this when I had the date of his expedition moved forward. I expected him to try something as foolish as this, though I'm sure it wasn't his sole idea."

Christine rose, making sure to keep her hands clenched into fists by her side. She put herself in front of Erik and directly in Philippe's path. She wasn't afraid of him. He couldn't touch them. "You've seen he's not here! You'll have to search for him elsewhere, though it is no wonder he seeks to escape from you, as controlling as you are!"

"Who is this, then?" Philippe asked, as he craned his neck to get a good look at Erik. "Another conspirator in your plan to ruin my brother? I would see your face, churl!"

Erik's head snapped up at being addressed and Christine immediately realized their mistake. She'd removed his mask and now his face was visible to Philippe. When they'd been crouched down, Erik's deformity had been hidden; now, not so.

Philippe reeled back, crying out in horror. Christine felt Erik flinch and the barely-checked anger inside of her burst forth. "Get out!" she screamed, rushing forward. "You're not welcome here!"

"Monster," Philippe shouted, raising his gun to point it at Erik's face.

Christine leaped at his arm, heedless of her safety. She heard Erik cry out a warning. Philippe cursed as she latched onto him, yanking down with all of her panicked strength. He twisted, trying to get free. Christine wouldn't let him.

He gave a great shove with his free hand, sending her careening backwards. The edge of the table dug into her spine, and she cried out in pain. Erik lashed out at Philippe with a punch that sent the noble in Christine's direction.

He crashed into her, upending the table and sending the candle and oil lamps flying. Christine screamed as the fabric of her costume skirts went up in flames as she landed on the ground next to them. Her underskirts caught and she rolled away, only to be stopped by Philippe. He flailed at the flames engulfing him, climbing to his feet with an agonized shriek. He ran, igniting a tapestry and another curtain as he careened about the room in search of a way out.

Erik batted at the flames along with her, his breathing ragged. Christine coughed as acrid black smoke tore at her nose and throat, making her eyes flood with tears. Erik coughed into his elbow and pulled her farther away from the flames.

The fire spread quickly. Christine remembered the tales of ballerinas who burned to death when their costumes caught fire from coming into contact with the gas footlights of the stage. She didn't want to end up like that. Philippe's screaming faded as he finally found the door that led to the main body of the island, his fiery form illuminating the darkness.

Erik pounded out the last of the flames on her skirts. Her legs were burned, but not badly. She gasped for clean air, the smoke twining in her lungs like a serpent. She pressed her face to the floor. She could barely see for the tears streaming down her face. Everything felt too hot, too close.

"Christine. Christine!" Erik's face was above hers, his body shielding her. His brown eye was blown wide, pupil eating up the iris with his fear for her.

When she focused on him, he sighed with relief. Coughs wracked his lean frame as he sheltered her. "Come on. We have to get out of here."

He pulled her up, half-supporting her. She could barely place one foot in front of the other; it felt like he dragged her beside him more than she walked. Erik held burning tapestries away from her, ushering her through with encouraging words and gentle tugs. She wanted to move faster, but couldn't get her body to work right. Her head swam as she breathed in more smoke, coughing at the rotten taste of it in her throat.

The heat grew more intense as they approached the door Philippe had exited. They were both coughing horribly, staggering at the lack of breathable air. She almost didn't hear the cracking noise, only noticing when Erik's head snapped up. She screamed as she saw the roof begin to cave in on them.

With a cry, Erik picked her up as if she weighed nothing. He heaved Christine through the door just as the ramshackle roof of the house on the lake fell down. She landed hard, her head slamming into the ground with a force that rocked her. Stunned, she watched dumbly as flames flared out from the ruined building.

Understanding hit her as her head cleared. "Erik!" she screamed, clambering to her feet.

Racing toward the burning building on shaking legs, she saw no signs of him. The heat was intense up close, but she kept going. Christine dropped to her knees, desperate to find him. She clawed at the debris with her bare hands.

There!

A pale hand reaching out from beneath shattered wood and rubble. Heedless of the flames, Christine crawled closer until she could grab it. Erik's skin was still icy cold as she grasped it. Hauling backwards with all of her strength, she slowly felt the slide of his body along the ground. Her lungs burned and her back and shoulder muscles shrieked in protest, but Christine didn't care.

All that mattered was Erik.

His face was slackly unconscious and smudged with soot. Blood streaked what little skin she could see beneath the black mess of his hair. Some of the length had burned away in the fire.

"Please!" she shouted, praying for more strength as her own flagged. He was half out of the flames, but she was exhausted and it was so hard to pull him free with the heavier debris weighing him down.

He groaned weakly and her heart leapt into her throat. Wading in, she tossed what she could lift away from him. Her hands and arms burned with pain, but she ignored it. If Erik died it wasn't going to be because she quit. He was hers, probably the only thing in her life that had ever been and she wasn't going to have him taken from her now.

She grabbed him beneath his armpits and heaved with everything she had left. Erik's long body slithered free of the fallen detritus. Christine fell backwards at the sudden lack of resistance. She scrambled back to her feet to drag him further from the burning house. She patted out the flames that licked at his clothes and skin. When they were doused, she pressed her head to his chest to listen for a heartbeat.

When Erik moaned in pain, his weak breath stirring her hair, she wept in relief.

CHAPTER 27

IT WAS SEVERAL WEEKS later when Christine, cloaked and hooded, knocked on the door to Raoul's Paris lodgings. She'd heard that he'd been forced to delay his trip to the Arctic indefinitely upon receiving word of his brother's death in the lake beneath the Palais Garnier. Philippe's body had been found, badly burned, on the other side of the lake. He succumbed to his wounds and drowned. How he'd ended up down there and why no one knew.

Christine knew. And she wasn't interested in telling anyone.

Well, except for one person.

The burns on her legs and hands still gave her pain, but they were slowly healing. She'd have scars, but that didn't bother her, not anymore.

She'd only been back to the opera house once since the fire, to collect her things when no one was watching. The tunnels she and Erik had traversed for months led her unerringly where she wanted to go. Now her purse was fat with francs from Philippe's check and she had a train ticket out of the city. She would leave behind everything else. Paris held nothing for her anymore.

Raoul met her in the salon overlooking the garden. He looked tired, his blue eyes washed out and faded like rainwater. He still dressed sharply, but there was an air of unkempt frustration to his hair, almost as if he kept sliding his hands through his tight curls. His generous mouth was pinched at the ends, and Christine felt a moment of sadness for his loss. She didn't miss Philippe, but it was evident Raoul did.

"My condolences," she offered.

"Thank you." He remained standing. Christine watched him as he walked over to the fireplace. "I am assuming that's not the only reason for your visit."

"I came to say goodbye." She wasn't entirely sure why she'd come, but she'd listened to her gut that told her she should at least speak with Raoul one final time. "And to beg you to forget everything you know about the opera house, the ghost, and me."

Raoul's gaze turned vacant, detached. He nodded once, almost haphazardly. "It's better left buried," he whispered. "Did Erik kill . . .?"

Christine shook her head. "No."

Raoul gave her a long, assessing stare. Christine pursed her lips to fight back a smirk. He was growing up, becoming more suspicious. And he certainly harbored no more misconceptions about her innocence. "I didn't either," she assured him. "It was an accident."

"An accident." He raised in eyebrow in elegant doubt

"He saw Erik's face and knocked over a candle. The whole place was ablaze in moments." She didn't think Raoul needed to know all the details. "He came looking for you."

"I know." Raoul rubbed the back of his neck. "He didn't approve of you—of us," he told her.

"Yes," she said with a snort. "He made that abundantly clear." But seeing the pain in his eyes, she added, "He cared about you. He only wanted what was best for you." She brushed her palms down the front of her skirt. "Which I think we've all agreed was never me."

"What will you do now?"

Christine forced herself not to clutch her bag too tightly, a dead giveaway for the francs stashed there. She took a few steps closer to the door instead. "I think I might return to Sweden for a time. I miss home."

"No more singing?"

"No more singing," she said and did not think she would miss it at all. There were only two people she enjoyed singing with anyway. She checked the mantel clock. "I should go. My train leaves shortly."

"I'll see you out," Raoul said, joining her at the door. His blue eyes searched her face for a long moment. "I did love you, Christine."

She put a hand to his cheek, brushing the skin beneath his eye softly. "I know you did, Raoul. But you deserve someone who loves you back."

"And you could never?" he asked, the faint stirring of hope in his voice.

She smiled at him, a real one, not the simpering smirks she'd used to draw him in. Christine watched as realization dawned, and his eyes narrowed in scrutiny. "But you could love Erik?"

Christine's face fell and she lowered her gaze to her shoes. "I could." She cleared her throat of its sudden tightness and did her best to explain. "You called him a monster for the way he looked, but he was never that, not really." She raised her head and met his eyes, gaze fierce. "We are alike, he and I. His outsides match my insides."

They walked in silence to the front door. Hand on the handle, Raoul paused. "What of him?"

Christine's heart seized at the name. The ache in her chest threatened to overtake her until she sank to the Turkish rug in tears, but she fought against the emotion. "The opera ghost died in the fire that killed your brother," she managed to choke out, blinking back tears.

Erik had saved her again. But at a cost.

Raoul's fingertips brushed the back of her hand. "I am sorry, Christine."

She pulled away. "As am I. Goodbye, Raoul. I hope, one day, you'll think of me fondly."

CHAPTER *28*

Ireland, 1901

BASTIEN STARED AT CHRISTINE'S serene face as she finished her tale. She lifted the whisky glass to her lips, pink tongue sweeping out to capture the last drops of liquor before setting it gently back on the table. She folded her hands and looked back at him expectantly.

"That was quite a story," was his only response. He could think of nothing else to say, his brain still trying to make sense out of everything she'd told him.

"One hardly would believe it," Christine said, leaning back in her chair wearing an arch expression. "But it is true. Every word."

"You don't come off very well in it," he told her, surprised at her forthrightness.

Her laugh sounded like bells. "Still surprised even after what Raoul told you of me?" Her lovely little smile grew quite a bit wider. "I doubt he forgot the lesson I taught him."

"I thought he exaggerated." Bastien did not tell her of the look in the Comte de Chagny's eyes when he spoke of Christine, of the aborted love that lingered there. He suspected Raoul would always love his version of Christine. He might even have been capable of loving Erik's version, though now no one would ever know.

Christine sobered. "He did not." She pushed away from the table, and said briskly, "You've had your story. I've had my drink. And now I must be going."

He stretched out his hand, entreating her to stay just a moment more. "But the music box?"

Her curls bounced as she shook her head. "I do not want it. Tell Raoul to keep it or burn it for all I care. Christine Daaé is dead along with the opera ghost."

Bastien rose as she came around the table and took her hand. "Thank you for speaking with me, Mrs. Spöke. I appreciate your time."

Christine slipped her hand from his grasp after a brief shake. "Of course, Monsieur Beauchamp. It was lovely to meet you."

He heard the door to the public house open, heard people greet the newcomer enthusiastically. A pleasantly husky male voice responded to their calls. Christine's face brightened, her blue eyes dancing and full of joy.

"What will you tell Raoul?" she asked, but she sounded distracted, almost as if it no longer mattered.

"I will tell my employer that Christine Daaé is dead, just as you said."

"Thank you." She stepped away to join the tall man with the dark hair who had just entered.

Bastien walked closer to the pair, curious. As he watched, the man helped Christine on with her heavy shawl. He leaned forward and whispered in her ear, saying something that made her throw back her head and laugh freely. Bastien realized how false all her expressions had been with him as soon as he saw this one.

As the man turned, Bastien caught a glimpse of his face, obscured as it was by his shaggy black hair. Dark red scar tissue covered half of his face and ear. A black eye patch covered the eye on that side. Even the hand on that side of his body showed burn scarring. The man had obviously been caught in some kind of fire. Bastien gasped.

Christine waved to the barmaid, and the man shook the hands of several patrons in the pub before he tucked Christine under his arm and the two departed. Bastien threw some money on the table and followed.

As he exited the pub, the two crested the low stone wall separating the pub from the road. He heard Christine ask, "How were the lessons today? Any particularly horrible students?"

The man chuckled, pulling Christine into his side. As Bastien watched, she stood on her tiptoes and kissed his scarred cheek. "They were all quite capable, though only one seems to have true talent."

"None of them were as good as me though." She sounded smug.

The man's voice was fond as he said, "Of course not, my dear. But you were always incomparable." He smiled down at her.

"I love you." Christine wrapped an arm around his waist.

"And I you."

Christine hadn't lied, exactly, though she hadn't told the complete truth either. Raoul probably expected nothing less, now that Bastien thought about it. Erik had survived the fire, and he and Christine lived here as husband and wife. Erik and Lotte Spöke.

He walked a bit further so he could lean against the stone wall and watch the two of them. He wasn't sure what he was going to tell his employers, but he had time to come up with something. Christine and her opera ghost were lost in a fire. Two phoenixes emerged. Bastien found he couldn't begrudge them their new lives.

The two continued down a rock-strewn path toward the main part of town. As they went, he heard Christine's lilting soprano rise like a bird on the wing, followed moments later by Erik's silvery tenor climbing to meet it as the sun sank below the horizon.

AUTHOR'S NOTE

Even though this is a retelling, I still had to do my homework. The first stop was the source material—the original Phantom novel by Gaston Leroux. The age difference between Erik and Christine always felt uncomfortable to me, especially with how innocent she is in the novel. I wanted a Christine and Erik that were much closer in age and understanding.

As I reread the novel, I noticed some strange things about Christine's father that I failed to notice before. He and Christine travel widely after the death of her mother, making a point to follow the country fairs. Then Pappa manages to find a man who makes it his life's work to proclaim his musical genius and invites them to live with him and his wife. This struck me as suspect, which led to me reworking Christine's father into a consummate grifter and confidence man.

The next hurdle was reconciling the musical, which most people know far better than the novel. I wanted to have a few nods in this story to that interpretation. The chandelier scene is such an iconic moment that I decided to scrub it altogether and went with history rather than fiction. A counterweight did fall and kill an audience member during a performance; Leroux reported on it. I used that instead of the chandelier falling to keep the body count low.

The Paris Opera House does have a lake under it; if you are interested in architecture, read about the construction of the structure. While you can tour the Opera House, the lake is inaccessible these days. Operas and ballets mentioned in this book came from known performances of the time period and at the Opera itself (where available).

Mentions made of the Exposition reference the Exposition Universelle of 1889. The food and dishes referenced came from menus found during that same period. Place names and street names come directly from Leroux's novel.

ABOUT THE AUTHOR

Jeanette Battista is the award winning and Amazon best-selling young adult author of The Moon Series, These Violent Delights, and the Books of Aerie series. She received her MA in English literature with a concentration in medieval studies. She'd been a technical writer, a software release project manager, and a freelance educational writer. She's taught college freshmen how to write and occasionally still talks writing with high school and middle school students.

Her household includes several humans and three cats, one of whom is missing an eye. He is unfortunately not named Odin, a choice that will haunt her forever. When she's not writing, she's having the crap beaten out of her in a ring during Muay Thai class, reading anything she can get her grubby hands on, and playing Unstable Unicorns. She lives and works in North Carolina.

www.ingramcontent.com/pod-product-compliance
Lightning Source LLC
Chambersburg PA
CBHW031017120726
47905CB00007B/1948